GILLEAN CHASE

TRIAD MOON

gynergy
books

COPYRIGHT © 1993 GILLEAN CHASE
All rights reserved. No part of this book may be reproduced
or transmitted in any form or by any means without
permission of the publisher, except by a reviewer, who
may quote brief passages in a review.

Thanks to Lynn Henry, my editor, for her thoroughness (and patience)
and to Louise Fleming for her courage in publishing this unusual love story.

COVER DRAWING:
Uprising by Janice Udell

PRINTED AND BOUND IN CANADA BY:
Webcom

gynergy books acknowledges
the generous support of the Canada Council.

PUBLISHED BY:
gynergy books
P.O. Box 2023
Charlottetown, P.E.I.
Canada C1A 7N7

DISTRIBUTORS:
Canada: General Publishing
United States: Inland Book Company
United Kingdom: Turnaround Distribution

CANADIAN CATALOGUING IN PUBLICATION DATA
 Chase, Gillean, 1946-
  Triad moon

  ISBN 0-921881-28-2

 I. Title.

 PS8555.H431T74 1993   C813'.54   C93-098653-9
 PR9199.3.C42T74 1993

CONTENTS

ONE • 1
TWO • 9
THREE • 18
FOUR • 28
FIVE • 36
SIX • 41
SEVEN • 49
EIGHT • 56
NINE • 66
TEN • 71
ELEVEN • 78
TWELVE • 85
THIRTEEN • 91
FOURTEEN • 99
FIFTEEN • 109
SIXTEEN • 116
SEVENTEEN • 124
EIGHTEEN • 133
NINETEEN • 141
TWENTY • 150
TWENTY ONE • 156
TWENTY TWO • 167
TWENTY THREE • 176

To my Spirit Guides who helped me write this novel,
and to my life companion who assisted them with patient
and persistent editing and criticism.

CHAPTER ONE

Brook Thiebault gazed at the light spilling from Tracy's apartment window, breathing deeply to calm the butterflies in her stomach. It was difficult to walk up to the intercom and punch up Tracy's suite number, more difficult still when Arlan's voice responded, "Hello?"

"It's Brook," she said, trying to sound relaxed. The door clicked open. All the way across the lobby she avoided the full-length mirrors. As the elevator closed on her replica and carried her up eighteen floors to Tracy and Arlan, Brook wondered why she thought she was ready to see them again.

Tracy answered the door, looking tall and dramatic despite her nondescript clothing. She was wearing a grey turtleneck sweater and black slacks. Her hair was tousled and in need of a trim, natural brown waves speckled with grey at the temples. She looked overworked. There were dark, purple shadows under her eyes.

Just behind her Arlan stood, hands in the pockets of her pleated beige slacks. Her hair was orange-red and shaped to flatter an already attractive scalp. She wore a tan leather tie and a green shirt and moved like Pan about to pirouette. Brook felt Arlan's amusement like an unspoken challenge.

Tracy showed her excellent teeth. She had a well-balanced grin that dimpled her cheeks, a smile that won the instant trust of clients who came to her for therapy. "It's about time," she said.

"In its time." Tracy recognized Brook's rejoinder as an admonishment — slightly she bowed her head. In honour of February Eve, Brook handed her a branch of mountain ash. Tracy passed the branch to Arlan, who placed it on the altar in the living room. Following them into the high-ceilinged room, Brook was introduced to Ruth, a black woman from Georgia with sad, distrustful eyes. Her expression was cryptic as an onion, layer upon layer of silence. Brook extended her hand to Ruth and then to Tabatha, who clasped her fingers firmly. Although she looked to be in her mid-twenties, Tabatha was small and muscular, as if still growing into her adult size.

For a while the five women chatted, then gathered up their coats, candles and ritual paraphernalia and headed for Ambleside Park. On the beach they built a fire and stood around it, hands joined, their bodies forming the shape of a pentacle. Tonight Ruth would serve as High Priestess, channelling the energies of February Eve. The first of the Celtic Sabbats, this one would honour the Triple Goddess in her Crone aspect. In the twilight Ruth welcomed the four elements, soliciting the protection of air and fire, earth and water. She placed an enamel pot on the fire: they stood watching the water boil. Ruth poured in dried mint and steeped the leaves, inviting each of the women to dip a cup into the pot.

Brook was grateful to do so. The wind blew damp from the ocean and cut through her cable knit sweater. She heard gulls crealing and listened to the fire as it spent itself in a great burst of heat and light. Swaying, the women joined hands and began to chant.

"Rid yourself of the old," Ruth said. Tabatha dropped a jockey's whip into the flames, saying in explanation: "I injured my knee. Never again can I ride horses competitively. So be it."

In unison they chorused: "So it is."

"What will you do now, Tabatha?" Tracy asked. Her counsellor's face was alert.

"Work the stables and teach dressage," Tabatha said quietly. "Until the horses themselves ask me to leave." She made a ritual jump over the flames, a symbol of her willingness to leave behind what she could no longer do.

Across the fire Tracy met Brook's eyes. She spoke clearly. "I ask the forgiveness of my ex-lover, for my failure to love her as she deserves." There was sadness in her voice and some strain. Eyes swivelled towards Brook. Uncomfortably, she gazed down at the fire, memories of the rupture between them festering like flesh torn by blackberry bushes. Hardest of all for Brook to accept had been the weight of Tracy's judgement — that she was an impractical idealist with dangerous beliefs. Nor had it been easy to learn about Tracy's involvement with Arlan, from someone who thought that Tracy should be confronted. When Brook had asked some direct questions, Tracy cried. She wanted time to work out her feelings, time to discover what Arlan meant to her life ...

What Arlan meant to her. Whatever makes a person enter a new relationship when there are problems with the old one, it had been quite clear to Brook that Tracy needed space. And it was certainly easier for Brook to move out of the house shared by the two of them than it was for Tracy to relocate her practice. For whatever reasons, however, Tracy had chosen to move to a high-rise apartment. Perhaps she preferred soundproofing her walls to being surrounded by unwelcome memories.

Unpleasant as enemas, the months of their separation had come and gone. Brook had been determined to apply her "impractical beliefs" by learning to like and respect the woman with whom she shared Tracy's love. She invited them both for dinners or to concerts, soon enough realizing that the problems between Tracy and herself had very little to do with this other woman. Tracy responded by occasionally spending the night with Brook — through a misplaced sense of gratitude or guilt? Whatever Tracy's motives, Brook had work enough to keep clear about her own.

Then had come the morning when Arlan manouevred them into a ménage à trois. When they made love, however, Brook had the sense of letting herself down, badly. She did not and could not love Arlan. Chemically and psychologically the woman was anathema to her. Brook's solution had been to avoid intimacy with either of them, a solution of dubious value to an already blighted relationship.

It was only a matter of time before Tracy moved in with Arlan, telling Brook about it only after the fact. Still, her sense of injury was nothing but an albatross rotting around her neck. Candlemas was the time to bury the old. Her love for Tracy was timeworn, nothing but a habit of heart and mind.

Proudly Brook tossed back her head. "There is no blame. I believe that we agreed to experience this together. You know that."

Tracy looked bewildered in the way she looked so often by what she called Brook's spiritual fatalism. She stammered, "I regret the failure of my honesty."

"It is finished. Give it to the fire of the dead year." With some difficulty, Brook said the ritual words. It very clearly was not finished. Tracy could put their impasse down to a failure of honesty, but the failure of love belonged to both of them.

Leaping over the flames, Tracy touched fingers and thumbs to Brook's. In unison they said "I release you," and stepped back from one another.

Resolute, Arlan lifted her shoulders. "I was not careful of your child in defending my own. I made you my rival for Tracy's love."

Like a five-pointed star, the coven joined hands. Ruth said, "Embrace your child. She needs your love."

Graphically, Arlan held herself. "I embrace my child. There is enough love for each of us." Arlan jumped the fire and held out her palms to Brook.

Brook covered Arlan's hands with her own, speaking quietly. "I relegate the spirit of reproach to the dead year." Minus the pronoun, five voices carried the chant into darkness.

"Thank you." Head lowered, Arlan took her place next to Tabatha, her body language self-conscious. She need not have worried — what was discussed in the circle never went beyond it. Each woman in the coven was bound to listen with open ears and clear heart. When they could not, they left the circle, as Brook had. She had found pride an empty emotion, however — missed celebrating the new and full moons with a coven, missed the rituals and the discipline of witchcraft.

Now she said: "I am happy to return. I lost faith in my own beliefs. That is a personal failure. I thank Tracy and Arlan for helping me bring my crisis of faith into the open, where I can deal with it."

Tracy whispered: "How we like to throw sand in our own eyes and in one another's."

With an acute glance at them, Ruth spoke, relinquishing her father to his death. Gently she honoured her memories of him. She called the ancestors to listen and guide. They were needed now, to help him find his way home. "I ask the fire to teach me to let him go," Ruth said. "I am keeping him here with my sorrow." Sap bled and hissed as flames devoured birchwood. The firelight cast red and yellow hues into their clothes and giant shadows strode among them. Shivers crept up their spines: the spirit of Ruth's father walking. They chorused: "We invite his guides to help him home."

"So be it," Ruth murmured.

They returned the ritual words, "so it is," chanting until the embers began to dull. Darkness had fallen like shards from a broken bottle. Cold, distant stars winked. For the second half of the ritual, Ruth brought forward a cardboard box with twigs and wood. From the embers of the old, they kindled a new fire. Legs warmed by the blaze, each talked about her goals for the season when life would quicken again.

Brook said: "I'll be living on a writer's grant, so I can't afford to keep my apartment. I need a cheaper place to stay."

"Put up a note at the library," Tracy suggested. "You still work there?"

"Until April, when the grant starts. Though I'd like to live with children. The central character in my book is a nine-year-old boy."

Tracy teased, "Can't you remember what you were like as a child?"

"I was never a boy," Brook said ruefully, and made them laugh.

"Would it be easier to make your central character a girl?" Tracy asked.

"That might be easier," Brook agreed. "But only a boy can become a violent man." She shivered. She felt compelled to write about her father, who had attempted to live with his mistress, his wife and the children of both relationships. But this was not the forum to discuss the problems of a ménage à trois, especially since Brook was still suffering from the pathos of her own efforts.

Ruth continued. "To the main concern. Visualize the house you want, Brook, room by room. Don't limit yourself to what you can objectively afford."

Brook grinned. "A fireplace, of course. Freedom of the house and certainly of the kitchen. An aquarium would be nice. A shower, rather than a bath. And a garden, where I can grow herbs and vegetables."

Linked hands rose and fell. "So be it. So it is." Brook's desire had been "sent." This gathering of energy would help it to manifest. Brook almost snorted. Here in the witches' circle Tracy, too, believed that the ideal could be made real. Outside the coven, dreams were only wishes and too esoteric for her blood.

Before the next Quarter Day, Arlan wanted to make a rock video of a song she had written. Tabatha asked for strength to be celibate until she and her lover could stop reproaching one another every time they made love. Tracy's eyes diagnosed the problem as "distance to compensate for intimacy," but as usual kept her own counsel, especially when she caught Brook looking at her satirically.

Yes, Tracy. I wish that you were a better critic of your own emotions, but letting you go is the only act of love that I can make.

Her mind stinging, Brook looked at Arlan. *The desire to make a rock video or to write a book. Contrasted with Tabatha's sharing from the gut, these are egocentric concerns. I wonder if we're antagonists, Arlan and I, only because we're so much alike.* But this was not a therapy session. It was a ritual for letting go and engendering, for rest and cleansing before the season of growth.

To loosen her shoulders, Brook clasped her arms behind her. The ritual was ending. Soon she could go home and gratefully close the door to the implosion of feelings brought on by seeing Arlan and Tracy. Wistfully, she thought: *I feel like a fish caught halfway between salt and fresh water, gasping to death on the beach. How melodramatic. Like the salmon, I can survive that change of environment. My grief is struggling against its own death. I am ready to let it go.*

She freed herself and walked to her Datsun, politely offering a ride to anyone who needed it. Ruth came with her, quiet on their way into Vancouver. Brook was grateful for her silence. It felt generous and more communicative than talking would have been.

At Broadway and Arbutus, Brook dropped Ruth off. She watched Ruth run up to her storefront apartment, wave from the entrance. Her brown-yellow eyes cryptic in the mirror, Brook released the clutch and sped into the night.

With an armload of books, Brook left the library, walking into a drenching February rain. She ran towards her Datsun, dumped the stack of books unceremoniously into the back seat. Rain slashed down, obliterating anything beyond the windshield. She decided to warm the car and wait for a break in the weather.

Condensation and the mere act of breathing created a thin film on front and rear windows. She turned on the defrost, confident that the heater would soon dispense with the misting. Beneath the overhead light she read. Patience, however, did not stop the rain. If anything, the storm worsened.

With a sigh she reached for her wet poncho. The cafeteria lights glimmered directly to the right, guiding her race through the quadrangle. Her feet were soaking well before she reached the entrance, as were her cotton slacks from the knees down.

Obviously her entrance had coincided with break time. She joined a line snaking slowly towards the cash register. Balancing a small container of peach yogurt and a black coffee, she found an isolated table.

A brightly coloured poster on the bulletin board caught her eye. "Woman to share home with woman and two children, ages twelve and eight. Private entrance, room and bath. Ideal for student; non-smoker preferred. Located in Kitsilano; close to beach. $300 a month; laundry facilities included."

Three hundred dollars a month? That kind of rent might make it possible to lease the word processor she wanted. And here was her opportunity to live with young children. Would the children be noisy or go through her files and notes? Deliberately she stretched out her legs. No purpose would be served if she invented roadblocks. This home might or might not be appropriate to Brook's needs. If it were not, she must only be more specific in what she visualized. She believed in Wishcraft, if Tracy did not.

Finally the rain abated. In wet shoes and slacks, Brook was chilled and impatient to be home. Almost as an afterthought she copied down the telephone number on the poster, along with its invitation to "contact Lila" afternoons between four and six o'clock. What the lady in Kitsilano would think about "exposing" her children to a lesbian Brook did not care to worry about.

While she warmed the car Brook became aware of the whine of an ignition, of light pouring from the open door of a dark blue Volvo. A woman got out to look under the hood, then scanned the parking lot for assistance.

"Dead battery?" Brook queried.

Cloaked in rain gear, the woman nodded. "I have jumper cables if you would — ?"

"I would." Brook angled her Datsun towards the raised hood. Not wanting to lose her battery in the process of assisting someone else, she got out to supervise the process of attaching the cables. But there was no fumbling; quick, able hands connected both batteries. In a moment, the ten-year old Volvo was humming.

In a gesture that Brook found both vulnerable and endearing, the woman ran her agitated hands through short, windswept hair. Sounding rueful, she said: "I've been meaning to replace the battery. I never make time to do it."

Brook grinned. "Sounds like your battery is making the time." Briefly the woman held out her hand. A firm handshake and she got into her car.

Suddenly reluctant to part from her, Brook placed her arm on the car door. "Should I follow you for a while?"

"No. I'll be fine." The woman's smile was businesslike, but somehow it reached into Brook, made her feel that her lungs were expanding. Something about her seemed gentle and strong and familiar.

For a moment Brook hesitated. "You're researching Anaïs Nin. I've hunted down references for you at the library."

Humour tranformed the woman's narrow face. "You've got me indexed by subject matter, I see. Research must be getting to me. I dreamed about you handing me books that went all the way to the attic."

Brook grinned. "Maybe that's why you have battery problems. Yours needs recharging."

Lightly, a gloved hand rested on Brook's bare skin. "Thanks for your concern. And for your help. Good night." Like a garage door her expression closed.

Clearly dismissed, Brook stepped away from the car. The woman signalled her way out of the parking lot, leaving Brook staring after her Volvo like a gawky kid. Embarrassed, Brook got into her sedan. For a brief time their routes coincided. Then the woman signalled a turn onto Macdonald and her lights faded into distance.

Loneliness became a passenger in Brook's car. Briefly met on a rainy night, a woman had touched her hand and activated her need for companionship. Her mouth crinkled. For most of this Tracy-less year her libido had been dead. Why did it choose to stir in such foul weather? Obviously she would have to steer a collision course between fantasy and need, until once again someone appropriate was in her life.

In front of her, the road swirled into mist.

CHAPTER TWO

Focusing energy on each of her chakras, Brook chanted her way through vowel sounds — ooo oh aw ah eh ih eee om — until her throat vibrated like a musical instrument. Root chakra. Belly chakra. Solar plexus, heart, throat, third eye, crown and Higher Self. Methodically she cleared her body of pain, anger and fear, ranging through the spectrum of sounds and colours until she felt bathed in the violet ray of well-being. Her spirit eye opened.

In one such meditation, Brook had received her name. She was to be fluid in the world and non-resistant. As water wears away rock, so she must be, finding her way over and under and around obstacles. She wanted abundance — health and energy, loving, supportive friends and the rewards of creative work. None of those things required an imposition of her will, a fearful bulldozing, a pushing against a life force that could not be trusted. Like water, all things flow and shift. Brook did not have to be afraid that change would carry her hard against rocks.

Finally she was done. Getting up from her cross-legged position on the floor, she flexed her knees. Now from a place of power she could call Lila and enquire about the room in Kitsilano.

The telephone was answered by a young girl, who noisily put down the receiver and picked it up again. Almost irascibly she said: "Mom's cooking. Is this about the ad?"

With a distinct smile in her voice, Brook said: "Yes. Is the room still available?"

"Mom says — Mom! Please take this call. I can't rent the room, you know."

The adult picking up on the call was slightly breathless. "Forgive my bad manners. Cyndi is right of course. You want to talk to me."

"Shall I call back? This is obviously a bad time for you."

There was a pause filled with ambiguity. "No, let's talk now. I'd like someone quiet but not dead. I appreciate that as an adult you have friends, so I can also make a sitting room available."

"That's generous. You'll need references, I suppose."

Lila chuckled. "Why don't we eye one another and decide what we're getting into? How is Thursday evening around seven?"

"Thursday is fine. Oh — my name is Brook Thiebault."

"Unusual names, one so English and one so French ... Sorry. Does that sound rude? We're near the southwest corner of Kits and Macdonald." Lila gave the number and courteously hurried Brook off the line.

Well, Brook thought. *What an intriguing voice, full of sinuous inflections like the slope of muscles in a sun-warmed cat. Interested in me and yet so protective of herself at the same time.*

Lila's home was miles from Brook, but when Thursday came, she decided to bicycle. Between writing and a sedentary job, her muscles felt stiff, unused.

As usual, she found riding through the familiar East End a juxtaposition of opposites: the core of the so-called lesbian "ghetto" existing cheek by jowl with Italian machismo, cappucino shops and pool halls. The East End was made up of unaesthetic warehouses, inner city schools and residences with shrunken lots. Yet every spring, Brook's immigrant neighbours planted gardens, bordering their small, bright houses with flowers and vegetables.

Brook liked their pride, their sharing. It made so much more sense than the pretentious walls of self-sufficiency that she associated with Anglicized Canada. However, Lila seemed very much the Anglo type, private, even if on the phone she had been quite intuitive. Brook was caught between two cultures. Growing up in Alberta as a displaced francophone, she had become almost ashamed of her emotionality, shielding herself from the quicksilver expressiveness of her Latin parents. And no doubt she had become far more like the English, caught up in the mystique of individualism. As she had learned only too well, in isolation there is only isolation, no matter how socially elaborate.

Soon enough Brook was in Kitsilano, gazing at comfortable old homes with columned porches, bay windows and landscaped yards. Given its proximity to various beaches, "Kits" was popular with renters and prices reflected the prestige of living there. So. Either Lila was offering incredibly low rent for the area or she had over-represented what she had to offer and the room was no more than an unfinished basement. That suspicion, however, was given the lie by Lila's voice on the phone. Unless Brook was sorely mistaken, that woman was both accommodating and honest.

In the vicinity of Lila's home were few neighbourhood stores or shopping centres, which was no surprise to Brook. These residents would shop in trendy green grocers and boutiques, or at the farmer's market on Granville Island. For Brook, proximity would require discipline. Set loose in Granville market, she would be tempted to purchase exotic ingredients for recipes from a potpourri of distant lands. She grinned. Exercise on an empty stomach certainly was activating food fantasies.

Not only hunger made her glad to arrive at Lila's. Even inside woolen gloves her hands were cold and damp air was finding its circuitous way through her windbreaker. With a toss of the head she took off her helmet, releasing her brown curls from confinement. Pushing her bicycle, she started up the walk.

Between the cracks in concrete slabs grew straw grass. On broken trellises overgrown with ivy, a few hardy roses struggled to survive the austere breath of winter. The entire yard cried out for a gardener wielding several kinds of tools.

When the door opened, Brook felt a curious lurching of the heart. She was facing the woman whom she had helped in the parking lot. Her surprise was followed by matter-of-fact acceptance. Of course this woman would be Lila.

Lila's expression mirrored a gentle irony. "So Brook Thiebault is the good Samaritan. There's a character reference for you. Please — bring your bicycle into the alcove."

Lila's back, however, was less relaxed than her tone. Brook followed tense shoulders into the living room.

Seated on the carpet behind the pages of an illustrated book about World War II aircraft was a young boy, his bony knees drawn into his abdomen. His hair was black and almost fiercely curly, his skin olive dark even in the midst of winter. At eight years old, he was already large-boned and tall, growing too fast to be graceful. With singular absorption, a pubescent girl chose a record for the stereo. Even from the doorway Brook felt "keep your distance" vibrations hitting her like gravel spun from the wheels of a car. This young woman would take time and patience to know.

Lila introduced them with a wave of the hand. "My offspring, Mark and Cyndi."

Cyndi muttered, cross. "Oh, Mom. You make us sound like fish you spawned."

Stifling a chuckle, Brook managed to draw a suspicious glance from both Cyndi and her mother.

"My apologies," Lila drawled. "I don't mean to make you feel like guppies. Speaking of which, Mark —"

"I fed them, Mom." With a grin and a stretch, Mark put his book aside, preparing to be polite.

So there was an aquarium. And there was most definitely a fireplace. Made of sturdy grey stones, it occupied the centre of the living room and was ablaze with crackling logs. At opposing ends of the mantelpiece were glassblown swans, their curving necks reflecting yellows and reds from the fire.

A grey leather arm chair and a matching sofa graced the hearth, "protected" by a blanket long since thrown askew. Magazines threatened an ornamental vase sitting on an oak coffee table. A single orchid in each mouth, the vase spiralled into an open lemniscate. The room was replete with scattered records, sweaters and hardcover books. A forest of plants provided a panoply of green. In the corner of the living room was an old upright piano. Brook wondered who played and how well.

While Brook evaluated the room Lila waited, quiet. Crisply she asked: "Can I get you a drink? I could make something hot — or join you in a glass of wine?"

Brook drew a breath. If Lila wanted to know whether she drank, both of them should agree there was no problem with that. Though she would have preferred herbal tea, she said, "Wine. Please."

"Sit." Lila offered the armchair, her inflection disarming the ungracious, single word. Brook watched her disappear, then gratefully stretched cold legs towards the fire. On the turntable, Corey Hart began to sing.

"Are you a student?" Mark asked, adjusting a hearing aid. He searched Brook's face for signs of discomfort at his deafness.

Enunciating clearly, Brook said: "No. I'm a writer, Mark."

Spontaneously Mark grinned. "A writer? Of plays? My Dad always goes over scripts with me. When he's home," he added in disgust.

Lila came back with a tray of wine cheese, crackers and grapes. On a wheeled trolley she had stem glasses, a decanter and a pitcher. Silently she offered tomato juice to Cyndi and Mark. "Jack is in Los Angeles, making his rounds at TV studios, " Lila explained. "Mark is not happy about it. The children haven't seen him since Christmas." Gracefully Lila folded her legs beneath her on the couch. So there was a husband.

With a smile Brook reached for the glass in Lila's outstretched hand. "I write nothing so exciting as plays, Mark. Mainly I hunt up old letters and photographs. Right now I'm writing about my father, who was an immigrant farmer in Alberta."

Mark pondered. "I like history. If someone can make it seem real."

Brook laughed. "I know. It's like understanding that your parents were once children. That doesn't seem real either, does it?"

Cyndi twittered. "That is hard to imagine. Why would you *want* to write about your father, anyway?"

"Because I always thought of him as my father, not as a person. Now I have all kinds of questions I wish I had asked, about who and what mattered to him outside the family. I thought time began for everyone in the year I was born."

"Hmm." Lila said. "I wonder how much of our lives go by, before we're able to analyse our own experiences to others. Perhaps your father could not easily have answered those questions. However. The children are used to leaving Jack alone when he's working. In this house we respect a closed door, don't we, Cyndi?"

The girl shrugged. A current of strain between mother and daughter worried Brook. If she did move in, could she comfortably provide a buffer zone to each of them, some way of mediating without interfering in what was essentially none of her concern? Lila's brows arched. Some of Brook's sympathies must have spoken through the silence.

"You have a grant, I assume, that will allow you to quit your job at the library?" she asked.

Brook sipped. The wine was highly palatable and chilled. "Yes," she shivered. Contemplatively, she circled the rim of the glass with her finger, unaware that the gesture was sensual. With a click Lila set down her glass, her grey eyes the colour of wet slate. Abruptly she asked: "Would you like to see the room?"

The air was so charged that Brook wanted to ease Lila into the armchair. Her solicitude made Brook feel comical. Lila's demeanour did not encourage familiarity. In that regard Cyndi and her mother were alike — fierce and protective. Adolescent pudginess and her explorations with make-up might speak to the girl in Cyndi, but there was a core in her that was like iron being slowly tempered. In Lila the tempering process was a lot further along.

As if he were Brook's contemporary, Mark said: "I'll leave you alone to look at the room. See you down here." Stonily, Cyndi remained where she was.

Brook was aware of the lithe stretch of Lila's muscles taking her effortlessly up the stairs. Her walk made Brook feel transplanted to a still forest glade where light and shadows intermingled with the sound of birds. With an act of will, she focused her attention on the banister. It was made of handcrafted oak, with a dark finish. Through a glass door at the end of the hall, she caught a glimpse of lawn and the sprawling branches of arbutus trees. The ground was littered with dead leaves and peeling bark, but if Lila would allow it, there was room for herb beds. "Do you garden?" Brook asked.

Lila chuckled. "The lawn is wasted on Jack and me, much to the disgruntlement of our neighbours, I might add."

"Would you mind if I were to grow herbs and flowers? Cities make me itch to plant things."

"Perhaps some of your herbs could end up in our salads. With your approval, of course."

Lila opened the door to the East bedroom. The room was high-ceilinged and spacious, huge windows providing natural light. Stained glass made prisms of the sun's dying rays. Oak panels and beams ran from floor to ceiling, the design both simple and grand. Rich, dark shelves waited for books, c.d.'s and tapes. Hooks in the ceiling invited plants. The room felt well-ventilated and quiet.

Quelling her excitement, Brook searched for flaws. She tried the windows. They opened easily and had working security locks. There were several light fixtures in the room and a number of electrical outlets. Brook liked the sturdy appearance of the cream-coloured radiator but wondered if it would make the room overly hot. As though reading her mind, Lila turned on fans in the ceiling. Brook smiled.

Closet space was more than ample. She would probably have to store some of her dishes in there — better to put away the kitchenware than hide her sculpture. The carpet was a neutral colour: Brook would place over it her more colourful Navajo rug. Silently, Lila watched the swift play of expression in Brook's face.

Delighted, Brook said: "I'd like to take it. Unless you need more time to decide?"

Lila seemed oddly chagrined, as if she could not imagine that an adult woman would settle for this. She said slowly: "You do have furniture?"

"Of course."

"Let me show you the sitting room. The room is heated by wood but there is space for a stereo and television." She trailed off as Brook went to stand before the wood heater, placing her hands on the cast iron beast as if she were about to stroke it.

"You'd provide your own wood," Lila said hesitantly. "I know someone you can order it from. The children don't come in here — they find the room depressing."

It was a small room and almost shabby. But Brook's imagination had taken hold. She could place the Kachina sculpture next to her armchair, set up her medicine wheel and cover the walls with Sante Fe tapestries ...

Smiling gently, Lila eased Brook downstairs. "You'd have to share the kitchen of course, so we'll post some sort of schedule. I can clear a few shelves for you. There's a refrigerator in the basement that Jack used to stock the bar, if you want to store your groceries there. I'm sure that the kids would not disturb them in any way." Her voice trailed off.

She led Brook to a well-lit utility room which contained a recent model washer and dryer. Next to it was a rec room with gym equipment and dumbbells. In one corner was a billiard table; along another was a well-stocked bar with arbourite counters flanked by tall, naugahyde stools. Barbershop glass and antique guns lined the wall. The whole basement was too masculine for Brook's liking, but overall she liked what she was getting into.

Lila opened the door to a small bathroom. "There's a shower stall. You could put in shelving for your toiletries. I can't think if there is anything I haven't told you, except about keys and entrances."

Brook felt Lila's hesitation. Perhaps in her enthusiasm for the place she was moving too fast. "Please don't let me hurry you. Would you like to consider other people?"

"Thanks. It's a relief to be given an option. But how dangerous can a librarian be?"

"Lila." Brook felt her pulse accelerate, even though she resented having to put herself at risk. "You should know that I'm a lesbian. Is that a problem for you?"

Lila put up a hand to stop Brook. "No," she said. "My husband is an actor, remember? The theatre is full of gays. I don't expect you to be any more discreet than I would ask anyone to be around children. Affection is a fine thing to see, but I believe sex belongs in private locations. I've taught my children to be aware of sexual overtures from strangers — and from so-called friends. That is the only way I can protect them from harm." She could not conceal a slight shudder.

Sympathetically Brook touched her arm. "Goose walk on your grave?"

"I ... don't understand."

"Did that raise an unpleasant memory? I'm sorry, my question is intrusive."

Lila freed her arm. "No. I'm glad that you're aware of my signals. I don't like living with strangers any more than my children do."

Kindly Brook nodded. "Thanks for your candour. I'll be a friend at a discreet distance, then."

"Is that agreeable to you? People need to know what is expected, if only so they won't be disappointed. If you are, we'll talk about it. Okay?"

No doubt that conversation would be brief, Brook thought. This woman is a small explosion, ticking towards a sudden hour. Why then didn't her alarm bells go off? Because frankly this woman felt like a friend. And Brook trusted her instincts.

"I do have one concern. How often will Jack be here? Your ad said 'woman to share with woman and two children.'"

For a moment Lila's colour flared. "If I didn't understand from my friend Helen how uncomfortable many lesbians are about living with men, I'd find your question way out of line. You know — or you should know — that the room will be available to you for no more than a year. And Jack, well, Jack has the rights of any owner." With her foot she worried the rug. Pluckily she met Brook's eyes. "Nonetheless, he's been absent for all but eleven days in the last six months. Can you live with that?"

Brook grimaced. She shouldn't worry about Lila coming on like gangbusters. It was Brook who was being aggressive now. "Sorry. I'm used to living alone. I'm having transition anxiety."

"I'm anxious, too." Lightly Lila brushed Brook's hand where it rested on the banister, her touch soothing though her eyes were clearly distant. "I hope we both know what we're doing."

Brook echoed her laughter. "I've given you a lot to handle, and you haven't closed me out."

"I admire your honesty — though you encourage me to be just as direct. While we're sharing our 'druthers,' I'm renting the room to one person. I expect to have to deal with only one person, except for occasional overnight guests, of course."

"I have no lover," Brook said clearly. That reality had to stop causing her a flare of denial.

Lila guided her to the kitchen, a large room with a track of spotlights above a counter inlaid with blocks of wood. Part of the L-shaped counter was a breakfast nook featuring several high-backed wooden chairs. The fridge and stove were huge and avocado-coloured. Beside the stove was a unit with a grill and a rotisserie and a mammoth butcher's block, evocative of another century and obviously an antique. Brook stretched out her arms with delight. "It will be good to turn around in a kitchen and not bang into the opposite wall."

Gentleness lit Lila's eyes. She returned Brook to the living room and sat her down to the glass of unfinished wine. "I'd appreciate it if you can stay a couple of hours. I do want all of us to know what we're getting in to."

"I brought my bike light," Brook said. "Sure, I'll stay."

"What kind of bike?" Cyndi asked, without turning around.

Brook chuckled. "It's no Schwinn, although professional racers might get more out of it than I have. Do you race?"

"Yeah," Cyndi said. "To Spanish Banks — when Mom lets me go alone. Why don't you have riding pants?"

"Because I'm not serious enough about racing. You're about my height — would you like to try my bike?"

"Be careful, Cyndi," Lila said sharply. "It's dark outside."

Silently Cyndi nodded at Brook.

"Here. Use my light. But you're being asked not to go far. Okay?"

"I won't," Cyndi sing-songed.

Brook handed over the helmet. "I like riding to Spanish Banks, too, by the way. Why don't we go there sometime. I don't write much past four in the afternoon."

"Alright!" Animatedly the girl tucked her hair under Brook's helmet, hesitated and then hiked up her blue jeans. "Do you like picking shells?"

"Ah! I have a whole collection," Brook laughed. "From the Oregon coastline, from California and from here. I'll show you my local hunting grounds."

"And me!" Mark inserted. Wordlessly, Brook smiled at him.

"Well!" Lila said, when Cyndi had clumped happily down the stairs carrying the bike. "What makes your old bike so special?"

Brook drawled. "The opportunity to get out of the house, of course."

Like six-year olds they stood grinning at one another, sure suddenly that they would become friends.

CHAPTER THREE

"Beloved," Jack's letter brought him suddenly into the room. "What shall I do, darling? I can't hide in L.A. until the Yanks consider me for a big-time role. We need to talk. Fortunately the director wants to film a segment in Tanzania, without me. I can fly to Vancouver and stay for nearly two weeks. Oh, to act like a husband again and to curl up behind you in bed, my hands cupped over your breasts or on the smooth, round curve of your pelvis ...

"You can see that this is the part where television would cut to a fireplace with bright logs burning, or focus on anything but the sight of man and woman exultantly humping. Sex on television has fallen from grace, you know. If American producers become any more repressed, they'll bring back skirts for the legs of pianos.

"Oh, Lila. I can't even write tonight. I feel as though a thousand miles have washed between us. No joke, they have. And I am talking to myself. You know how actors are — we have to play to an audience. However, the last phone bill staggered me.

"You told me in your call that The Lesbian has moved in. My dear, I do hope you're not trying to tell me something. Think of the children and all that. Just teasing. You're so oblivious to the sexual charms of anyone, male or female." *Oh? And how did I become a mother, Jack? A double dose of immaculate conception?*

"I'm making reservations for Easter. That should please the kids. I expect that Adera will sit with them the first night. Oh, that's not fair, is it? Parents can't ever want to be alone. Oh well. If I'm away any longer the kids will have their own social plans. And be taller than I am."

Oh Jack. How can I share this — communique — with Mark and Cyndi? They miss you so desperately and you sound as though you don't even want to see them. And what, pray tell, are you suggesting between the lines — another six months, this time kicking around in Toronto looking for Shangrila? In her temples anger throbbed, spreading almost at once to the back of her skull and settling there. Remember, Lila, you encouraged him. You surely did not believe that it would take less than a year to establish himself elsewhere.

Lila sighed. No. But I also did not realize how hard this would be — to teach days and research nights and "be there" for Cyndi and Mark. I know that I'm resenting Cyndi for resenting me that Jack is not here. I hate how she locks me out. I'm losing my own daughter, losing any bridge I have to reach her. How do I bridge a gap that just keeps widening? Over Spring Break I'll limit the work I do on my thesis. Somehow I'll get close to her again ... And close to Jack? Is he calling me frigid because he's having an affair? If so, this won't be his first ...

Why shouldn't Jack notice that lovemaking was a game she played, in this facetious world that narrowed down to the walls of their bedroom and inevitably to the walls of her vagina? Each time he entered her, she would plan ways to leave him. What she would pack, what kind of note she would leave, if any. Did she expect to vanquish her coldness, to make him oblivious that she was dreaming of ways to be free?

How long had it been since she had fantasized that she was kissing a woman, a very specific woman with Helen's face? Nights of twisted limbs when she had tried to make Jack come or go away or become a shadow or become real and she never knew which. Sometimes the woman, the doppelgänger in her bed, hid behind Jack's hands or his mouth when he discovered with delight how to please her. Unfamiliar to her and terrifying, orgasm was like climbing a dark, spiral staircase to a place where the sun burst inside her. At last she understood why Jack fell so soundly asleep after sex, his mouth relaxed and smiling. What she did not understand was her feeling of guilt. And her aversion to this man whose only crime was loving her.

She had begun to close off the erotic fantasies that included Helen. Surely loving Jack was a simple matter of discipline and fixed intent. And pregnancy. Once conceived, however, Cyndi had taken over her body. She was morning sickness and nausea, acne, skin rashes and swollen ankles. She was watermelon-or-pumpkin hard and round in Lila's abdomen, not to be disguised by artful clothes or wishful thinking. Sudden kicks from within, lower back pain and nights of rolling on the mattress, making Lila feel like a beluga whale trying to find a place to beach.

Nor had Cyndi been a solution to anything. She was just part of a larger and larger problem, a fetus the doctor called She. Lila had begun to fantasize about strangling the baby with her umbilical chord, or drowning her in an amniotic sea. She woke sweating from nightmares and sobbing in Jack's arms.

"It must be awful to feel like your body is being taken over by someone else. Every mother must feel resentful," Jack had reassured her. "You'll love her when she's born — you know you will."

Lila did not know that she would. Guilt expanded with her girth until she was fighting for her life, her umbilical chord stretching like rope around Cyndi's throat. How many hours was it since her water broke, how many dry heaves before Cyndi was born by Caesarean? In her narrow hospital cot, Lila lay swathed in bandages, waiting for the flaps of her stomach to knit together, for the piercing ache in her torn genitals to finally stop. If this was giving birth, she wanted no further part of it.

On her second day in hospital Jack came in bearing flowers, his skin smelling of wine and second-hand smoke. He looked downcast, bleary eyed and rumpled. With tears in his eyes, he whispered: "I am so close to hating myself for having the power to do this to you."

"Wait a minute!" Lila teased. "You're not responsible for a malfunction in my plumbing."

Jack grimaced, his smile inverted like a clown's. "Haw — haw." Impatient, he measured the days until Lila's bandages were removed, following with his fingers the scars which marred Lila's skin. Then, abruptly, he turned on his heels and left the hospital. Hours later he phoned, playing the witty, considerate and self-contained husband. To Lila he sounded tired and very drunk.

For how many months had they danced their elaborate ballet of sexual avoidance? Had Jack wanted to make love Lila would have, for she had no desire to hurt him. But she plainly also had no desire. Being a new mother left her feeling encircled, trapped by routines of feeding and tending a colicky infant. She needed time, to draw towards herself and away from the needs of both Jack and the baby.

Not surprisingly, Jack had an affair. As he put it, "a man needs to feel like a man." Red-faced and stumbling with contrition, he told Lila about sleeping with the female lead in one of his plays. Perversely, she laughed. "That's one way to protect me from pregnancy, I suppose."

With uncustomary frustration, Jack shook her. "Lila. I'm not saying you're to blame for my affair. I'm the one who made the moves. And God knows I won't blame her. She wanted me and she let me know it. But you know things are wrong between us. Damn it, Lila, I don't want to have to leave you. Can we get past this one?"

Eyes smarting, she shrugged away his icy hands. "Because of the child," Lila whispered. "Because of your sense of guilt."

Jack winced, his expression both resigned and sad. "You need my sense of guilt. It protects you from making love with me."

Lila was recalled to the present by Adera's voice in the corridor: her mother-in-law had returned from taking Cyndi and Mark swimming. Quickly she tucked away Jack's letter and said, "Jack is coming home at Easter, for two weeks!" Cyndi's habitual pout reversed itself; Mark whooped outright. "Oh boy!" Then his small face was transformed by disappointment. "You mean he called when we were out?" Hating herself for the deception, Lila nodded.

With an astute glance, Adera gathered up soggy towels and bathing suits, heading wordlessly for the washing machine. When she came upstairs again, Lila had not moved from the landing. In the kitchen Adera put the kettle on for tea. She called, "Are you coming down — or practising suspended animation?"

"Yes," Lila said vaguely. "I've done all I can for one night."

"Good!" Adera Tennant was a young-looking fifty-six year old, thirty pounds overweight for her five-and-a-half foot frame and delicate bone structure. She dressed in clothing of her own design and — at the moment — had jet-black hair which fanned out attractively around her cheeks. As usual, she wore an elaborate necklace, several strands of it wrapped around throat and bosom. Three or four expensive bracelets decorated her wrists. Lila found it astonishing how much Cyndi copied her grandmother's sense of fashion, even allowing Adera to make her clothes. To Lila, the two of them seemed more like mother and daughter than she and Cyndi could ever be. Unfortunately, Adera also gave Cyndi home permanents and helped her apply eye liners and mascara. Lila did not want her daughter to learn so young the ploys of adult sexuality. Surely there would be ample time in Cyndi's life for growing into that.

Having grilled Lila on Jack's plans for Easter, Mark went to his room, to work on constructing yet another mini-mall with his Lego set. Lila heard Cyndi clicking the channel changer, looking for something on television. Cyndi hated sitcoms and called police stories "stupid fender-benders," sneering at the over-use of car chase scenes. Lila sighed. Be that as it may, Cyndi would probably be proud enough to see her father in just such a "fender-bender."

Fondly Adera touched Lila's shoulder. "Well? Tell me. How is Jack — and how are you in this upteenth month of his absence?"

Lila's smile was a thing of smoke and mirrors. "He calls. You must know how he is."

"Evasion?" Adera sing-songed. "Come on. I deserve better than that."

Like a diver risking the bends, Lila plunged into the truth. "He's confused about working in the States. Adera, unless I miss my guess, he wants to live in Toronto, not here."

"Oh. I've heard of grass widows, but this is ridiculous. Jack needs to 'find himself' all right. He needs to find himself without a wife who does his parenting for him." Adera's tone was certainly not that of a doting mother.

"He's an actor, in a crazy country where acting is something people give up with high school." Even to her own ears Lila sounded resigned.

"And what are you giving up? You're thin and the bags under your eyes could be used to carry home groceries. Lila, you've got to stop being Super Woman."

"Stop classes you mean? You know I —"

"Please." Adera waved a hand with eloquent distaste. "Did I ever say that your only career should be motherhood? No, Lila. You've protected Jack since your marriage. You made his career as an actor possible. You also made it possible for Jack to see his children less than a babysitter does. Don't you *want* him home? Isn't it time to make some ground rules?"

The television went off in the living room — was Cyndi listening to her grandmother's voice? "Come on," Lila said guardedly. "I'll show you the cabinet Brook is making downstairs."

"I saw it," Adera said, before she noticed the direction of Lila's glance. Silently she followed her daughter-in-law to the basement.

"And how is *that* working out?" Adera gestured skyward with her thumb. "I assume that your tenant has moved in at last."

"Yes. Would you like to meet Brook?"

Adera obediently re-examined the cabinet. "Sure. It's a tight job. The woman obviously knows how to use a level and a saw."

Lila chortled. "Talk about damning someone with faint praise." In front of the door to the East bedroom, however, Lila's amusement died. Her stomach twisted, as though she had suddenly catapulted from a ride at the fair grounds. Why should it intimidate her to disturb Brook, who was barely five feet tall and had the soft brown eyes of a cocker spaniel? She heard the restful sound of classical music and Brook humming softly. Almost inaudibly, Lila knocked.

Tonight Brook was dressed in faded denim, her jean jacket enlivened by a red cotton shirt. On a silver pendant around her throat was a shela-na-gig, a moon face which Brook had told her was associated with fertility. Surely that was a strange pendant for a lesbian to wear. From the corner of her eye, Lila watched Adera track the walls of Brook's room, looking for clues to the woman's personality. Adera's neck swivelled from Brook's queen-sized futon to her settee with knotted pine arms to the matching chair which fronted Brook's pine desk. At the desk, Adera perched demurely; Lila sat cross-legged on the bed.

Calmly Brook went back to work, placing softcover books on shelves made of interlocking pine planks. The unit, Lila thought, would be as easy to dismantle as it was to construct, a who-cares-how-often-I-move piece. The sound coming from Brook's speakers was superb. Yet it was a portable Panasonic that created the technical effects of stereophonic synthesizers. Lila glanced at her mother-in-law. She felt like a rolling camera on a movie set, following the filmic eye of Adera, recording titles like *Positive Magic, A Book of Pagan Rituals,* and *Ripening: An Almanac of Lesbian Lore and Vision.* When Adera got to the *Holy Book of Women's Mysteries* she glanced towards Lila, who chose that moment to look "casually" around the room. Brook's taste was certainly unusual, from wall-mounted and floor-standing ceramic sculptures of women to Navajo tapestries and a Gitskan button blanket. A white and blue Navajo rug was, quite apparently, another one of Brook's more expensive design choices.

Clustered at Adera's elbow were sheafs of paper and several books of dry research on the subject of Alberta immigrants. A typewriter was conspicuously absent from Brook's desk. Perhaps the machine was still packed in one of several boxes neatly stacked to one corner of the room.

Shyly, Lila asked: "Please tell me to mind my own business if you like, but what are you planning to do for a typewriter, Brook? You do have one?"

Brook grinned. "I have an Olivetti in the repair shop. I keep dreaming that when I pick it up it will have become a computer and I can join the electronic age."

"I have a Macintosh 512K. You're very welcome to use it. For most of your work day, I'm not even home."

Brook crowed. "You have a Mac? That's the kind I dream of using. It's at my level of technological illiteracy. I'd be very happy to reimburse you for materials."

Brook was sun to Lila's heavy rain: faced with the other woman's cheerfulness, Lila felt ponderous and heavy as an old rusted anchor.

"Some dreams come true then. I'm glad to have something to share with you." Aghast at her own gentleness, Lila hurried Adera out of the room. "But we mustn't keep you from unpacking."

Ironically, Brook blew Lila a goodnight kiss from her open hands, as though sending a butterfly into the air between them. Lila felt her ears turn deep red.

In the corridor Adera breathed: "My dear, is it clear to you that Brook is a lesbian?"

Lila heard Adera through a haze. Part of her was still in Brook's room, not here in the corridor. "Very clear." she said vaguely. "Are you shocked, Adera? Surely she's not the first one you've met."

Exaggeratedly Adera coughed. "She's the first one my daughter-in-law has invited to move in. Have you told Jack about this?"

"Yes," Lila was satiric. "He asked if I was trying to tell him something."

Adera turned to look at her. "Are you? And moreover, Lila, what are you telling your children?"

A drumbeat of anger pulsed in Lila's head. Stiffly she said, "I'm telling them that sexual preference is not a thing to fear. Brook is a woman just as we are. I refuse to perpetuate attitudes of repression and shame about sex. Feelings are natural, Adera."

"Lesbian feelings?" Adera persisted.

"Should I not rent to her because of that? Adera, your family went through Nazi prison camps. What is the difference between Jew or gay-bashing?"

Brook, on her way to the washroom, paused, irresolute. One look at her vulnerable mouth and Lila knew that she had heard some, if not all, of the unfortunate exchange.

Instantly she acted. "Brook, can I disturb you once I see Adera out?"

"Ah. My exit cue," Adera said, shamefaced. "Don't worry, Lila, I know how to find the door. I'll talk to you on Monday. We are still meeting for lunch?"

"Umph," Lila conceded and returned to Brook's room. Horrified that Brook had overheard, she paced, until with a playful push Brook seated her on the futon. Her expression attentive, Brook sat beside her. The woman's energy field made Lila tingle. It was not that Brook was sitting too close but that her charisma was overpowering.

"How much of that did you hear?" Lila asked tremulously.

Brook's eyes twinkled. "Enough to know that I'm supposed to be imperilling your children. Forget it, Lila. You defended me admirably."

"Adera isn't a bigot. She's just frank; you'll see. She'll get to know you and like you as I do." Suddenly she felt like the most gushy child.

Brook sobered. "I'm so matter-of-fact about being myself that I forget how volatile that can be."

Lila grimaced. "Adera's worried about me. She thinks I've been alone too long."

Brook turned slightly pink. "Do you mean what I think you mean?"

"Yes. I might react to the charms of anyone, according to her. But that's not all I wanted to discuss with you. I know you don't want to hear this, but Jack's coming home for two weeks around Easter."

"Thanks for telling me," Brook clearly looked worried and vexed.

Feeling like a clumsy fool, Lila whispered, "We won't interfere with your writing, I promise. I know you've already lost a week to moving in."

"Tell me, Lila," Brook asked with an almost scientific curiousity, "why do you give a damn how Jack affects me?"

"Because you made your conditions clear. I thought I could abide by them. But this is not only my decision to make."

Like a rainbow Brook's thoughts ranged through her face. Then she said the most surprising thing. "Don't give it another thought. I'm sure Jack's a fine man, Lila, or you wouldn't be with him."

"He's — How can I prepare you for him? He's theatre, the clown of the ancient Tarot deck. You know what I mean?"

Nodding, Brook pointed to an illustrated book on the Tarot. For a while Lila flipped through it, absorbed and quiet. Her angst was suddenly gone; she felt warmed by Brook's serenity. For some reason, that thought made her anxious again.

"I should leave you to unpack — unless I can help?"

Silently Brook accepted the offer. From a box marked "altar" Brook removed candlesticks, a silver goblet and two busts, one made of plaster and one of teak. Squatting, Lila puzzled over them.

"That's Pele, the Hawaiian goddess of volcanoes. She's very powerful, since She rules visions and sudden changes."

Lila shivered. "I'm not much for exterior gods. I think God is within, if He is anywhere at all."

"I agree. We give everything whatever meaning it has, both words and objects."

"I guess so. Though that makes spirituality so private and personal."

Brook placed a bright serape over her Rosewood table. Then she set Artemis on what was apparently to be her altar. She took the plaster bust carefully in her hands. "The Goddess of the moon. You probably know

Artemis as the 'flake' who hunted Acteon with bow and arrow for spying on her while she bathed?"

Lila chuckled. "Yes — I've always thought that was a heavy toll to pay, even for voyeurism."

Brook sounded whimsical. "Well, compare that to how Catholics feel today if a woman enters the inner sanctum, where she is still forbidden. In an age when women were the spiritual leaders, men were similarly allowed in the temples only after rites of purification. Acteon didn't take the time to purify himself, which would be a little like a Catholic swallowing the Host without going to confession."

"Oh!" Lila said. "Now I understand."

Again Brook reached inside the cardboard box, this time emerging with an Oriental statue carved from the bone of a fish. "Meet Kwan Yin. Yin means woman, while the word Kwan means earth. So we have Woman as Earth Mother, sometimes pictured riding on a dolphin. Kwan Yin wanted to become a nun, but her father insisted that she marry. Grudgingly he sent her to a temple hoping that a dose of poverty and hard labour would change her foolish notions. When she grew to like the austere life of the temple and wanted to remain there, he killed her. Needless to say, she became the Goddess of Mercy."

"I suppose she learned the need for mercy from her father," Lila mused. "There does seem to be such a male attitude of force towards people of other races, women and the environment. War just caps off the ideology of conquest. I honestly don't know if men can change. And I'm raising a son, in a manner of speaking. Sometimes I think the world is raising him for me no matter what I do … " Heavily she sighed. "Anyway, you were talking about your altar."

Sympathetically Brook nodded. "Sensitizing Mark isn't all up to you, Lila. Soon enough your son will be responsible for making his own choices." Without further explaining that remark, Brook set out small shells, dried flowers, acorns and the feathers of eagles, arranging the objects around the circumference of a brown plate. "The altar must contain something representing the four elements — fire, air, earth and water, which are essential to life. I've never lost my respect for Nature's ability to move and shake me if I do not honour her."

Between manners and honesty Lila hesitated. "That sounds … primitivist. Isn't that like saying that floods or earthquakes can be controlled by observing certain rituals?"

"Perhaps. But then scientists observe an equal number of rituals — commonly held agreements about the nature of time and space and matter. The new physics calls into question everything we term either real or imaginary." In a smooth motion Brook rose from her knees. "There is a spirit in things. A life force in rocks and water and trees. I am part of these things. I am born and I will die. Perhaps that is the only knowledge worth having. It certainly makes humanity more humble."

"You're very eloquent, Brook," Lila said weakly. "But what kind of world would exist without some agreements about the nature of reality?"

"I'd like to find out," Brook said softly. She placed candlesticks on the altar, her expression speculative.

Lila snorted. "Each of us learns that a stove is hot, with no mass delusion involved. Oh, I know: how would I explain those who walk through fire without getting burned?" Hollowly she laughed, getting up from the bed. "But I'm intruding. Thank you for sharing your altar with me."

Brook's tone was firm. "Lila, you don't know how to be intrusive."

Feeling ridiculously flattered, Lila struggled to control a broad grin. "You must meet Helen. She meditates, too."

Brook nodded. "Meditating with someone else can be powerful."

Lila carried Brook's quicksilver smile with her into the corridor. The faint scent of Brook's cologne teased her, an aroma as light and heady as the dying strains of Vivaldi.

Her last glimpse was of Brook turning to her altar and reverently lighting beeswax candles.

CHAPTER FOUR

Immersed in writing, Brook became aware of an ache in her wrist, of a dull throb of pain along the nerves of her neck. Rotating her arms and shoulder blades, she bent and stretched until her body unclenched. It was definitely time to end the long, quiet pattern of her day. Perhaps Cyndi would go riding with her.

Doors opened and closed. There was the sound of running water and laughter she did not recognize. As she reached the landing the piano sprang into a medley of pieces from "Oklahoma," the light-handed touch of keys counterbalanced by someone's slightly more hesitant stroke. Splashing water on her face, Brook hummed along. "Oh, what a beautiful morning ..."

At the archway to the living room, she paused. Cyndi was hunched over the keyboard with a woman whose hair reminded Brook of a raven's plumage in the sun, shining blue-black. Her face and neck in profile were slender and graceful, her eyes dark blue. Something in her was poised, as though her muscles would be comfortable only in motion.

Smiling, Brook tiptoed to the kitchen where she found Lila putting together a tray of drinks, her sandy hair gathered in a cameo on her neck. Sometimes Lila looked Grecian, the curve of her chin and brow a sculpted setting for cool and noble eyes. The sight of Lila evoked some awkwardness in Brook. Both of them acted a little like clumsy children in the presence of one another.

"Oh, good, you *are* home." Lila sounded animated and warm. "You were so quiet I wasn't sure. Now you can meet Helen. She's here, giving Cyndi a piano lesson."

"So *that's* the Helen of myth and legend," Brook said lightly. "She's very beautiful."

"Yes." Lila sighed almost wistfully. "She is."

Brook wanted to ask if Lila believed herself to be less beautiful than Helen. But Lila was wary of compliments, no matter how sincerely they were meant. So she said simply: "I was going to ask Cyndi to ride with me. I guess she'll be occupied for a while."

"Quite a while — she'll be staying overnight at a friend's. Oh, by the way, I've invited Helen for dinner." Whimsically she laughed. "Mark tells me he won't eat if you're not invited, too."

Brook chuckled. "Yeah, I arm wrestled him the other night and let him win. He owes me. Do I have time to cycle? Writing stiffens me more than I like."

Lila grimaced. "I know. Stiffness is the body's revenge on us for living in our heads. By all means, ride. I have the whole evening to do as I like."

Brook's fingers identified ropes of tense muscle in Lila's shoulders. For an instant Lila stiffened beneath her touch, then she let her shoulders relax. Briefly, Brook patted her. "You and I have a date tonight for a massage, and no argument." Then she went to free her bicycle from the porch railing.

For nearly an hour Brook rode, farther and farther past Spanish Banks. Leaving her bicycle chained to a young maple, she was drawn to the shore by the familiar sound of raucous crows fighting over carrion. With each incoming wave, they hopped and fluttered into the air.

The ocean was high with the odour of dead fish and seaweed. On the sand were the shells of mussels, littleneck clams and rose tellins. Desultorily Brook sorted through them, a beachcomber missing the flotsam of tidal pools and mud flats and the more stony beaches of the Pacific shoreline. Here were small purple shore crabs and the common ochre starfish, no chitons or bright red and yellow anenomes, no pale moon jellyfish, no wheeling sunfish or cream-coloured moonsnails ...

Just over her head noisy crows swooped, stealing a rock crab from the beak of an irate gull. *Crows.* Brook felt a tingling across her heart, like a tear line opening scar tissue.

> ... Her mother lay beneath the willows by the creek. From a distance her body looked like a Raggedy Ann doll flung casually aside in play. Sounds carried to Brook, tearing sounds interspersed with screams of rage, like the sound of a bull on a chain. Brook clenched her fists. She could do nothing. Nothing but question her loyalty to her father, whose actions apparently caused such pain.

At fifteen she knew why her mother cried. One evening, while dreaming in a field of wheat, she had awakened to the sound of her father's laughter, to whispers and moans and the rustling of grass. A woman's voice said, "Please, Jean, please don't torture me like this." Brook, who was not Brook then, sat up, about to make her presence known. Her father's hand bared the breast of a woman who lay with neck arched, her hair a tumult of auburn in the setting sun. Elsa. Brook watched his hands descend importunely; the woman's hips rose and there was a patch of black silk discarded in the grass. What Brook saw then was riveted on her consciousness. She sank weak-legged into the grass. With black humour a crow cawed, settling on a willow branch and swaying, finding its equilibrium.

Growing up on a farm, Brook had not been slow to learn the movements of sex. But this woman was Elsa, her mother's friend, who sang at socials and sitting in the cool evening on the porch told anecdotes, actively encouraging Brook to be a writer. "You really have a way with stories, you know," she said, an animated lilt in her corn-husk voice. And so, dear Elsa, do you, that you so successfully played my mother's friend.

As though she held a mouth full of stones, Brook clamped her teeth around the unwelcome secret. No one noticed that she was stand-offish. They already called her the Lady In the Tower and put her behaviour down to adolescent hormones and to the dreaminess of one who wants to be Someplace — anywhere more romantic than Here.

Sympathy for her mother did not destroy Brook's loyalty to her father. She trusted the open-faced look of him, his flamboyance of voice and gesture. Sensitive about being French, he avoided his own language in order to "Canadianize." But there was no Canadianizing the rhapsody of his Latin blood. He was hot and vital, his body a weaving dance of muscles and exuberance. Like her mother, Brook loved the dark-eyed brash boy in him, even the impulsive anger which flared like a grass fire through their noisy and active lives.

Would her mother have understood a brief affair? Would that have been easier for her to accept, her husband's repentance and a break with Elsa; painful recognition of treachery from a so-called friend, given up to "save" a marriage? A marriage which perhaps should not have been saved at all. Her parents' midnight confusion:

tears and half-smothered recriminations hurtled at one another under cover of the dark.

But giving up his mistress had not been her father's choice. Nor Elsa's. Not one quarter of a mile from the house, her father constructed a cabin into which he helped Elsa to move. In a few brief months there was a child, the sound of her crying carried on the wind to the main house. The baby had her father's long brown eyelashes and wavy hair — his face replicated down to the shape of nose and mouth.

Brook's mother, always emotionally effervescent, did what she could to control the situation. She went mad. One afternoon, burning with fever, Brook asked a neighbour to drive her home from school. The house was eerily dark and still. Dreading what she would find, Brook followed her inner radar to the creek. She found her mother lying beneath pussy willows, one arm in the water bleeding red onto the rocks. The water babbled oblivious, Spring run-off from the mountains. Her mother was not dead. But they took her away for a long time.

Impatiently Brook raised her head. She was no longer that girl tormented by adults who were tormented themselves, setting the forces of the heart in motion like the grinding cogs of a giant wheel rolling inexorably over Brook's life. Her father claimed the freedom to love as he would. For that her mother collected emotional ransom, holding her husband responsible for the horror of her own imaginings. How harshly Brook judged her. Until Tracy taught her compassion for the woman in herself who was her mother's daughter.

... Tracy telling Brook: "You leave me alone too much, when you know there are problems between us."

Brook's teasing response, insouciance constructed in front of pain. "You mean I could have prevented Arlan, if only I had forced you to be with me?"

"Yes. No. Do you realize how much I resent you for being so reasonable about everything?"

"Is love supposed to be unreasonable? I want you to talk to me, even about difficult things. Tracy, you don't need to pretend to feel what you don't."

Tracy gazed out the window, her back to Brook. "If you 'need' to be so deliberate about things, perhaps we should part." There was a jagged edge to her voice.

Soon enough Tracy went away with Arlan. All that weekend Brook dealt with her fears about losing Tracy's love, yes and her jealousy too. In the darkness jealousy was hydra-headed, tentacles reaching out to engulf her. Rather than lie awake she went to a midnight feature of The Rocky Horror Picture Show. For however long it lasted, she enjoyed the songs and the raunchy sexuality of it. More in touch with her sense of life she returned home, only to find Tracy making love with Arlan in the bed they shared.

Did Tracy want Brook to lose respect for her, to think her insensitive, arrogant? Did she need to hurt Brook in order to leave her? Or finding the house empty so late had she merely assumed that Brook was away for the weekend?

Through a haze of tears, Brook fumbled with the lock on her bicycle. Nothing was pointless, certainly not pain or grief or the difficult, necessary letting go. Memory was a crucible, distilling events and emotions into finer and finer powder. Perhaps that was why Brook wrote at all, to leave her marks in the sand before the incoming tide took everything away, including her fallible memory. She pedalled fast, lungs and legs stretching with the effort to leave her despairing thoughts behind her on the beach.

She came home to the sight of Mark throwing horseshoes on the lawn. From the porch she said: "Can't wait for spring, can you, Mark?"

"No." Concentration puckered his mouth. He threw one shoe, then another. Both clanked as they hit the peg.

With a grin he handed her the horseshoes, waiting through her trial throws. When she began to hit the peg, he murmured, "All right!" and reached to take his turn. They played until Brook became aware of feeling chilly. She was wet with perspiration from her reckless ride. Impulsively she put her arm around Mark's shoulders, then walked back to the house.

From the window, Helen murmured, "Look at this scene of domesticity."

"I know," Lila whispered. "She's quite wonderful with the kids."

"She looks like one herself," Helen giggled. Brook had a youthful stride and a curious and open expression that Helen did not associate with adults. Her mouth looked both puzzled and expectant, a volatile chameleon mouth which spoke to her wordlessly from across the yard.

It was a while before Brook joined them. She showered and changed, feeling oddly hermetic, until guilt about not helping prepare dinner drove her to the kitchen.

Gaily, Lila introduced her. "At last. This is my friend, Helen Winters. Brook Thiebault."

Helen's smile was winsome. "Lila has been raving about you."

"And vice versa. I hope we can live up to our mutual reputations." Brook shook Helen's hand, liking the firmness of her clasp.

Helen chuckled. "I don't worry about living up to mine. It's not my fault that Lila has an elevated opinion of me." Her voice was rich as chocolate, a seductive, intriguing voice. On the trail of her painful memories, Brook wasn't ready to be seduced.

Lila smiled calmly. "Would you like a drink?"

"Do you have Scotch and soda? It's by no means my 'usual,' but I'd like something stiff right now."

Lila placed ice in several glasses. "You had a rough day?"

"Gruelling," Brook moaned. "I've been thinking about mistresses and wives and love triangles, my own and others."

Helen laughed. "Well! What an icebreaker you are. Never mind the preliminaries, like how-are-you and what-do-you-do-for-a-living. Lila tells me that you're writing about your father and your life in the midst of his ménage à trois. What did you feel for him, sympathy or antagonism?"

Brook's mouth made an O. "Both. Though he needed my sympathy more — he was caught between a rock and a hard place."

Helen raised an eyebrow, quizzically. "What about your mother? Pardon me but your dad sounds like a fucking opportunist. Pun intended. But then I tend to judge men harshly."

Brook made a face: how like peat was the taste of Scotch. "I'm still mulling about my mother, and about people in general who try to force others to be faithful. What makes people stay with someone — love and guilt, duty and habit — and the fear of going loveless if one leaves." Brook sighed. "Leaving takes courage. I wonder if my mother had it."

Lila's brow furrowed. "But isn't a triangle the interim stage between one coupling and the next?"

"For my parents, perhaps it should have been. But nothing is inevitable. Maybe ... maybe there's a simple way to love more than one person at a time, if only we had the heart for it."

"Maybe. But any triangle I've seen is held together by two people desperately trying to win the love of the same person. I call that a loaded experiment," Helen said bluntly.

Brook made a wry face. "Hey. Love is a loaded experiment. It's painful to be honest, especially when a lover is not meeting our needs."

Lila's brows wrinkled. "You think love is cumbersome, then. A liability, to be endured only when other options are in place?"

"In some respects, everyone is a liability. We all come to one another dragging our very noisy pain. We can choose to shake it like a child's rattle, hold it up to everyone — until one day we finally put the pain behind us like that child's rattle. At some stage we commit to be happy, no matter what, or we continue to worry our misery like dogs with a bone. At least my father took some risks, knowing he had everything to lose and nothing clear to gain."

Lila looked frankly perplexed. "Why would your father try to keep everyone happy in a situation like that? Leaving his wife would have been simpler, and certainly more honest."

"What about jealousy?" Helen exploded. "I don't know about you but I'm plainly possessive about lovers." Her down-to-earth pragmatism made Brook and Lila chuckle.

Brook felt drawn into Helen's blue eyes as though she had just entered a long cave. She struggled for words to break the spell. "Jealousy. All that serves to do is obscure the fact that we have a whole range of other choices. Like understanding and listening. And a little creative compromise."

"Brook — " Lila looked clearly baffled. "Aren't you being idealistic? Maybe that would work for couples without children. But children don't understand adult complexities."

"I disagree, Lila," Brook said gently. "Children learn to be as fragile or as resilient as we expect them to be."

Helen drummed softly on the counter. "So we're children, but we're conditioned to monogamy. Anything else has the potential for disaster."

Brook poked at her drink with a swizzle stick. "So does life. Does that mean we should avoid living?"

Helen's expression was comical. Then she said roguishly, "Hmm. Lila, are you free later tonight?"

Lila swatted her arm, vigorously. "You're presuming on our friendship."

Laughing, Helen set down her wobbling glass and cradled Lila, rocking her gently back and forth. How beautiful they were together, Brook thought, this striking dark-haired woman and Lila with her hair the colour of a sandy beach and eyes the exact shade of a storm cloud. With equal curiosity, Lila returned Brook's glance.

Brook paced to the window away from those eyes and watched Mark, who was still playing on the lawn. She was annoyed at herself for being attracted to a heterosexual woman and annoyed again that she could not just accept the flow of her feelings. "May I call Mark in now? I think he's dressed too lightly. The sun is going down."

Lila heard the closure in Brook's voice. "Yes," she said. "Call him in. He'll need a shower, and I need some help with making the salad, Helen Winters."

"Aye, aye captain." Helen saluted smartly.

Brook drew the task of stirring the clam and mushroom sauce, adding sage and butter and milk until her mind was clear again.

With a flourish, Lila served escargot garnished with baked parmesan, a large Greek salad and home-made fettucine al dente, with Brook's sauce. Not surprisingly, Mark refused the escargot and picked through the fettucine, leaving his clams to one side of the plate but eating the mushrooms. His appetite returned, however, for the last course — he ate the apricot mousse with alacrity. Then he made himself a peanut butter sandwich, cutting up bananas to put on top of it. In silent commentary, the three women raised their eyebrows. Brook swallowed a smile. Mark might have food fetishes, but he didn't monopolize the conversation or demand undue attention. And in the absence of his father he might well have done more "acting out."

After dinner, Mark challenged them to a game of Scrabble, and Brook was hard put to match his moves on the board. Drawn to this peaceful boy-man, she put her arm around his shoulders. She did not notice Helen's talking eyes, nor her sidelong glance at Lila. Nor did Lila notice. Her gaze was fixed on Brook.

Hmm, Helen thought. Could Lila love a woman? That was an old and dangerous fantasy on her part. Perhaps Lila trusted the language of the body more than she trusted words, but her attentiveness to Brook — or to Helen — had nothing to do with desire, though to Helen in her loneliness it might seem so. Still, Lila seemed less quiet and controlled than she had been for most of the past year. It might help her to have someone in the same house, since she didn't take much time to reach out. She was far too responsible for her children and her work, and far too indifferent to her own needs for renewal. Brook, with her unconventional attitudes, might help Lila to focus more on her private needs.

Brook. What a name. Helen was determined to listen to her in the same way she listened to water — quietly — until she heard its voice chorusing. Coursing. Brook seemed so clear, but she might be as emotionally illusive as a fish gleaming silver in the depths of a pool. Espousing sexual "freedom" usually meant that someone felt unable or unwilling to make a clear commitment. The thought stirred Helen to an odd disquiet.

CHAPTER FIVE

In a straight-backed chair her mother sat, agitatedly rocking back and forth, a plump hand cradling her missing breast. By the dresser stood her father in carpenter's overalls, deep lines carved into his face. He had the crow's feet and wrinkles of a man ravaged by strong sunlight and long resentment.

"You have no business in my life anymore," Lila said. "I told you never to come here again."

Her father gazed at the steel tips of his work boots, mumbling without moving his lips. "There is something wrong with you or I wouldn't be here."

Telepathically Lila answered him. "No. There is nothing wrong with me. You're the defective one."

Her mother motioned from her breast to Lila's, the gesture both a warning and an attempt to console. Then she took her husband's arm and they faded from the room, worried ghosts on a mission peculiar only in the caring they revealed for her.

The strength of Lila's panic awakened her. Like an insect with antennae, she felt her way through the darkness. On the street there was the momentary gleam of headlights. Tires whooshed on pavement; she heard rain in the leaves. Chill night air swept from the open window towards her large and solitary bed, settled in her hair and made the tip of her nose cold. The terror of her dream made her reluctant to get up and close the window. Impatient, she switched on the bedside light.

Despite the illumination in the room, some malevolent energy hovered, permeating her bed with a sickly sweet odour reminiscent of the living carcass of her mother rotting from the breast inward to her vital organs. Dully Lila became aware that her hand was clutched fearfully around her own breast, as if to protect herself from the harm of that time that festered still, that time of decaying flesh and unspoken blame ... Suddenly she felt an overwhelming need to cleanse herself from some extraordinary grittiness of the soul.

Needles of water drove into Lila's pores. Jostled awake she adjusted the faucets, the concentrated spray of cold water massaging her neck and shoulders. She felt uneasy, as though she had forgotten something that she must remember. Night images came like pieces of a jigsaw puzzle, the colours muted into one another and indecipherable. Shampoo running towards her eyes, Lila swabbed despairingly at her brow. *They weren't really here*, she thought. *They're dead and all that is behind me, the abuse and my mother's silence* ...

The dream had played on her major fears like an illusionist works an audience. Her fear of dying, cancer transmitted from her mother's amputated breast down through the chromosomes to claim her daughter. And the old red fear — that to go to sleep at all meant subjecting herself to attack and injury. More than two decades later, her father still inserted himself into her bedroom, although now, at least, she had found the defense of words: she had told him to leave, that there was nothing wrong with her. If only she could believe that when she was awake.

She towelled herself vigorously, glad for the streaks in the mirror which prevented her from reading the expression in her eyes. In the bedroom, she donned powder blue slacks with a white belt and a shirt with blue flowers which she knew hurried the season. This morning she needed something as bright and promising as spring.

In the corridor was the smell of cinnamon and the whirr of a juicer. On tiptoe Brook stood, gazing through the kitchen window at something in the yard. Sunlight haloed her hair, which glinted auburn red. Impulsively, Lila touched her shoulder. Brook flashed the crooked grin that tugged at one side of her face more than the other. To Lila she looked tender and inordinately safe.

Lila still was not used to having alternate mornings free from getting the children ready for school. Why Brook wanted to spell her off Lila did not know, especially since that meant accommodating Cyndi's morning grumpiness and Mark's absent-minded search for something not totally inappropriate to wear. Brook rose early to meditate, she said, and liked to begin her day in the half-dawn. The result was a household smelling of slow-baking granola or muffins, mouth-watering aromas which titillated Lila into a natural waking. When the school board did not call her to substitute, Lila now had the luxury of extra time in bed. How Brook kept the children out of her room in the morning — and quiet — Lila could not imagine. But no longer was she jarred into waking by the ring of an alarm. Brook's sharing of "school detail" reminded Lila a little of the better part of living with Jack.

"Grapefruit juice?" Brook asked, pouring herself a glass.

Appreciatively Lila murmured, "You've got me totally spoiled. I'll never drink concentrate again."

Once again the grin sparkled in Brook's eyes. "It's my neurosis — to disarm criticism before it happens."

"In the way of all women," Lila said wearily.

Brook fingered the smudges under Lila's eyes. "Didn't you sleep well? It isn't like you to be cynical."

Fiercely, Lila rubbed at her cheekbones. "I had unwelcome visitors last night."

"I didn't hear anyone." Brook sounded puzzled.

Lila put a muffin on the plate. It was still warm and bursting with blueberries, making her mouth water like an eager dog's. "Only memories. No one of flesh and blood. Forget it, Brook. Sometimes mornings make me feel old."

Hands cradled Lila's temples. "Mornings make you feel old, or memories do?"

Beneath Brook's touch Lila stiffened. An unfamiliar current of desire stirred in her genitals, made her tone sharp. "Oh, Brook. You're such an earth mother. I'll bet you even bake bread."

"Sticks and stones," Brook said calmly, pressuring the medians of Lila's skull. Hands cupped her head at the diagonal, lifted her by the chin until Lila felt a bone snap into place.

The jagged ache dulled. Lila had the sense that her body had given away a secret. "Why are the people suited to motherhood the ones who don't have children?" she asked, querulous.

"Because the child care I do is not obligatory."

Lila opened her eyes to the sight of carnations on the counter, pink and white and vivid red blooms in the midst of winter. The flowers, like Brook's voice, reeked of health and optimism. Lila inhaled their fragrance. "Motherhood may be its own reward," Brook was saying, "but no woman believes she does it well enough. At least Jack is coming home for a while. That should take some pressure off you."

"You make him sound like a premiere," Lila grumbled. "Coming soon to your local theatre."

Brook continued the slow exploration of Lila's skull. In a few moments she stepped back, her tone too polite. "I'm ready to get to work, I think. You're welcome to the coffee."

With difficulty Lila met her eyes, feeling apologetic and disoriented. For an instant the features of Brook's face seemed to reassemble, the eyes mocking and imperious, a face from another dream about a Dutchman who bent to kiss her rudely beneath sprawling, leaf-laden boughs.

Lila shook her head. Brook as an impudent and sexually domineering male. The idea would be laughable, if only Brook's face would stop going into and out of focus like someone reflected in the ripples of a pool.

Brook was staring at her. "Strange," she whispered. "I just saw you as a dark-haired woman with high cheekbones and snapping eyes. You seemed angry."

Lila blurted: "And I saw the Dutchman, again. You know — in the dream I had, where he was striding around the East bedroom and then he turned into you handing me books piled all the way to the ceiling — "

"Well," Brook tried for levity, "if I see him in my room, I'll certainly invite him to leave."

"Unless he's you. Oh, I don't know what I'm saying. You must have slipped drugs in the juice."

"Don't blame drugs," Brook was wry. "Reality can be very flexible."

"So is madness," Lila replied.

"Lila, my mother spent years in a psychiatric ward. People call one another 'mad' at the slightest provocation. I don't."

Lila turned to look at her. "Brook, I'm sorry. My mother was one of those people who used the word too often. She made me feel borderline, especially when she denied what I saw even when it was there plainly to be seen ... " She bit her tongue, which suddenly felt huge in her mouth.

Keen-eyed, Brook nodded. "What did you see, Lila? Sometimes you remind me of a cat thinking he's invisible behind the leaves of a plant. Are you sure you're as hidden from view as you pretend to be?"

Instinctively Lila recoiled. She did not enjoy being rendered transparent by Brook's psychic radar. It felt too much like voyeurism into her soul.

She was literally saved from responding by the jarring ring of the phone. Brook answered it and handed the receiver to Lila. "You asked me to call the next time I design an Alpine garden," Adera said. "Can you meet me at Murray's Landscaping?"

Lila glanced helplessly at Brook, feeling like she was being torn in two directions by wild brahma bulls. How could such disparate realities of past and present share yoke and rein? Better to step carefully around moss and bracken in some nursery than explore these weed-filled gardens of the mind. "Sure. Do I meet you there or —"

"Yes. You do remember how to get here?"

"I think so." Lila checked out a landmark with Adera and hung up. Absent-mindedly, she slipped into a plaited corduroy jacket and located the keys to her car. She gazed mutely at Brook, who was herself again, with her lopsided, gentle smile. Like a well-bred princess, Brook waved her hand. "Go."

Feeling unsettled, Lila stumbled away from her.

CHAPTER SIX

Brook decided that she did not like Jack. He was too lean and bronzed and blond. Moreover, his mouth looked indolent and sneering. He treated Brook as though he were enjoying a private joke.

Nor did Lila look happy. If they were having sex, it was alienated sex. Brook found herself saying that to Helen, before she could censor the thought. With both hands, Helen turned Brook towards her. "You sound jealous. Are you?"

To the roots of her brown hair Brook blushed. "No. We just never finish a conversation. Not that Jack has made a difference to that — Lila seems leery about letting people get close. But the other day we had a strange experience. I don't want to wait 'til he leaves to deal with it."

Expressively Helen sighed. "I don't think she wants to slow down long enough to feel. Lila is drifting, Brook. And restless."

"Has she said anything to you about what's bothering her?"

"No, and her body is paying for the silence — that jaw of hers. So what else do you think of the illustrious Jack Tennant?"

Uncomfortably, Brook laughed. "I lied. I *am* jealous of him. I've been having erotic dreams about Lila, or about someone who seems to be Lila in another body."

Helen looked at her with eyes like fingers sculpting Brook's face from wet clay. "What a pleasurable fantasy," she said softly. "It's so polymorphous perverse."

Brook chuckled uneasily. "If I'm going to fantasize, I don't want it to be about a woman with two kids and a husband."

"Don't write her off on that account. I was married, Brook. I even have a daughter."

"But she's not with you?"

"No. It was a messy divorce. By the time the judge awarded custody to Tony, my lover was tired of being the Other Woman in the case."

"You mean she didn't stick by you?"

"No, baby." Helen's rich voice was both teasing and weary. "She didn't stick with me. To get custody, I would've had to promise never to see her again. I couldn't promise that, but my chivalry didn't matter."

"It sounds like you made a choice between losing your arm or losing a leg." Impulsively Brook reached up to hold her. With equal spontaneity, Helen kissed her firmly on the mouth. Motionless, Brook allowed Helen to probe her lips, her tongue, even her teeth. Dimly she became aware of Helen's laughter.

"Is this an experiment for you? You can open your eyes now. I'm done."

Brook flushed. "Helen, I'm sorry. I haven't been kissed in a long time. I didn't mean to be scientific about it."

"No harm done. I would like to go dancing, though. My body feels super-charged. You have a very sensuous mouth."

"Why, thank you, ma'am," Brook drawled. "Shall we go to *Street's*?" It wouldn't hurt to work off her own excess energy in disco dancing.

Once seated in Helen's car, Brook laughed, confused by her inexplicable response to Helen. "I think I've been celibate too long."

"Meaning?" Helen got behind the steering wheel, adjusted the mirror for traffic and backed efficiently out of her stall. She was a confident and relaxed driver. Her fingers on the wheel were long and tapering — musician's hands.

"Meaning that you're attractive. It would be so easy to become involved with you."

Helen looked pleased and very droll. "Falling off a log is easy, too. But would you want to? I had a crush on Lila, once. Something about the challenge of converting a straight woman to the fold, I think. I wanted to show her what she was missing. Fortunately I didn't act on the impulse."

"Why didn't you?"

"You mean aside from feeling opportunistic?" Helen smiled, languorous. "Simple. I'm greedy. Lila has clear commitments. There's her work as teacher and student and mother. I want to be the centre of a lover's attention. And I need a community — of lesbians."

"Hmm. Have you noticed that every community wants to approve of who we sleep with, and rarely does? I wish we didn't legislate to one another, so love could be openly given and freely received."

Glancing sidelong at Brook, Helen said: "I do too. But your father tried that, and you weren't very happy with his experiment."

Ruefully Brook laughed. "Or my own with Tracy and cohort. So now I vacillate between celibacy and desire, work and friendships. I hate getting hung up on love. I guess we all do."

Briefly Helen touched Brook's hand and returned her grip to the steering wheel. "Oh, yes — you attempted to share your lover. That's noble."

Brook grimaced. "Would you be amused if I say I try to be? I want my life to be rainbow coloured, even though I end up a little monochromatic, from my point of view."

Helen veered into the right lane and parked behind the Dufferin Hotel. "Rainbow colours. We'll find that at *Street's*, refracted light on the dance floor. Somehow, I like your rainbow better."

Generally Brook avoided gay bars. She had come to regard them as human meat markets where people came to select tender loin and spare rib. Helen must have noticed her uncertainty because she clasped Brook's hand, with an ease and assurance that calmed her. Whatever Brook expected to find in this bar, including a potential run-in with Tracy and Arlan, it couldn't be that bad with Helen beside her.

Street's was its usual hodgepodge of straights, gays and lesbians. Smoke circled under the spotlights; prisms of colour vibrated in the clothing of dancers gyrating on an opaque floor. Wearing muscle shirts and leather armbands, gay men flaunted their hips at one another. More sedately, lesbians danced, repressing their sexuality in this space shared with men.

Helen put her arm around Brook's shoulders, clearing a way for them through the crowd to a table in the back. They ordered a pitcher of margueritas and sat for a while until Brook acclimatized. Helen tucked Brook loosely against her shoulder. Her arm felt warm and safe, an oasis in this disorienting place.

"Ready to dance?" Helen shouted and firmly drew her into a medley of tunes. The music was characterized by a hard, driving drumbeat and words that said "I want you" in hypnotic variations of the hustling theme. Palling clouds of smoke invaded Brook's lungs and settled into her clothes. The volume was so loud that the music vibrated through her feet. So long as she accepted that this was not a place to get close to anyone, that it was a place to dance and try not to drink too much through sheer nervousness, she and Helen should have a good time. There was quite evidently no point in trying to talk.

Lithe and sinuous Helen moved, her eyes calm. *If only Lila had such physical ease* ... The unwelcome thought intruded, making Brook glance down at the rotating floor. If only's. What was she doing to herself — and to Helen — by always wanting something else, someone else, somewhere else.

And this indistinct sighting of Lila's other face, wavering like a special effects image in a movie about the supernatural — what was that about? The interlude in the kitchen had been abruptly terminated, not by the phone but by Lila's own ambivalence. Nor had Brook been blameless. She had given Lila the choice of getting back to her later, instead of asking some hard questions. Like why Lila assumed that Brook might be the Dutchman. And, if they had shared a past life, what it meant for them to be back together again. Such an old connection certainly explained her willingness to help Lila. Might it also be at the root of her jealousy about Jack? Somehow she had come to see herself as a co-parent, involved in the decisions of Lila's household. Jack's arrival had put that fantasy firmly in context.

Helen interrupted Brook's musings to draw her into a slow dance. For a moment, Brook allowed herself to feel the rhythm of the waltz, the sense of being part of a couple. People wanted — needed — to go home with someone.

Over Helen's shoulder she saw Tracy slow dancing with Arlan. Arlan's mouth had the kind of leer in it with which Brook was familiar — the hot 'let's go to bed' glance which had been directed at Brook on so many jarring occasions. She stumbled and drew suddenly away from Helen, saying simply: "Tracy." Helen followed her eyes and drew Brook once again into an embrace. Sooner than attract attention to herself by struggling, Brook burrowed her face in Helen's bosom, hoping she would not be noticed by Tracy or Arlan. No wonder she hadn't pursued the drama of the Dutchman. The past was difficult enough to resolve when it was merely a year old.

When the dance ended, Brook made a beeline for the table. They were barely seated, however, before Arlan's indolent voice requested an introduction.

"Tracy McIvers. Arlan Tominuk. Helen Winters," Brook said mechanically. She tried not to feel uncharitable towards Arlan, who looked smoothly confident. Helen cupped Brook's hands in hers. As though reaching for a life raft, Brook returned her clasp.

"So how long have you two been an item?" Arlan asked, seating herself without being invited.

"An item of what?" Helen's blue-violet eyes smouldered with phony innocence. She was astonished that Brook could be shaken by this arrogant woman. But Brook's amusement struggled with a far more unwelcome memory.

Hands in the pockets of her shirt dress, Tracy gazed imperiously at Brook. "Let me get this straight. You believe that we choose our parents before we're born. That we choose the time and country of our birth and things like skin colour and economic class. All so we can learn from these ... chosen experiences."
"Yes, I do." Brook said staunchly.
"And I suppose we choose whether or not we're born handicapped. Or raped by our fathers or killed in senseless accidents."
"Yes. For reasons that have to do with our own growth."
Tracy snorted. "How transcendental. So that's how astrologers cast a birth chart. Everything is already foreordained."
Smarting at her tone, Brook said, "Do you need to be quite so ... sarcastic? I nearly said narrow-minded."
"On the contrary. I'm being 'quite' restrained. But then my clients are survivors of sexual abuse. They've already experienced too much blame for what they could not help. I don't think that any of them chose to be objects of violence."
Under the lashing of Tracy's tongue, Brook stood quiet, feeling like she had been caught suddenly in a torrent of rain.

How much of that argument could they have avoided? Suddenly Brook felt a tingling along her spine. That would certainly explain why she had not been eager to keep Lila from joining Adera on that odd day in the kitchen. Even discussing the possibility of a past life connection with Tracy had torn them apart. In Lila's case, however, Brook had not even mentioned the idea. Rather, they had been capriciously immersed in what seemed to be a common memory. Brook's inner conflict must have shown in her face, because Tracy looked concerned. Firmly she drew Arlan up from the chair, bent to speak gently in Brook's ear. "Call me sometime, will you? Maybe we can do something together."
Brook dispelled her monsters long enough to look directly at Tracy and smile. "Maybe. Like walk on the beach," she answered.
Gallantly Tracy kissed her hand, folding Brook's palm over the kiss as though to capture a bird. "We'll do more than survive this fiasco," she said. "We'll thrive." Serenely, she led Arlan away.
"You need some air," Helen shouted and piloted her outside. After

the heat and noise of the bar, the night felt cool and quiet. Wordlessly, Helen walked her around the block.

"Well?" she said at last. "Do you think the beach will help wash things away?"

Brook croaked, "Maybe — " and cleared her throat. "I believe love never dies. Tracy and I will get a chance to do things over and over, until we do them right. Even if it takes several lifetimes, we will come to understand one another."

Helen shivered. "That's optimistic. However, I think I prefer to work things out in a single lifetime. Periodic balancing of the emotional ledger, if you will."

"Yes. " Brook stopped walking and turned to face Helen. "We deserve good things in our lives, all of us. And we'd — I'd — have them, if I didn't expect to be unhappy. I'm standing in my own light."

"To stand in light. What a mantra, in this city filled with icons." Helen gestured at raindrops shining in the naked branches of trees, reached up to touch the tight buds which were beginning to do their yearly spiral into spring.

"You know," Brook concurred, as though she had been the one to notice. "Winter is really over."

In her light jacket, Helen shivered. "So you tell me. Who ever heard of Easter in March?" She checked her watch. "It's also late. Shall I drive you home?"

Brook hesitated. "I don't want to sleep alone tonight. And I definitely don't want to make love. How do you feel about that?"

"Like holding you," Helen murmured cryptically. She drove to a three-storey walk-up near South Granville. Clumsily Brook followed her into the building and stood blinking under the lights in Helen's living room. The apartment was like Helen — a soothing combination of earthiness and serenity. Cushions and high-backed rattan chairs waited invitingly for occupants. On a glass-topped table Helen had left a novel cracked open along its spine. Surreptitiously Brook closed it. She could not bear damaged books.

Lamps were placed discreetly for reading or relaxing. Against one wall was an upright piano, far newer than Lila's; near the other wall swam red and black and yellow-gold fish. Brook went to stand over the glass, watching. Smiling, Helen handed her some food for the fish.

"I'm going to make some chamomile tea," she said. "I presume you don't want coffee at this hour."

Brook nodded. She fed the fish and went to stand on the balcony, quieting her pulse by gazing at the few visible stars. The avenue was still, except for the occasional whoosh of tires.

Helen came in bearing a tray with cheese and grapes and fat strawberries. In silence they drank their tea. Helen put on an album by Mozart and lay flat on the floor with a cushion beneath her head. Dreamily she closed her eyes.

Like a small child Brook curled up beside her, not touching. Helen's hand glanced her elbow, lingered companionable there.

"Helen ... " Brook stammered. "Do you ever feel that you've said 'no' to life for far too long? There are always different ways to do things. I feel like I chose the hard way, when I could have made things so easy for myself just by making other choices."

Helen was silent for so long that Brook thought she was asleep. Then she got up on one arm. "Let's go to bed. At the end of a day self-blame is too easy. So let up already."

To hide her talking face, Brook placed her head briefly on Helen's raised knees. Sensuous fingers stroked her scalp.

Preparing for bed Brook was nervous. Not having a toothbrush, she rinsed with mouthwash and then stalled for time by asking to take a shower. The large bathroom mirror cast Helen's quiet reflection back at her.

"Sure. I'll join you." Smoothly Helen stripped.

"I said I don't want to make love," Brook warned.

"Nor do you want to sleep with a cigarette butt. Strip." Helen had the good sense to step into the shower while Brook disrobed. Brook heard the sound of water and Helen's peaceful movements.

"There's a towel and facecloth in the second drawer. Help yourself."

Trembling, Brook joined her in the shower. Helen soaped and rinsed her back and waited for Brook to return the favour. Suddenly Brook was too aware of the indentation of Helen's waist, of her slender flanks and statuesque legs. The bones of her spine showed clearly. Brook wanted to walk up her vertebrae one by one with her fingers. Being washed and towelled gently dry felt downright delicious.

"I should let Lila know I won't be home," she interjected nervously. "She'll worry."

"At two-thirty in the morning? She'd kill." Helen turned back the covers to her queen-sized bed and climbed in. Noticing Brook's nervousness she reached for a book, which made Brook feel silly. Carefully she crawled in beside her. Helen placed an arm beneath her neck and continued to read. Studiously Brook closed her eyes and tried to sleep.

"Fake," Helen said cheerfully.

"And your reading isn't?" Brook turned to gaze down at her.

"I'm waiting for you to ask," Helen said.

"Ask what?" Brook stammered.

"To be held."

"Oh," Brook whispered. As she had done on the dance floor, she buried her face in Helen's breast. Her arms reached awkwardly to cradle Helen; she felt her gentle returning embrace. Bare, soft, warm skin.

Helen kissed her glancingly on the neck and was still. Only when Helen began to breathe deeply did Brook realize that she was asleep. "Thank goodness," she whispered in relief. She held Helen firmly in her arms and wrapped her legs around her.

For a while she was too keyed up and astonished to rest.

CHAPTER SEVEN

Carrying a breakfast tray, Jack kicked the bedroom door closed behind him. The sound awakened Lila to the arrival of pancakes and sausages, a thermos of coffee and a pitcher of freshly squeezed orange juice. The pièce de résistance was a yellow rose. Lila's eyes widened. From Jack, this was unusual pampering.

Perfunctorily, her husband kissed her on the cheek, wriggling to sit comfortably upright against the pillows. Judging from his grey sweats and his warm body, he had been lifting weights in the basement.

Teasingly she said, "All this attention. Are you making up for something I don't know about?"

Jack blinked, his blue eyes almost wintry. "It's strange to be with you. Somehow, I can't get used to being here again."

"I know." Lila could not look at him. It was odd to deal with elbows and knees in the night, to wonder where on Jack's muscular chest to place her hands. She felt intrusive if accidently she brushed against his thighs. "I feel strange too. I guess we just have to become re-acquainted."

Absently he rubbed at his damp forehead. "How's your thesis coming on Anaïs Nin?"

Softly Lila chuckled. "You don't want to hear, remember? You loathe my 'obsession' with a dead diarist."

"Well ... Why should you care whether 'Ninny' slept with women, men or polka-dotted kangaroos? If you want to examine your eroticism, surely you don't need the excuse of researching a Master's degree. In real life, Helen would be more than willing to help you find yourself."

Play it again, Sam, Lila thought wearily. Like "Bogey" nursing a drink in some torpid bar, we nurse our grievances about one another. "Are you being fair, Jack? I care very much for you and for our children."

"Oh, you're a scrupulous wife and mother. I just wish you'd do something wrong for a change. You're so goddamn perfect." He sounded quite put out.

To shake him or to hug him? Timidly Lila placed her fingers around his thumb. "You're so silly, Jack," she said mildly. His grip was hard and fleeting. Then he disengaged his hand, ostensibly to pour coffee.

With a click he returned the thermos to the tray, his smile distant. "At least you can talk to the librarian about 'Ninny.' She probably loves vicarious thrills."

"'The librarian.' 'The lesbian.' Is the name Brook difficult for you to pronounce?"

"Sorry," Jack said. They were both silent, searching for a way not to argue. Jack looked at his watch. "Kids should be up soon."

Lila groaned. "Do we have another action-packed day planned? I'm finding you hard to keep up with."

"If you want to, stay home. I'm going to take the kids to the CBC. They can play movie moguls while I say hello to old friends."

"Thanks. I think I will." Relieved, Lila strained to hear sounds from Brook's bedroom. Perhaps today they could spend some time together. With Jack around she felt closeted away in a familial world.

"She didn't come home last night," Jack said astutely.

Annoyed, Lila turned aside her tattle tale face. "She was with Helen, I think. They're becoming good friends."

"They have sexual preference in common." Lithely Jack stretched, attentive to the resultant tip of cup and glass. His ears seemed to perk at the tone in Lila's voice — just like a dog's, she thought uncharitably. "You've become quite fond of her."

She looked at him sharply. Was Jack leading her on or merely coaxing her for more information about the style of her life without him? Oh, why did she give everything this subterranean meaning and not simply take his remarks at face value? "Yes," she said cautiously. "It's good to have another woman in the house."

"For your girlish chats, or because she has a crush on you?"

Ears burning, Lila felt like a teenager who has unexpectedly been told that someone she cares about likes her back. Carefully she put down her fork, the taste of compromise choking her. "Is it because she's a lesbian that you're so insecure about Brook?" she queried.

"Dear wife." Firmly Jack turned Lila towards him. "Have you noticed the way she treats me? She makes me want to plead guilty to some undefinable crime."

"Well, you do monopolize kitchen and basement. I'm sure Brook feels in the way with you here."

"I'm in the way here, not Brook," Jack blurted out.

Lila put on her robe and stood at the window looking out, trying to take wisdom from the taut buds on the branches of the naked arbutus. It was true, her feelings for Jack had cooled. He was now a mere habit of caring. The realization frightened her into denial. "Listen, Jack, I'm not the one who's avoided making love."

"Aren't you?" Jack bounded across the room, drew her into a cloying embrace. His mouth suctioned at her neck.

"I don't want to be attacked," she cried out. "Approach me gently, not like an ape."

Jack smiled, his expression both triumphant and defeated. Sighing, he moved the breakfast tray over to the dresser, sitting heavily on the bed and patting the mattress beside him. "Come over here," he ordered.

Apprehensive, Lila sat. Jack folded her in his arms and kissed her mouth. It was a long kiss and more and more intimate. She felt the rush of her pulse, reluctantly acknowledging her desire. After all, it had been a long time since she'd been touched.

Then Jack's familiar hands were on the aureoles of her breasts, the nipples stiffening beneath his seeking mouth. Her robe fell open and her closed heart and she lay down hopefully beside him. Smiling oddly, Jack stroked her mons.

Like a searchlight her eyes scanned, looking for the beloved in the face of this stranger. With her hands she traced the lines around his eyes and mouth — surely they were deeper. His cheeks, although somewhat more full, hosted yearning eyes. He looked unfulfilled, this her companion, her friend of fourteen years. Then it came to her that they needed simply to make love, not necessarily with one another.

Burying her face in his shoulder, she hid from the feeling that they would be merely scratching an itch. That she could be so calculating about the act of love sickened her. Perhaps if he used his tongue he could re-awaken her desire, make her feel alive again instead of alone and clinging to the edge of this dark, cold place.

From the tension of her hands Jack understood how she wanted to make love. Eyes averted, he turned Lila on her stomach; a practised mouth caressed her back and buttocks and thighs. With his fingers he entered her and Lila made way for him, trying not to crawl into a fantasy that had nothing to do with him. How long ago was it since she had begun to imagine softer lips, smoother limbs, women whose hair and breasts grazed enticingly along the skin of her back? A band tightened around her forehead, throbbed inside her skull. Always these damned headaches when she made love with Jack.

"You're not using birth control are you?" It was so responsible a thing for him to ask, and spoken so dispassionately, that Lila started.

"No," she whispered. Defensively she wanted to add: *You're not home for months. Why should I take birth control? It's my body that gets pumped with chemicals.* His weight rolled away from her back, easing the vitriol of her thoughts. She watched him search through the closet, turn something out the pockets of his suit pants. At once pragmatic and graceful, he inserted a rubber over his penis, abandoning his sweats behind him on the floor. Uncertainly she welcomed him back into her, feeling the kind of aversion she felt when taking castor oil. This act might clear out her body, but there must be something less obnoxious on the market.

Frustrated by the chattering in her head, she tried not to close him out, not to eject his cock as finally as an oak door closes on a great hinge. Why wouldn't he use his tongue? Surely she had made it clear how she wanted him.

Covertly she glanced at Jack. His eyes were lowered and his fine, sensuous mouth looked grim, as though he needed to prove a point of some kind. Judging from his unhurried breathing, he would take forever to come, if he came at all. And, yet again, she would not. Of its own volition a tear rolled down her cheeks.

Impatient, Jack launched away from her, scissoring his knees up to his chest. With pity Lila thought: *If you were a child, Jack, you'd be reassuring yourself now by sucking your thumb.* Side by side and eons apart, they lay silent. When Jack spoke it was matter-of-factly, as though nothing at all had happened. "I'm supposed to phone Ritt Cutler today. She's negotiating a regular part for me in the series."

"Your agent," Lila said woodenly. "Can she pull it off, do you think?"

"Yeah." He twisted to get comfortable on the pillow, looking away from her as though he thought his expression could be dangerous. Almost speculatively he said, "She wants me to stay in Los Angeles."

Jack's tone clamoured in her like an alarm. "I don't understand. I thought you were disenchanted with the States. Are you going to stay there after all?"

Their eyes locked, his pale and lidded, hers wary and searching. In the shadows from the lamp his nose was aquiline, a hooked eagle's beak. Lila felt suddenly like a rodent paced by the shadow of gliding wings. Opaque, his eyes surveyed her like a winged hunter imagining warm entrails. "I don't know, Lila. I'm a Canadian. I can't shed the feeling that I'm selling out to stay there."

"So?" Lila prodded. "What's the next move? A return home?"

"I think not. Rumour has it that funding for the CBC will be cut again, which makes working for them professional suicide. You know that."

Whimsically Lila smiled at him. "I'm extremely tired of single parenthood. I'd like us to live together before we become complete strangers."

Through half-lowered lids Jack peered at her. "Look, what would you say about me moving to Toronto? We both knew it would take the better part of this year for me to find something else."

Lila stared. Why did he want to leave the U.S. when his agent was negotiating a contract for him? With quiet rancour she drawled: "I didn't consent to meet you between stations as you explore the world."

Jack swallowed, his Adam's apple jumping almost painfully. "You needn't be sarcastic. What do you want, Lila? For me to come here and be unemployed?"

Lila slapped the mattress, shocking both of them. "After nearly seven months you want to leave Los Angeles! Jack, you're not yet a household commodity. It takes time for the industry to know your work."

He reached over to pat her on the head, which only served to increase Lila's sense of grievance rather than to mitigate it. Suddenly his blue eyes were conspiratorial and uneasy. "I've been a bad boy, Lila. There's a woman pursuing me in L.A."

Lila sat bolt upright. So that was why Jack had been so removed, his mind endorsing an act for which he did not have the consent of his body. Her voice too loud, she croaked: "Pursuing you for what?"

"Shhh. You're broadcasting to the whole street. It's — she's a married woman, Lila. Well, don't you see? I thought it was safe to have fun together. She has a husband; I have a wife. I didn't know she'd get so involved."

Lila blinked. She had to find some way to be logical, to find out just how "involved" they were, Jack and his new mistress. How else could Lila know what she must do?

As though telling his children a story, Jack said breezily: "She wants us to divorce our partners and marry one another. Now do you understand? I've got to break off with her, for Cyndi and Mark."

Lila wet her lips. So Jack was prepared to stay with her for the sake of the children. What a charming reason to cohabit. Just one more duty undertaken for daughter and son. He got lonely. Well, so did she. Living was increasingly an act of alienation to her. "What belated integrity you have," she murmured. To her own ears, she sounded enervated, even indifferent. Could she really be this casual about his confession unless somehow she had expected it? With the flat of her hand she rubbed something invisible out of the bedspread, back and forth and back. "Los Angeles is a big city, Jack," she whispered. "Surely you can avoid your lover there, if you care to."

Dejectedly, Jack raked at his hair. "I can hardly avoid her. She's my agent."

Lila began to laugh. "I thought you learned last time not to mix business with pleasure, Jocko."

"Don't call me that. I'm not a jock. I wasn't being opportunistic, either. We just hit it off."

Suddenly too hot, Lila walked to the window, cooling her forehead on the pane of glass. "So how do you propose to solve this one, Jack?" she murmured judiciously.

"I told you." His voice was hesitant, almost coaxing. "By leaving L.A. You do see that it would be best."

Lila felt her vision clouding. She peered at Jack who lay spread-eagled, his shrunken penis still bearing the ridiculous coloured rubber. Coldly she looked at him, her eyes filling up with storm. A muscle in Jack's mouth twitched. "Lila, I want to save our marriage, don't you see?"

"No. I don't. I see that no matter what choice you make now, other people are going to deal with the consequences. Your mistress, our children and me."

Jack demurred uneasily. "Look. Let me check out Toronto. If in half a year I still haven't made it — "

"You'll try New York. Broadway." Lila snickered. "And other agents."

"Do we really understand one another so little?" Jack padded across the room to her, climbing into his discarded sweats. His hand dropped clawlike on her shoulder. She stood rigid like paralysed prey. "Lila, you're a good woman. We have two wonderful kids. But I've known for a long time that I don't fulfill you sexually. Oh, I please you." He raised a hand to halt her interjection. "When I make love with you like a woman would." Furiously she whirled towards him. "No, it's true, Lila! You've got to stop fighting yourself. Maybe it wouldn't be a bad idea if you had an affair with a woman. Maybe you just need to work this out of your system so you can start to want me. So that I'm not your father to you, taking something he had no business to take —"

In an intense burst of distrust, Lila cried out. "Stop it! You can't rationalize your affair by getting me to have one." Lila did not want Jack's leftover feelings; her own, or his, holdover loyalties. She couldn't unravel the skein of her emotions for him — her sympathy for his predicament and her sense that Jack could not, must not be trusted ever again. And what of Ritt Cutler in Los Angeles? What about this woman who was prepared to leave her own husband to live with Jack, who loved him that despairingly? The only clear realization she could muster was that she had to think apart from him. "I want you to leave, Jack."

"Leave? You mean give you time, or — "

"Go. To your agent. I want us seriously to think about divorce."

"You can't mean that. The kids aren't a meatloaf we can split up and share."

"They will continue to be split between the two of us whether you return to Los Angeles or go to Toronto. I would just ... respect you more if you went back to finish what you started."

Jack inclined his head, smiling nervously. "How magnanimous of you. Don't you hear what you're saying? You're inviting me to go back to my mistress."

"Yes. And you're inviting me to take one. Take your ... opportunism ... and your confusion elsewhere. I can't deal with your emotions and mine."

"Lila." For a long time he was silent. Then Lila heard the door close softly behind him.

She shoved her index finger between her teeth, staring out the window into a yard she did not see. Furiously she began to swing at the glass and caught her arm just in time. She must not hurt herself. She, at least, had to provide stability for Mark and Cyndi.

"And for myself," she heard a whimper and started to cry without making a sound. "And for myself. If only I can be enough." *Who will I be if I'm not Jack's wife and my children's mother? I'll be a Master's thesis walking around campus. I'll be the daughter my father raped.*

Since the time she was Mark's age she had lived with incest, with her sense of being a cipher, a Pandora's box. She could no longer live with the guilt of it, with her sense of being bad. She needed help. Help no one could give her except a therapist.

Lila smiled, quite without humour. *He has the affair and I seek out a shrink. I need a shower. I have to get clean.*

She wished that it were possible to slough the whole noxious, confusing business like a snake does its old skin. *Well, do it, Lila,* she lectured, adamant. *Change, before you do yourself harm. Before any more harm is done to you.*

Impatiently she rubbed at her eyes, staring at the wetness on her fingers as though never before had she seen her own tears.

CHAPTER EIGHT

Early spring pretending to be mid-summer. Tall hedges alive with the chirps and flutters of juncoes and vari-coloured sparrows. Cedar boxes lying in wait for flowers. The pungent smells of dirt and moss and weeds.

Hearing movement, Brook turned to accept a bowl of café au lait from Helen, whose glance was so unabashedly direct that Brook blushed. Together they stood gazing from the balcony, the remembrance of their mid-night exchanges making them gentle with one another.

In the silence, Brook said lamely: "I've only seen bowls of café au lait in Quebec."

Helen grinned. "Before the Parti Québécois purged les anglaises, I contemplated living in Montreal. I was madly in love, and taking French immersion courses in order to stay. But alas, I didn't become bilingual quickly enough."

Brook knitted her brow. "Do you often make jokes at your own expense? You surely don't feel great about losing your lovers."

"No. But then humour protects me from being tedious. One is quickly expected to cope, and spare other people the need to be supportive."

"Listen, Tough Guy," Brook drawled. "You deserve better from life — and love."

Helen waggled her mouth. "So you keep telling me. Drink your cafe au lait. I didn't undergo such — loving labour for you to let it go cold."

Brook sipped. How to relate to someone so languid and teasing on the surface whose unmined depths promised the Mother Lode? The air between them seemed charged with potential, whether or not that potential made Brook feel comfortable. As for Brook's recent and unnecessary fear of intimacy, there was no sense in letting it grow wild. After all, she couldn't very well scold Helen that she deserved better if Brook did not believe that herself. With genuine warmth she said: "Thanks for last night."

Helen shrugged away her gratitude. "Hey, listening is cheap."

Unable to contain her restlessness, Brook mumbled: "I'd like to get away for the weekend. Of course, to a resort that costs nothing," she chuckled wryly.

Like a fairy godmother Helen snapped her fingers. "I have just the thing. A cottage on Mayne. It's too late to make this morning's ferry, but then we'd have to pull together some supplies anyhow. And I'd need to find a sitter for my fish."

"You have a cottage?" Brook said wistfully. "On the waterfront?"

"On the waterfront. With a fireplace and electricity. And no phone. The beach, however, is rocky. Perhaps I didn't visualize thoroughly enough when I was looking for it," she mugged.

"Talk about 'looking for it'!" Brook swatted Helen's arm, making her yelp.

"Brute. So? Will that do for 'checking out'?"

Caught like a rabbit in briars, Brook hesitated. "Should we take the car, or go as foot passengers? How important to you is convenience?" Her objection, however, was not financial. She was in danger of getting close again. *Serves me right*, she thought satirically, *if I choose to shower with a relative stranger.*

Dismissively Helen waved. "Money is never so green as Mayne Island. Be my guest. Besides, I always spend at least a week there during Spring Break."

With sharp teeth Brook worried her bottom lip. "It would be better than putting up with Jack," she muttered. "He's so male."

"Men are. I wonder how Lila is doing."

A shiver ran along Brook's arms. "Let's not discuss them. I think Lila could do so much better."

"With a woman, no doubt," Helen said rakishly. "Let me see if I can make a reservation for the ferry on such short notice." She must have been able to, because she hung up with a pleased flourish. "Come on, let's go shopping in Granville Market. We can breakfast there at one of the concessions, while we stock up on what we want to take."

"I know what I'll have for breakfast," Brook grinned. "A hot breaded oyster on a stick. Or sushi."

"For breakfast." Helen raised her eyebrows. "If you want, we can harvest oysters on Mayne as well. It's actually a good time of year to eat them. As for sushi, at the cottage you can help me make some with crab meat and avocado. If you'd like that?"

Brook crowed. "Like that! Come on! Let's raid the food stalls."

"One moment. I'll see if Liz is in and give her a key." While Helen arranged for the care of her fish, Brook cleaned the cappuccino maker, the milk pan and the two now-empty bowls. Then, tugging playfully on Helen's arm, she hurried them out of the apartment.

Fresh from their adventure at the farmer's market, they headed for Lila's to pick up Brook's clothes. She also wanted to take along her *Encyclopedia of Women's Myths and Secrets*. "Since we'll be celebrating Eostre, I want to do a rite to the Goddess."

The wind rippling through her hair as she veered towards Kits, Helen tossed back her head. "Easter," she drawled. "Good old eclectic Christianity, totally made up of pagan rituals. I've forgotten — which ones relate to Eostre?"

"She had a sacred hare who laid the golden egg of the sun. Did you ever wonder how rabbits are supposed to lay eggs?"

Helen laughed. "Only in passing. I reserve my angst for more personal events."

"Okay, smart pants. Don't ask if you don't want to know."

"You'll tell me anyway — for my edification?" Helen sounded content to listen to Brook talk about anything.

"Alright, but only because I'm forgiving. For the Persians the solar year began at spring equinox, when they presented one another with coloured eggs, usually red, to symbolize the rebirth of the year."

"Hmm-m," Helen said.

"The Goddess is important to me, Helen. All this obsession with a male god gives women no images of the divine as female. We are regarded as sinful, not sacred, and in patriarchal religions are denied a place, except as obedient wives and dutiful mothers." Was she sharing with Helen or merely attempting to create a barrier in philosophies between them, because of her own need to maintain distance? Brook frankly did not know.

Helen touched her hand briefly where it lay on the seat. "We agree. It's important to you. So Brook, how will we celebrate Easter?"

Brook chuckled. "With eggs of course. Red food colouring. And an egg hunt down on the beach."

"Sounds wonderful. Under the full moon, no doubt."

"No. Easter is always after the full moon. In this case eighteen days after. We'll need flashlights if we do this at night."

"Could we?" Helen sounded like an adventurous child. Tenderly Brook smiled at her, glad for Helen's attention to her driving.

When they pulled into Lila's yard, the house seemed deserted. *No doubt the Tennants are involved in a Daddy-centred family foray.* Why this acute resentment? Brook tried to tell herself that she was merely disappointed, that now it would be a few more days until she could find out how Lila was, or simply enjoy the sound and sight and smell of her. Simply. There was no simplicity to such a complex of emotions. She seemed to be hovering on the brink of a crush on either of two women, which seemed downright capricious.

Morose, Brook left a note for Lila on the kitchen table, explaining where she was going. Preparing for any kind of weather, she packed shorts and sweaters, rain gear and summer blouses; took candles, incense and her three Ugandan goddesses. They were portable and made of speckled stone, shapes merely hinting of arms and legs with round eyes and ears carved into their heads. There were thousands like them distributed throughout archeological digs, the record of nomadic peoples whose "altars" travelled with them. Where Brook was the goddesses were, blessing the temporary homes she made. All homes, she thought, are temporary. Gently she held the goddesses in her palms, feeling the hum of stone talking. Her harsh emotions quieted.

Murmuring, Helen handed her a package of matches. "You'll need that for the candles."

On their way out, they passed the closed door to Lila's bedroom. Neither of them realized that Lila slept, exhausted, having awakened throughout the night listening for Brook's return.

Aboard the ferry they braved the wind at the railing, their clothes and hair snapping, gazing in wonder at an ocean which stretched far beyond them to the horizon's rim. Gulls scolded one another, perched on floating logs and flying off again, skimming the surface of the water for silvery fish. Others divebombed the ferry for scraps. Delighted, Helen and Brook watched an employee from the ship's kitchen hurtle pieces of stale bread upward, bringing sea gulls creeling and clustering from all points of the compass. At the sky's edge sunlight gleamed, red swirls glinting in the water.

Too soon, the bow ground harshly against the pier at Village Bay. "Do you want an overview of the island?" Helen asked. "I can point out the two stores, the pub, the lodge and the motel. Oh, and there's a restaurant and a hardware — sometimes. Mayne is small, but then I come here for the inlets. Tomorrow in the light we can explore them thoroughly."

"Yes, let's leave the tourist hang-outs for another time. Which bay are you on?"

Helen leered. "Oyster Bay, of course. From the cottage we'll have an excellent view of the sunset. I even have a love seat from which you can watch it."

Brook sighed. "Oh, Helen. You do love your mask of frivolity. Let's go."

"D'accord," Helen said dubiously, and headed down the narrow road towards Oyster Bay, avoiding pot holes and soft shoulders. Even with a small car, she seemed justifiably nervous about staying on her side of the road.

Pavement and gravel wound soon enough to the cottage, an octagon with cedar siding, skylights and many windows. From the patio Brook had a panoramic view of the inlet, of sandy beach which graduated to pebbles and rugged sandstone boulders standing like sentinels in the bay. Tall cedar and fir trees leaned towards one another, encroaching into the clearing around the house. Brook heard the creak of branches rubbing. At cliffside a winch stood ready to let down an absent boat. Facing out to the water was a brick barbecue pit, a picnic table, stools made from rough-hewn logs and the love seat about which Helen had teased her. A horse's head was hewn into the soft wood, its nostrils flaring. Welcoming her, the west wind ruffled Brook's hair.

In silence Helen switched on the yard light and they unpacked the car. Hauling groceries into the kitchen, Brook stared curiously around her, until Helen took a bag away from her and led her by the hand on a tour of the cottage.

"O-ohh," Brook said of the fireplace. Three centrepiece tiles featured kachina dancers in a glorious triangle wearing bright oranges and blues and vibrant whites, enriching the earth red of clay tiles.

Smiling, Helen gathered kindling and lit a fire in the glassed-off hearth. "That should deal with the chill," she said. "The nights are still quite cold."

Brook gazed at an L-shaped couch, at coffee and end tables and a driftwood-based lamp with a shade made from lace agate. Overhead was a loft with a ladder leading up to it.

Brook pointed. "Is that where you sleep? In the loft?"

"No, my pet." Helen led her to a room facing out to the ocean. One whole wall was glass, with red and yellow draperies which she opened to the view. A wood heater and black and white framed photographs of the Mayne landscape occupied another wall. "I took those," Helen said shyly.

"You have an unusual eye. Move over, Ansel Adams," Brook teased.

"Not quite, though it's nice of you to say so. I like photography. It's a real hobby of mine."

"That's apparent," Brook said. "You have an intriguing visual sense."

"Gee, thanks, ma'am. It's good to have my photographs appreciated."

Brook gazed at a queen-sized mahogany bed, watching Helen fiddle with a thermostat. Suddenly she was anxious for bedtime, wanted to press close to Helen's nakedness and kiss that graceful gazelle's neck of hers. *With numerous places to sleep*, Brook thought, *don't presume that you'll luck into an invitation to share her bed tonight.*

Somberly she accepted a glass of champagne from Helen. "Mumm's?" Brook laughed. "Don't tell me the liquor store was out of Dom Perignon."

Without comment Helen drew her over to the fire. Heat climbing up their legs, they sat listening to the crackle of wood, the hiss of sap. Then, as she had done at *Street's*, Helen put her arm around Brook. Trembling, Brook burrowed into her shoulder, betraying her desire. Gently Helen lifted Brook to her feet.

"Bring your champagne," she whispered and with the flashlight guided Brook between boulders to the ocean's edge. "It's customary to offer something to the Goddess, isn't it? When one receives an unexpected gift?"

Her throat constricted, Brook nodded. Helen took the glass from Brook's nerveless hand and poured the Mumm's onto a boulder; handed her long-stemmed glass to Brook, who with a sense of ritual drama poured the contents between them in the sand.

Drawn to Helen's sensuous mouth, Brook grasped her by her raven hair, in every pore answering Helen's need. Steadily Helen gazed into Brook's face, then made her feel crazed by nibbling at her ear lobes and eyes and mouth. Brook captured that erotic tongue and sucked at it hard. Helen gasped, gently reaching to stroke Brook's clitoris.

Weak-kneed, Brook wrapped her arms around Helen's shoulders, then grasped her soft, round breasts in a kind of wordless plea. Helen's nipples hardened. She groaned Brook's name.

For a while as Helen stroked, Brook stood listening to the sound of the loon, to the swishing feet of the waves coming ashore. Then she felt her own wave, crawling in a red flush along her body, twisting like a blow.

Helen's fingers danced, circled and thrust Brook into the most primal responses. Raggedly Brook cried out, frightening the loon. Feeling the collapse in Brook's legs, Helen made room on her lap, sank heavily against the cold, solid rock and held Brook — as if letting her go would be self-amputation.

Above them the sky was pregnant with winking stars. Under the crescent moon Helen shivered. Like sleepwalkers they headed back for the warm and lighted cottage.

In front of the fire Brook removed Helen's clothes. With her tongue she circled the aureoles of Helen's nipples, sank her teeth sharply into Helen's soft neck. Deliciously Helen moaned. With nibbling bites and kisses, Brook caressed her way down Helen's back, around Helen's buttocks and inside her thighs. She explored Helen's vagina, carefully orchestrating pressure and tension, licking the hollow of Helen's spine with a skilled tongue. Wetness charged along her hand. She followed the living walls of Helen's desire, the opening and closing of her, reaching to twist thumb and index finger together. Helen gasped, her breathing sharp.

Brook felt the exultant, raw power of sex. For nearly a year she had not made love. Now her desire was focused, concentrated. She would not stop, though Helen begged for respite. Adopting the rhythm of Helen's body, Brook rubbed against her, feeling her own clitoris become full once more. Brook's wetness gave Helen a reason to turn, to bring her lover to the same state of trembling terror which Brook had not heeded in her for what seemed like hours of deliberate torment.

This time release made Brook cry. Helen wiped away Brook's tears, stroked her wet hair. "Under my hands your head feels fuzzy and sweat-streaked and delicately round," she whispered. Then she lay on Brook and cried too, as the fire bellowed its way into bright red embers. "I love you," she murmured and held Brook tightly in her arms, perhaps afraid that her words were sudden and rash. But Brook clasped her by the buttocks and pulled her still closer. It was nearly dawn when they fell into sleep, exhausted by their harvest of joy.

In the early afternoon they awoke and gazed at one another shyly, as people will who are stripped bare of their defenses. Sunlight crawled through the muslin drapes. Naked, Helen went to let in the day. Light flooded her in a kind of benediction.

"I want to cook for you," Brook murmured. "What would you like to have?"

"Muffins," Helen said. "With dried apricots and raisins. And a huge fruit salad. I'm starving."

"Sounds lovely." Uncertainly, Brook stood to put on her clothes.

"No," Helen whispered. "Wear this if you're cold." She handed Brook a bright coloured silk kimono and slipped into a floral wraparound, which ended at the beginning of her thighs. Brook could not take her eyes away from Helen's black and generous crotch. Her pubic hair continued up her stomach and along her thighs, which Brook found far more arousing than if she shaved. Helen seemed disconcerted by her brown stare, her hot and disturbing eyes. "Oh, don't," she pleaded. "I'll starve to death if we make love again."

Brook knelt to kiss her labia. Then she went to the kitchen and studiously mixed the batter for muffins, while Helen fished into fridge and cupboards. Together they poured yogurt over the fruit salad, sprinkled it with allspice. Carefully Brook placed the bowl in the fridge. "We have half an hour until the muffins are ready," she murmured, "and I would dearly love just to cuddle."

Helen took the time to put eggs on to boil and reached to take down the red food colouring. Drawing her to the mattress, Brook laughed softly ...

They ate at the picnic table under the boughs of a linden tree. The tide was extraordinarily low, which inspired Helen to drive to one of the island stores for salmon heads. She baited the crab trap with the heads and tossed it over the pier. "Crabs are clumsy," she said. "They wait for the incoming tide to carry them towards food. Or do you know that?"

"I know they're fussy," Brook said. "They prefer fresh to frozen heads."

"Well," Helen grinned. "If you feel guilty for sleeping in, we could always dig for butter clams. That act will make up for any misplaced sense of sloth on your part."

"We were slothful?" Brook drawled. "But let's dig. I want to trade fairly — our labour for their lives."

"Oh, we'll earn every bite," Helen laughed and went for shovel and trowel. "Let me show you their blow holes, unless you want to dig up every geoduck on the beach." She screwed up her nose. "They are not my idea of a taste treat."

"Hey. I live on the Coast. I know what I'm looking for."

"I noticed," Helen dead-panned, and headed demurely down the beach.

While Helen dug for clams, Brook drew bright red eggs from her pack, placing them casually behind boulders. Then she watched surreptitiously, shovelling with apparent absorption. At last Helen found the first egg, whirling towards Brook, her mouth agape. Brook hooted. A geoduck took that occasion to spray her and to dig swiftly away from her shovel. Glancing down at her runners, Brook noticed that they were completely encased in wet sand and mud. As they stood leaning on their tools, a gusty wind ballooned their clothes and caressed them.

"Have you ever seen limpets this large?" Helen yodelled. With a Swiss knife she forced the limpet from a boulder to show to Brook, then carefully placed the creature back on the rock.

The incoming tide hurried them away from the beach. Reluctant to abandon their adventure, they made their way back to the cottage via a woodland trail. To clean out some of the grit, they placed their catch of oysters and clams under running water. Then, like diehards, they went out in the rowboat, combining sunset with the retrieval of their crab trap. Inside the trap were five adults, three of them males. Carefully they extricated the females and threw them back into the bay. "So here's sushi," Helen said.

Brook grimaced. "Let's make tomorrow a 'kill nothing' day."

"Want to throw them back?" Helen offered. Spontaneously they freed the males, then reached for one another's hands, feeling both tender and shy. Overhead the wings of an eagle cast a shadow across the boat. Aimlessly they drifted, until a north wind motivated them to seek shelter.

Back at the cabin Helen boiled the clams and oysters until their hinges opened, serving them in garlic butter with lemon and basil. Then they drank chilled white wine and danced to music played on Helen's portable compact disc player. "My hands feel hungry for you," Helen whispered.

"Let me feed them," Brook muttered back.

"I'll never have enough of you."

"I sincerely hope you won't," Brook said, and tongued her out of her senses. They went to bed, not knowing if it was early or late, falling at last into a blissful sleep.

Then Brook had the dream. In sunlight she and Helen walked on the beach. Out from a great, swirling mist Lila emerged, blundering sightlessly near a precipice. Beneath her the ocean foamed as she walked somnambulent closer and closer to the edge.

"Lila! Don't!" In the dark Helen heard Brook cry out, saw her sit bolt upright in bed and struggle to regain a sense of where she was. "Helen, she's going to kill herself!"

"Easy." Strong fingers captured Brook's wrists, twisting them until they hurt. "Lila is not suicidal. Brook, I've known her for over four years."

Ferociously Brook freed her wrists to rub at her temples. "Something is wrong. She needs us. We've got to go back."

Helen turned on the light. She looked as though she had been living inside a bubble and Brook had taken a cruel prick at it. Over the last three days she had fallen deeply in love. Without more shared time, Brook could jeopardize that love. Yet Lila was not a friend that either woman could or would abandon.

Sadly Helen whispered: "If you feel this way in the morning, we'll take the ferry back. Now lie down and let me hold you. You must not let a dream disturb you so."

Leaning into Helen's warm scent, Brook allowed herself to be held. "Listen, dreams are a whole other level of reality. They link us with ourselves, and with other people."

"Ye-es," Helen said slowly. "I've had dreams about people I care for. When they're in need, or troubled. But dreams can be no more than our own projections and fears, Baby."

Brook sat holding her own knees. "Maybe. She really is self-reliant. But Jack must have done something — "

Helen chuckled, uneasily. "Really, my love. You do like to see him as a villain." With gentle fingers she caressed the roots of Brook's hair.

Like a child Brook clung to her. Helen smelled like spring, flowers and musk. The undercurrent of their loving. Brook inhaled her until once again she felt able to sleep, closing her eyes to the feeling of Helen's fingertips gently stroking her scalp.

CHAPTER NINE

Lila stared, mesmerized by the flames in the hearth. Heat inched out to where she lay, wrapped itself in her clothing and threatened to blister her skin. For a moment she ignored her discomfort and listened: to the snap and roar of fir as it burned, to the wind as it made its whooing way down the chimney. The marvellous voice of Maureen McGovern sang tunes from Gerswhin, inviting Lila simply to lie back and rest. Cyndi and Mark had long ago gone to bed, and where Jack was Lila did not know — or care. On some level she felt both chattering and silent, her mind too keyed up to shape coherent or linear thoughts. She wondered at the clutch of loneliness in her throat, wished she felt less like a squirrel carrying ideas instead of nuts — along boughs where all her possible options fell into some cache, to be bartered over or defended with nasty and nebulous squirrely chatter. Who heeded the wishes of squirrels, no matter how busy they were or how annoyed.

Always a throat full and sore and empty of words. Jack informed her that Ritt was willing to have Cyndi and Mark spend the summer with them in Los Angeles. They had to meet his mistress, of course. Lila could hardly protect them from the facts at this stage. Their parents were parting.

More words came from Jack's mouth, arrows curving towards her heart. Arbitrary and non-consultative words. And from Lila's mouth flint and gravel and twigs, but she was sure words did not rival the sparks in her eyes. She felt incendiary, hot and urgent as a comet burning itself up in the atmosphere.

Lila struggled to acknowledge the sensibleness of Jack's plan. Did it matter who was to blame for ending this, when it had needed to be ended for so very long? She wasn't innocent and neither was he. The shame of this — the shame of staying together without love — belonged to both of them.

Impatiently Lila climbed the stairs, searching for something to distract her from her gnawing thoughts. In front of the door to Brook's room, she felt impelled to enter. Brook still was not home. Standing in her room, however, Lila could feel her there, making all of this comprehensible. And not because she was an "academic," too, searching for copy from the real lives of other people. She wouldn't discount the validity of Lila's scholarship like Jack did because he had no use for her studies. Lila had to have something to rely on, some work in the world. Sexual love was too unreliable.

Was it important to her not to be sexual? That day in the kitchen, Brook massaging her shoulders. Warm hands like electricity making its way through water to jolt her. But she wasn't going to become a lesbian just because she had lesbian fantasies. Still, that did not explain the rawness she felt when she read the note from Brook, that she and Helen were gone to Mayne Island. She knew they were attracted to one another. She even dreamed about them making love. The dream was explicit and set her teeth on edge with longing. It ended with Helen holding red eggs in her hands, arms elevated to the sun. Lila did not understand. Eggs were an obvious symbol of fertility. Her psyche found lesbianism fertile? Imaginative, creative and intelligent. But she knew that. She knew that she would be lucky to have such a relationship in her own life.

Stabbed by sharp pains in her chest, she sat hard on Brook's bed. Jack was right. His penis did make her tighten up, close her eyes and think of England. Of anything at all, except Jack and what he was doing to her. She lay beneath him remembering the plunder of her child's body by an adult male. Jack's rhythms were similar. The sounds he made. Gasping, tearing cries as he came inside her. The sense of being strangled and unable to breathe, crushed beneath his slack, sweating body. Feeling dirty.

So. She had lost him. Did she deserve to? Surely there was room in the world for the victims of incest, some allowance for the time it took to recover. Little children ran to their fathers for protection. She ran away from hers and got beaten. Her mother just stood there while he stropped her with his belt. *"You mustn't run away again,"* she said helplessly. *"Don't you understand that it makes your father angry?"*

Everything made her father angry. How she ate. Whether she ate. How slowly she tied her shoelaces. Why she cried when she had to be alone with him.

On impulse she lit a candle to Kwan Yin. Brook had called her the goddess of mercy. Mesmerized, she stared at the flame, seeing the aura of light through tears. Suddenly, wrenchingly, she was back in her father's house.

She woke to the sense of lying in something wet, nightgown clinging to her. He must have come to her while she slept; he must have put it inside her. She felt sticky and warm there. No! He couldn't have done that. Surely she would have wakened.

Quickly she snapped on the night light. He was not in the room. There was no telltale white discharge on her sheets. There was blood. The bleeding came from inside her, from the place Nurse Pruett called the vagina. What had she said? That bleeding turned a girl into a woman. She said that when that happened a girl must be careful if she did not want to become a mother. And she clipped some diagrams to the board, of what she called a penis and a clitoris. For the first time Lila knew the technical names for what her father had been doing to her. It was called penetration. And the white stuff was semen. Semen joined a ripe egg to become a baby. She could have his baby. She held her pencil so hard that it broke and some of her classmates tittered. But she didn't have to worry yet. She didn't have the menses. How long would it be before she got her period? Nurse Pruett showed them pictures of tampons and sanitary napkins and taught the class how to wear them and how to dispose of them. She told them if they spotted they must wash out the blood immediately or it would stain. Lila's Health and Hygiene teacher, who seemed embarrassed, left the room for that part of the discussion.

Lila put on her housecoat, heart beating too fast. She would have to rinse out the sheets and her own nightgown. Incoherently she prayed that her father would not be waiting for her in the bathroom tonight. Waiting to clamp a hand over her mouth and push her face against the wall. The procedure was always the same. He rammed inside her from behind until he was done. She stood quietly with a full bladder trying not to pee. Once she couldn't stop herself and he swore, pushing her down on her knees. He stuck her face in the urine and mopped the floor with her hair.

She ran water into the sink, praying that he would not hear: scrubbed at blood in the sheets, rinsed and twisted them, heart beating violently. Then she opened the door to take the sheets to the laundry room. She would have to tell her mother that she wet the bed again. Her father would wonder why she was using their excuse.

When she got back to the bathroom he was waiting for her. He started to push her back and then noticed her nightgown.

He chuckled. "Well, I'll be. You're a woman now." His cock bulged through his shorts. He groped free of them. "We're going to have to do this a different way." He sat on the edge of the tub and made her kneel. "Put your mouth around it," he said. "And be careful. You hurt it and you won't see morning."

He wrapped his hands in her hair and pulled. She did as she was told. It was too big for her mouth. He kept moving it back and forth so that she gagged. She was strangling; could not breathe. He wheezed, too, as though running up a very steep hill. Then something warm and acidic shot into her throat. Involuntarily, she spat on the floor and wiped a hand across her mouth. It came away white and sticky.

"Lick it," her father said. "Put it in your mouth and swallow."

At last he was done. Back in her bed she lay sleepless waiting for morning. This would not, could not happen to her again. She would have to find a way to end it. This was Tuesday. The school nurse would be in. Maybe she would be able to stop her father from doing this. She thought about Nurse Pruett's grin, about the young woman's discerning blue eyes. Maybe she knew about menstruation but she wouldn't know anything about this. What if she told Nurse Pruett and the nurse decided to tell someone else? There had been a girl in her class until January about whom her classmates gossiped. They said the nurse found her on a fold-away cot "doing it" with a boy in Grade Nine. The girl — her name was Alison — had been expelled for a few days. Lila waited for her but she never came back.

Automatically, Lila accepted a bag lunch from her mother. At the normal time she left the house and walked head down towards the bus stop. At the last instant, she boarded a bus headed for West Vancouver. At Lighthouse Park she got off the bus and walked. She followed trails aimlessly until they led her to a rock-strewn beach. Lila picked her way over boulders and sat near a crevice in the rock, playing dangerous games with the tide. More than once the current rushed at her. She let herself slide forward into the vortex of water, shocked by the temperature into recoiling. Grudgingly she inched back to solid rock, salt spray on her lips. Splintered two-by-fours rushed past her ankles.

Above her, sea gulls wheeled, screaming. She opened the brown bag and fed them, throwing bread and chunks of meat into the water. They swooped and chased one another for the scraps. When her lunch was gone, she climbed, carefully placing her toes in the granite face. She felt the rush of menstrual blood and the dull edge of a stomach cramp. At cliff's end she teetered. Raising her arms in imitation of the gulls, she let herself fall forward. A branch caught at her blouse and held, just long enough. When she wrestled free, the courage to die was gone.

All morning she tried to jump. In the heat of noon, she rose like a sleepwalker and made her way at last to the nurse's office. Her loathing made the words come out. The despair of being able to trust no one else.

Miss Pruett did tell. She reported to the police. After more than four years of abuse, Lila was removed from her parents' home. The horror stopped. But not the dreams. They woke her screaming and made her afraid to use the bathroom. And never had she been able to go down on Jack.

She lay on Brook's futon and tried to sleep, weary beyond living. What was she doing in this room? And why wasn't Brook home to reassure her that everything would be all right, like she did with Mark when he broke her vase. As though Brook could — or should — mother her, too. How needy of her.

Lila dozed, dreaming of jagged rocks. She fell heavily and fast and then panic made her realize that she had wings. She was flapping slowly, gliding like a large, soaring eagle, finding pockets of wind on which to ride. I can't kill myself, she thought. See, there's Brook on the beach, standing with her arm around Helen. Then Brook took on the face of her mother, a grotesque caricature of eyes and mouth, jeering at her. Lila tossed to shake off the nightmare.

Abruptly she opened her eyes, at first confused about where she was. Resolutely she stumbled back to the living room. She had to stay awake, until the fire was safer to leave unattended. Stay awake, until she could trust that she was not back in her father's house waiting for him to sleep or to die. She would make a pot of coffee and watch a late movie. She needn't circle around in her head like a rock rubbed smooth by friction until she didn't recognize the gem that was herself at the core.

In her mind a clear thought crystallized. Only a therapist could help her to remove her deep sense of being ugly and broken. Or self-loathing would destroy her, more jagged and hard than the rocks in Lighthouse Park.

CHAPTER TEN

Reaching for comfort, Helen found Brook awake and gazing steadily back at her from the height of an elbow. Helen burrowed into her breasts, confused and moved by the gentleness in Brook's face. Then the memory of her lover's dream pushed aside her sleepy contentment. "What time is it?" she asked abruptly.

"Time to get up and pack, if we're catching the ferry."

Helen groaned. Cradled in Brook's arms, Helen was loathe to leave the bed, let alone the island. Would Brook's feelings for her survive a departure from Mayne? Maybe it was this place that exerted the magic between them, the reality of being one to one in a rare idyll. "You still think something is wrong with Lila," she said wistfully.

"I do." Brook lifted away the cover of Helen's dark hair: brown eyes and blue played peek-a-boo.

Helen refused to be lulled by the illusion of an intimacy which might suddenly vanish. She grumbled: "I need coffee." Wrapping the bedspread around her she padded to the kitchen.

"Addict." Still leaning on an elbow, Brook watched her. To Helen she seemed small and beautiful, unashamed in her nudity. Even after months beneath a winter sun her skin had an olive cast. She looked like a native of northern Italy, brown and healthy as a nut-laden tree.

With a deliberate attempt at lightness, Helen said: "Sticks and stones, Thiebault, sticks and stones. You can put the fridge on defrost and place the perishables in the cooler. Get useful."

Languidly Brook opened the fridge to pour two glasses of orange juice, popped bread into a toaster and peeled some of their red eggs. They ate standing, chewing slowly in a wordless and sensual communion. Helen felt pulled by her viscera through a narrow passageway towards the light in Brook's amber eyes. "I need a shower," she muttered darkly. "And I have time for one. It's barely seven-thirty."

With too much anticipation for Helen's taste, Brook said: "We'll be on the morning sailing."

"So pack fast," Helen growled. At the entrance to the bathroom she kicked away her wrap.

When she emerged from the shower, Brook had returned the wandering duvet to the bed and straightened the dishevelled sheets. No longer did the single pillow bear the indentation of two heads. And no longer was Brook languid and nude. She had pulled on a russet sweater, underwear and warm socks and recovered her brown cords from the pile of linen by the bed.

Reluctantly, Helen watched her empty the drawers of her clothes, wishing that Brook could leave them at the cabin as she did — as a promise of return. There was no reason to wrestle a future from their intimacy. Their attraction had bloomed like a cactus flower, as suddenly and with equal fragility. It might or it might not be something that could be tranplanted to the mainland and grafted onto their lives there.

She ran a brush through her wet, black hair, then hid her erect nipples beneath a striped cotton shirt and a lavender knit. The undistractable Brook set out to haul things to the car.

All too soon they were ready to leave. Silently Brook walked the Ugandan Goddesses around the cottage, blessing it. With a stick she drew a circle and coaxed Helen inside its circumference. Then she turned Helen with her to face each direction, calling on the winds of the North, South, East and West to protect the cottage. As if in response, a convection of breezes stirred at their shoulders. Wide-eyed, Helen whispered: "Such blatant witchery. No wonder I lost my heart." Suddenly she wanted to be careful of glibness, of the fear of rejection which led her to conceal her intensity. In love she had developed an armour, clunky as that which led knights to be hoist onto their horses because they couldn't mount by themselves. Somehow she had to learn to be naked in more than her body.

But Brook said only: "The winds favour us but I do not claim their power. It is a gift."

Hesitantly Helen answered. "This island feels sacred. It needs rituals."

"It's voluptuous. I'll never forget it, Helen. Goddess grant that we return here."

"Or construct the altar in another place," Helen murmured. "Isn't that the lesson of your portable goddesses?"

Still she worried about boarding the ferry. Among other people there would be the social need for restraint. But on the deck Brook clasped Helen's hand in hers, apparently unable to pretend for the sake of propriety that she was not this woman's lover. In this other world, it would seem, the absence of touch would have left both of them bereft.

The nearer they got to the mainland, however, the more tense Brook became. Wisely Helen kept silent as Brook edged the car into lanes of drivers who, to Helen's slowed-down perception, seemed diabolical. Island life and city driving were certainly poles apart.

At last Brook pulled into Lila's driveway. Despite the absence of the Volvo and the stillness of the house, Brook apparently felt Lila's presence, because she said with certainty: "She's home. And waiting for us."

Before Helen could knock, the door to Lila's room opened and Lila stood swaying. "Hi," she said with poignant relief. Undisguised tears gathered in her eyes. At the top of the stairs she sat down, hard, stifled the sound of grief in her throat. "Sorry," she said. "I need to talk. I'm having a hard time assimilating."

"Is it Jack?" Helen knew that it must be. A woman cried this way for one of two reasons: a lover had left or a loved one had died.

Lila nodded. "He met someone when he was in L.A. We're separating." The raw facts made her wail.

Brook's tone was an odd combination of tender and tough. "You'll deal with it, Lila. You won't be alone."

Silently Helen handed Lila a kleenex. She honked her nose loudly. "I sent Jack there. Can you beat that? An actor without work is half a person. I wanted him to have what he needs to be happy." Her laughter made Helen wince. It was humourless and hard.

Softly Helen said, "Try to hold on to that good will. He too must be hurting about this." She thought uncharitably: *Just where is my loyalty — with Lila or with Jack?*

But Lila leaned firmly back, resting between Helen's knees. After a while she began to murmur, barely audibly. "Oh, Helen. Thank goodness Adera has Mark and Cyndi today. They blame me that Jack isn't here, I feel it. How can I explain that he's leaving, permanently this time?"

Unsympathetically Brook snorted. "Is the job of explaining yours? What's Jack's responsibility in all of this?"

"Jack is doing what's necessary." On the inflection Lila's voice broke.

"He wants to take the kids to L.A. this summer, to try living with Ritt."

"She's the Other Woman, I presume," Helen inserted.

"His agent." Again the wedge of unutterable weariness in Lila's voice. "Ritt gives him the good sex I don't."

"Oh." Helen said. In her bowels she understood the pain of that. Lila twisted her face to the wall, away from both of them.

Hands in her pockets, Brook sat down on the stairs beside her. Quietly she asked: "Did he say so, or is that your fear?"

"Oh, he said it. I know I have a problem with sex. My father saw to that."

Before Helen could frame a delicate way to express what she thought Lila meant, Brook asked point blank: "Are you talking about sexual abuse?" Lila's ringing silence made Brook put her head in the woman's lap. From behind, Helen rocked Lila gently, back and forth, unable to speak. She could barely hear Lila's whisper. "How can I enjoy penetration? It reminds me of — that ... "

Firmly Helen shushed her. "You are a giving woman. Don't you see, what's happening with Jack is not your fault. It has something to do with that little girl who was hurt by her father. And it has something to do with Jack, with your mutual needs."

Wearily Lila leaned into Helen's embrace. "I don't think I'm guiltless in this."

"Nor, I'm sure, is he. Jack took the lover, not you. Nonetheless, something had to happen. You were both crying out for change."

Lila sounded grimly humourous. "Oh, I got change, Helen. I got so much I don't know what to do with it. Marrying Jack made me feel normal. Then we had children and I waited for Jack to do to them what my father did to me. But I never had reason to believe that he was capable of such an act. And I was a wife and a mother. The roles protected me from feeling monstrous. Now Jack wants the children to live with him for the summer, and that will only be the start. I don't know how we'll deal with custody; I know only that Jack has an equal right to the love of our children."

Helen saw Brook bite her lip and decide to speak out anyway. "I think Jack is giving up his rights with both hands. And that you, Lila, have to be a lot more concerned for your own needs than you are for the needs of others." Cryptically Brook embraced her, aware that Helen could see directly into the nebula of love for Lila which glowed in Brook's eyes.

Then she stepped quickly back and Lila's hands curled instead around the stair. "And now I don't know what my role is. The role of the betrayed wife? Of the abused daughter? No. It's my life I'm talking about, not the life of a victim. Still, how will I adapt if I don't have Mark and Cyndi to be strong for? They keep me from falling apart. They have always kept me from falling apart."

Gently Brook lifted Lila's hands and kissed them. "It sounds to me like the roles are getting in your way. Maybe not being responsible for anyone but yourself will help you discover who it is you really are."

So. Helen thought. *Brook, understand that Lila has to do this alone. Despite the support that we'll both give her, we all make it through alone.*

She focused on the sound of Lila's voice, which sounded unusually clumsy and strained. "Your friend Tracy is a therapist, isn't she?" asked Lila.

Satirically Brook grinned. "Now that would be ironic — you seeing her. One more reminder that the world is a place of overlapping circles. Still, the choice of a therapist is very personal, Lila. If you decide not to work with Tracy, you can get her to refer you to someone else."

Lila seemed uncertain though she nodded, her hair inadvertently tickling Helen's chin. "I have to complete my thesis this summer. I can't just let my life fall down like ... like a house of cards."

Brook's brown eyes continued to embrace her. "Therapy or your thesis — does one exclude the other? It may, but give yourself permission to come first, before anything and anyone else."

Suddenly Lila must have felt melodramatic, because she laughed uneasily. "Isn't that what I'm doing now? I haven't asked either of you even one thing about your holiday."

Tightly Brook clasped Lila's hands. "We'll tell you about it later. I'm glad you confided in us."

Helen felt rather than saw Lila smile back at Brook. "I dreamed that you were lovers," she said slowly. "Easter got mixed up in it, so I saw Helen holding red eggs over her head."

Brook's mouth fell open. Here again was this seam in space that knit their lives together like arms of the same sweater, binding them even when they were apart. But Lila was flushed and obviously feverish. Brook would have to be content with her large surprise for the moment.

Helen said carefully, "It wouldn't be a bad idea for you to get into bed. We'll bring you chicken soup, or something."

Obediently, Lila stood. "I am hungry. And so very, very tired." Helen helped her into bed and covered her with blankets to her ears.

"Rest now," she said. "We won't be long."

"Don't fix anything heavy," Lila whispered. "I couldn't keep it down."

From the door to the bedroom Helen thought about the wisdom of the body. It acted in literal metaphors. Lila must find all of this hard to stomach. Softly she closed the dark oak door.

Hoarsely Brook whispered: "Wherever he is, I hope Lila's father is miserable."

Helen kept her tone carefully neutral. "What I'd like to know is: do *you* feel guilty that neither of us was here to help Lila through this?"

Brook turned to cradle her. "No. I need what we share. There's something holy about raw, unadulterated sex."

Helen winced. Was that all this weekend had been to Brook — raw, unadulterated sex? She reached deep for a judicious reply. "Yes. And dangerous. I feel as though we're unleashing powerful forces, destructive ones."

"Really?" Brook seemed surprised. "Our energy may be powerful. But neither of us is destructive."

Visibly Helen shivered. "We all crash on our dark places, Brook."

Brook glanced at Helen's goosebumping arms. "Like my dream about Lila jumping off a cliff," she said softly. "Dealing with incest must feel like a plunge into death."

"Brook," Helen struggled between feeling objective and feeling far too involved to be. "It's not your responsibility to save anyone from either death or life. Besides, Lila won't allow you to take on her problems for long. You know that."

Looking drained of energy, Brook heaved a long sigh. "It riles me that Lila gets dumped and Jack gets his ego massaged by a new lover."

This time Helen arched an eloquent eyebrow. "Lila has given him a great deal of freedom to pursue his own life." She kissed Brook's cheek, which tasted of sea salt. They still wore the beloved, encircling ocean in their pores.

"I thought you were making chicken soup," Brook teased.

Automatically Helen went to the fridge and foraged for leftovers. "Be careful not to waste energy laying blame. You won't be very useful to Lila if you defend her like a devoted dog."

Brook's ears reddened. "You're right of course. But ... her dream, about you holding up the eggs? She and I keep weaving into one another's psyches, as though we're dreamers in the same dream."

"I don't doubt that Lila 'called' you back. I have the uneasy feeling that something here is just beginning."

"Do you, Cass?" Firmly Brook rested her arm on Helen's waist.

"You mean Cassandra, the seer? Hey, making chicken soup is simpler than fortune-telling."

Ruefully Brook chuckled. "Ain't it, though? Channelling takes real work."

"Hmm," Helen deboned the chicken. More than passingly she wondered if Brook felt woven into her life, as integrally as she did into Lila's.

CHAPTER ELEVEN

Like current in a lightning rod, Lila felt her distress pulse upward through Brook's arms. Slowly she felt the current change and her stubborn muscles unlock.

Hands bore down on the hollows in her shoulders, until relief brought involuntary tears to her eyes. Nervously Lila smiled up at Brook. "The kids are too quiet. I should be with them now, not Helen."

"Be here now," Brook whispered. Rubbing in lotion she pressed Lila's palms and fingertips, adjusted the blankets to keep Lila warm. Using the flat of her hands she kneaded Lila's spine like dough, circling up and in and down. Lila's body opened, water falling from rock.

Pressure in the hollows of her buttocks; Lila's resistance and consent to this unfamiliar intimacy. Hands exploring even the contours of her feet. Far from being eroticizing, those fingers awakened an implacable anger. Wanting to scream at Brook, Lila balled her hands into fists and hid them like weapons beneath the sheet. Oblivious, Brook alternated to the other leg, which was suddenly stiff and unbending. "Am I hurting you?" she asked softly.

"Yes. No," Lila mumbled.

Silent, Brook probed the pads of Lila's feet, the muscles of her shin and thigh. Suddenly Lila was listening to the persistent complaint of windshield wipers scraping away the mist of rain, to Jack's voice saying: "Well, I guess this is it ... " *This is it ... This is it ...* the wipers echoed. Caught between them, time twanged like a slingshot, breaking them apart between one moment and the next.

Above them loomed the sign for U.S. flights. Clumsily Lila got out of the Volvo and opened the trunk so Jack could get his bags.

In the midst of concrete railings, large vehicles and human traffic, she stood dwarfed. She did not understand the impulse which made Jack embrace her. For a moment she rested her head on the rough tweed of his shoulder, feeling like a sleepwalker or an observer in someone else's dream. Beads of rain gathered in Jack's hair, sank into Lila's scalp like bugs crawling for shelter. Awkwardly Jack said, "Well ... Take care of yourself."

Resentful, Lila stepped away from him. Too sharply she said: "I'll be all right. Now check in. I don't want to prolong this." Emphatically the driver of a Hustle Bus leaned on his horn. Relieved by this intercession of chance, Lila got quickly behind the wheel of the Volvo, driving away from Jack's hand while he was still wiping at the fog between them on the glass.

With only a cursory glance in the mirror, she changed lanes, heading for the Oak Street exit. Fortunately there was no driver in her blind spot to take advantage of her sudden destructive impulse. But she had better slow down. The on-ramp was winding and wet and constructed of very solid concrete.

Lila clamped down on the steering wheel, reminding herself that she was in control of her life, just as she was in control of this car. The world would call Jack's choice infidelity. But Lila was to blame that he had been driven to such a solution. In the final analysis, it had been Jack who was faithful to his needs. Faithfulness.

I wish I believed in God. What a farce it was, to believe in a deity who personally responded to petition or pain. Whatever the sex of God — Loving Father or Earth Mother — it was all the same. A reneging on the loneliness of being human, of making one's choices without benefit of the divine, which could neither bless nor damn nor intervene at all between act and consequence.

There's no one out there, Lila thought dully. Only some force waiting, pretending to be benign and caring. The best she could substitute for an absent God was her own conscience and some kind of concern for those who depended upon her. Did that make her a better parent than her mother had been to her?

She felt like a child, barely pubescent and very alone. Why did she persist in thinking that a mother — her mother at any rate — should be able to provide her child with love, even with caring from beyond the grave.

Lila shivered. That dream of her mother dying. Tubes in her arm and nostrils. Blue eyes blinking at something that Lila could not see.

Lila reaching to touch her mother's paralysed arm, fingers climbing along the ridge of bandages which covered her mother's labouring chest.

Somewhere in her skull her mother's voice saying: *You're nearly an adult. You don't want to cry, now do you?* Whether or not she did want to, she was certainly beyond needing her mother. Perhaps now she could forgive herself for wanting what her mother could not give her. After all, Jack had shown her what it was to think that she ought to be able to love someone and yet she could not. Better that she forgive herself for that glaring failure, rather than reproach her dead mother in a dumb and recurring demand for love.

The dream could be some kind of gestalt, Lila supposed, not about her mother at all, but about herself. Maybe it was her "breast" that was amputated, her ability to nurture and sustain another human person. To give nurture best, however, it was necessary to receive nurture oneself.

In a kind of cosmic nudge, Brook rubbed lotion into Lila's breasts. Sharp pain made her catch at Brook's wrists and cry out: "That's enough, Brook. I feel better, really."

Brook frowned slightly. "Lila. Will you talk? If you think your problems might burden me, I'm a big girl now. I'll decide my limits."

I'm a big girl now. Lila's mouth twisted into an ironic smile. Who was this woman that she lifted phrases right out of Lila's head before she even spoke them? And what defense could she erect against Brook's intuitiveness so that this did not continue to happen? Still, there was no need to turn Brook's empathy into an inappropriate act. Her smile wobbled. "What is the point of regurgitating, unless one is a bird? Perhaps I'm better off dealing with this alone. This pampering only makes me feel emotionally crippled."

With a contrite smile Brook patted Lila's blanketed knee. "Sometimes it helps to release feelings, no matter how self-indulgent that may seem to you."

"Melodramatic and selfish. Don't encourage me. Go back to Helen, won't you? You two are getting very friendly." Far from being teasing, Lila's voice was unbelievably staccato, at least to her own ears.

Like a miner's basin in a sunlit stream, Brook's eyes shone with gold flecks. Lila struggled to look away from them and could not. "You assume I want to be somewhere else than here."

"Well, you and Helen are lovers, aren't you? The whole world must not stop for my divorce." The words scraped in Lila's mouth. Did she need to — did she want to — know whether they were lovers, right now? Would that information help her to feel less like she was losing Helen's love as well as Jack's?

Like a Canada Day sparkler, Brook's lopsided smile flared and went suddenly out again. "You said I'd like her," she drawled.

Feeling inordinately betrayed, Lila turned her face away. Betrayed? What promises had she and Brook exchanged, what covenant had they made together? Lila was being ridiculous. What was wrong with her anyway that she expected to keep her friends in inaccessible towers, when she already benefitted so much from their efforts? No doubt she was just reaching out for love again, focusing on anyone who might give her what no one could give her, a sense of being lovable ... *What a deception it is to want love. Need catches me like a fly struggling in sticky goo. How am I to free myself from it?* But Brook was gripping Lila by the chin, giving her less, not more, room to get away from her. "You think that because you're my friend you aren't as important to me as my lover is?"

Like a round-eyed fly, Lila tried to focus on one of several replicas of Brook. Woodenly she said: "Lovers are blind for awhile. There's nothing wrong with that."

"There's nothing wrong with needing us, either. When your life is falling apart, the happiness of others can be pretty tedious." Brook's hands were too warm on Lila's shoulders, too solid for Lila, who felt pinned on cardboard and other-dimensional. Perhaps Brook would go away if Lila but closed her eyes. How silly. As though what she could not bear to see or hear could simply be wished away. Brook's tone became as sensitive as a thermometer placed beneath the tongue. "Have I let you down, somehow? Talk to me. Don't make me guess."

"I feel inadequate, as usual," Lila whispered. She supposed that that was an honest, if vague, statement of her condition.

"You're not inadequate. You're one of the brightest, finest women I've ever met."

"You don't know me," Lila said, hoping that she sounded jocular.

"I know there's a powerful link between us. Remember your dream about Helen holding up red eggs? That really happened. Just after we became lovers, we went for an egg hunt on the beach."

Lila's eyes narrowed. Was it a curse or a gift, to know what was to come or, perhaps more accurately, what had already been? Many of her dreams, however, were more violent than prophetic, dreams so upsetting that Lila knew she must deal with them. Jack's departure, it seemed, was activating a snake pit full of fears. Yet it was not Brook she must talk to, but Tracy. Otherwise Lila would only get mired in her love for this woman and in this misplaced and ill-timed need. Past her clenched throat Lila spoke. "I'm glad for Helen, by the by. I think you'll be good for one another."

Brook drew into the lotus position and waited, her amber eyes like x-rays into Lila's heart. "Let's celebrate at a more appropriate time. After all, you called me home so that I could help you to deal with this, didn't you?"

Lila blinked at her. "How did I 'call' you? I don't understand."

"I dreamt that I saw you walking towards the edge of a cliff. There were rocks below and a strong current and you seemed determined to jump."

Lila touched her, to see if Brook was really there, not just some apparition from a private, cherished dream about having the power to summon someone back to her. "I really did try to do that, when I was about twelve years old, after my father — " Eloquently she screwed up her mouth. "Lying in your room, I was remembering that. Perhaps you picked up on it." She flushed guiltily. "I'm sorry, Brook. I won't go in your room again when you're not home, I promise."

"Lila, I don't plan to punish you for being in my room!" As if to punctuate her words, she blew a strand of hair gustily out of her eyes.

Good. Bad. Sounds without meaning or purpose. Behind Lila's eyelids a giant iceberg drifted. She sat near the top of it, a small shadow concealed in its glittering conclivities. It was carrying her away somewhere too far to return. From an immense distance, Lila murmured: "Love is always conditional, and always elusive. I try to be 'good,' but whether I'm 'good' or not, things still keep happening to me. It's not even that I don't deserve what happens, because I do — " Words slid out of Lila's mouth, slithered across the mattress. She indicted herself to Brook, as alone she had indicted herself many times before. "When I was about four years old I had a nightmare. I went into my parent's room and crawled in between them. They cradled me and laughed and I went to sleep, feeling safe from harm. In the night I must have reached out because I woke up holding my father's penis in my hand and he was breathing funny. I started to whimper and my mother got impatient with me. She said if I was going to keep her awake I could go back to my own bed. 'I may as well take her,' my father said, and carried me in his arms to my room — "

Brook touched Lila's lips with a cautioning finger. "Are you telling me that you feel to blame, somehow, for your father's hard-on? Isn't it just as likely that you didn't touch him at all but that he put your hand there."

"I suppose. But if I hadn't climbed into his bed maybe he wouldn't have thought about doing that to me."

"Christ, Lila!" Brook swore. "You were a baby having a nightmare. Where else would you go for comfort but to your parents?"

"You don't understand. I can be as logical and 'adult' as I want, but over and over I'm still the child who made my parents quarrel. My mother said I did. Because of me my father hit her."

Brook clenched her hands, although she asked evenly enough: "And what is it you were supposed to have done to cause that, Lila?"

"I — I can't remember. Some of it I've blanked out. I remember coming home from school, to see my mother with a bruise on her cheek. She said she fell against the cupboard. But my father sneered: 'You know why you got that. By covering up for her. She's the one who should have got it.' My mother looked at me hard and said: 'Maybe so. Maybe I was wrong to cover up for her. I won't do it again.'"

This time Brook made no effort to disguise her anger. "What a gamy couple your parents were. Lila, why is it that you got to have all the guilt? Didn't your mother have any, for not sparing you from the abuse of Mr. God?"

Lila could not meet Brook's eyes. "I guess we let each other down. My mother died of cancer, Brook, and I know I wished death on her, so many times."

"Well, aren't you powerful! Did you also order the lump on your breast, to make up for giving your mother cancer?"

"On my — Is that why it hurt when you were touching me there?"

"Yes. Let me show you." Gently Brook lowered the blanket and placed Lila's reluctant fingers over her left breast. Above Lila's nipple was a furrow like one worn by rain into soil, and a fibrosity that no healthy breast should have. Brook said firmly: "The body listens to the kind of message you've been giving yours about being unworthy. Get a check-up. Even if you have a cyst or something, it can easily be removed. Just let up on yourself, Lila. Before you think of half a dozen more reasons that you're not good enough to live."

For a moment the room swam in thick, encompassing shadows. "Why is it our breasts ... " Lila whispered almost inaudibly.

"Well, guilt may be a common denominator between you and your mother — but I don't really think that you should die because of yours."

"You don't know how cold I can be. I pretended to Jack that I loved him, but all the while I schemed about leaving him. I was a coward, though, afraid of what it would mean to be on my own. So I deliberately got pregnant with Cyndi, thinking that would make me stay. Then I resented my own baby because I put myself in that kind of trap. I kept wishing that the umbilical chord would wrap around her throat and there wouldn't be a child to make me stay ... " No wonder people chose to lie to themselves. This filtering of facts was raw sewage. There was no way to stay clean or to look good. Lila was mired in her less than noble motives; sinking beneath the weight of her own judgement.

Brook's laugh was a rough cloak over her own pain. "If thoughts were corpses, we'd all have a garden full of bodies ... We either love someone or we do not. Love is almost larger than our ability either to give it or to withhold it ... Let go of your guilt, Lila. You've carried it around long enough. Or do you want to drown in old regrets?"

Her big confession and all Brook could find to say was that guilt, and not Lila, was horrible. As if simply getting rid of guilt would rid her of this unavoidable awareness that she had been selfish and unloving for so many years. It was time, however, to regain her dignity. No crisis should render her as helpless and small as this. "I'm sorry, Brook. You're right, this is quite sick on my part."

Brook's expression was animated by what could have been anger or a thin despair. Then she was kissing Lila on the mouth, passionately and very thoroughly, reaching in as though to exorcise a demon, to pluck it suddenly and inexorably out. Lila felt the beat of her own blood surging like a narrow waterfall through her temples. Then she tore her mouth free, turning an incredulous and humiliated face to the wall. If this was sympathy on Brook's part, it was strange and disloyal behaviour for both of them. Lila was too startled to move or speak.

Very slowly Brook stroked Lila's hair and crooned to her. Despite herself, Lila began to feel safe and tired and warm, drifting away from Brook towards a cocoon of sleep and blessed oblivion, where she could neither blame herself nor be blamed for anything she might have omitted to do or caused to be done ...

CHAPTER TWELVE

With a curious sense of having reached safety, Brook opened the door to her room.

"How's the patient?" Helen lay on Brook's futon, her limbs an open statement of fatigue. Relieved of shoes and socks, her feet looked narrow and long.

"I'm not sure." Jack-knifing to sit beside her, Brook clasped Helen's thumb firmly between her fingers. "Better if she has a breast exam ... "

"A breast exa — you mean for cancer?"

"I don't mean for the hell of it."

"Spare me the jokes." Helen sat up. "Whatever possessed you to buy a futon? I've slept on carpets more comfortable."

Like a small child seeking comfort, Brook inserted herself into Helen's embrace, wordlessly nuzzling into her neck.

"You know, I've figured out Lila's appeal for you." Helen's jaw shaped the words in Brook's forehead. "You think she's vulnerable. For some people, there's nothing more attractive than neediness."

Unwillingly Brook lifted her head, not ready to deal with any more emotion, especially the emotion of jealousy. She wasn't sure enough about what she felt for Lila to deal with that.

Helen insisted pluckily. "Self-sufficiency may not 'turn you on.' But don't fool yourself, Brook. Lila may be even more independent than you are."

With a fingertip Brook circled Helen's soft mouth. "Are you worried that I'm in love with her?"

"Don't arouse me. This is serious."

"I'm listening with my fingers, " Brook whispered.

Helen looked confused by Brook's tenderness. "Love has to be motivated by more than sympathy, Brook."

"Lila has a backbone of iron. I know, I massaged her," Brook wisecracked.

"Don't get me wrong, I *want* to help Lila. I just don't want to lose you because she's having a crisis."

"Am I lost?" From an elbow Brook turned to face her.

"I see the way you look at her. Like she's a rare object in some world-class museum."

Carefully Brook answered. " Perhaps you recognize the look because you care in the same way."

Helen let out her breath, gustily. "Unrequited love is tiresome. That being the case, friendship is far more valuable."

Sharply Brook looked at her. "Love is never lost. Or wasted."

With a stiff grin, Helen turned towards her. "Maybe I'm just not as optimistic as you are, Brook. Loving alone is loving alone. Period."

Unflinchingly Brook met Helen's torch-blue eyes. "I can't speak for Lila, but I can for myself. I don't want either of us — you or me — to fear being vulnerable. Or being independent."

Softly Helen cleared her throat. "If you and I weren't so new, I wouldn't feel quite so much like love is slipping away before it takes any kind of shape of its own. I mean, I barely have time to build up illusions about you. What kind of romance is that?"

Brook laughed softly, rubbing noses with her. For a moment she tried to comprehend just what kind of love Helen must have for Lila, to want her so deeply yet to settle for what Lila was prepared to give, a distant if steadying friendship. Suddenly she was aware that Helen needed protecting just as much as Lila did; the kind of protection that could come only from being deeply loved. "Shall we give it more of a shape, our romance?" she whispered.

Arms and thighs encircled Brook; there was the welcome pressure of Helen's mound of Venus. With the flat of her hand Brook felt her way along the bristling triangle created by Helen's generous pubis, followed her lover's pelvic bones, the hollowed valley of her stomach. She was filled with that curious mix of security and excitement that was always there when she touched Helen, an active soothing and seduction that occurred at one and the same time.

"How are Cyndi and Mark?" she asked gently.

"Oh, Mark is being hyperactive and talking too much — about anything and everything but what's on his mind. Cyndi is totally attached to her headphones. She's barely speaking at all."

"Well, if anyone can reach them I know you can," Brook said. "They really trust you."

"I'm blundering and moralistic. Whatever I do, I'm sure it's not the right touch."

"Can anyone protect them from their lives? With a little help, they'll no doubt realize that they still need — and want — their parents' love."

"Yeah." Helen sounded unconvinced. "What in their experience can I compare this to? I left my daughter. What do I know about how Mark and Cyndi feel?"

Thoughtfully Brook put her arm under Helen's neck. "Does it matter who leaves? Did you feel more powerful, Helen, because you left?"

"How can I describe that decision? For the first time in my life I was deliriously in love with a woman. With Tony I felt restless and impatient, almost claustrophobic."

Listening intently, Brook nestled into Helen's familiar scent. She felt rather than saw Helen turn her head away. "Did I feel powerful? No, I felt idiotic. By leaving Tony I lost my child. Reaching too far for that elusive brass ring called love won me the contempt of the court. And of my lover."

Brook gazed into Helen's dear face. So Lila's divorce was activating some of Helen's unresolved pain about her own ... Of course it would. "Nobody said freedom was easy." Did that remark sound "preachy"? Brook hoped not.

With a small sigh Helen closed her eyes. "Freedom is a twentieth-century mirage. Choices bind. Inevitably."

"Yes. But at least we make them."

"Do we? Love is renewed daily. There are spinoffs to sticking with nearly anyone."

"Hmm ... Had you stayed with Tony I wouldn't be here now. And that would mean that I'd lost something beautiful."

"Is my love beautiful to you?" Huge violet eyes widened.

"Yes, Helen." Brook said shakily. "It is beautiful to me. I'm trying hard to believe that I deserve it."

Without humour Helen laughed. "Deserving has very little to do with love ... "

"Yes, it does. When I don't believe that I deserve love, I sabotage it. Like Lila, I find it difficult to be cared about."

"I know. You seem perplexed whenever I'm tender ... Despite your belief that you deserve happiness, I might add."

"Is rising above my limits simply a matter of wanting to?" Fiercely Brook reached to embrace Helen, combatting her sense of being helpless in a separate body, at one and the same time both rewarded by — and isolated from — touch. She could accept neither the absence of Lila nor this merging with Helen, felt split into halves and disassembled somewhere between them both. Clouded by involuntary and blinding tears, Brook bore down with wrenching hands, pulling Helen up by her intestines towards a dangerous cliff.

Startled, Helen drew in to herself while Brook's fingers circled and thrust and insisted. Then Helen's hips rose and she moaned. Firmly, she placed her hands on Brook's chest, seeking to make her tender again. But all Brook could think about was controlling Helen, getting her lover to climax.

A ragged cry escaped Helen's throat, and another. She twisted her thighs, as if to expel the force violating her body. Brook was conscious that Helen must hate to be loved like this, to be a tool in the hands of an inexorable impulse. Why did Brook suddenly want to own her, to obliterate and control her? Her own violence left Brook terrified. Hoarsely she said: "Take me in. Let me in, Helen. Let me."

Letting, of course, had everything to do with it, but it was not Helen's letting go that had to happen. Brook waited through the pounding of her blood, through the sense of being a virago in motion. Repentant, she collapsed on top of Helen, feeling contaminated by a dark and sluggish force.

Helen rolled Brook away from her and unto her back. Then she seemed to find her music, her orchestra, and played Brook as though she were a conductor performing a concert with supple concentration and nuance. In some realm that had to do with inner sound, the notes blended and fell distinct.

Helen was gentler than Brook had been with her, more tentative but no less in control. A long time she played, elongating and prolonging Brook's numb resistance. Finally, Brook felt that if she waited one more moment for orgasm she would die. She stole an incredulous look at Helen. Her mouth looked serene — patient — as though she were meditating instead of making love.

Suddenly Brook's hardness disintegrated, the unusual cruelty that was her response to this contradiction. She felt discovered, found out, as if Helen had some key to a door that, since Tracy, she had locked on herself. Concretions of cynicism, of sexual pragmatism, dropped like weights away from her. It was as though she had been knocking, wishing somehow that a door would — and would not — open, and finally it did. In the dark behind the door, she was suddenly afraid of what she now might discover. Afraid of being her father's daughter, whose needs could not be simply met by one woman.

She grasped Helen's arm. Helen waited, motionless, no doubt feeling the clasp of Brook's vagina and the strong spasms in the walls of her. For a long time Brook would not let her fingers go. Gently Helen embraced her. Her warmth filled Brook, made her feel suddenly serene again.

With sudden alarm she asked: "Are you staying, Helen? After all, you love my futon so ... "

Helen snorted. "No. I'm going to put my clothes on and go home. Right after my post-sex smoke."

Brook looked up at her and held her very tight. "I love you," she said. Her throat filled with tears that would not fall. She thought about Lila, about the woman who even now could be choosing to snuff out her own life like a candle. For Lila, getting cancer could very well be a deliberate act of suicide. "Helen, do you think we choose how and when we die?"

"From 'I love you' to dying. What a Freudian leap." Whispering, Helen gazed into Brook's grieving face. "You need to ask me? I thought you believed in the immortality of the soul and its return through many lives."

"I do." Brook gurgled with self-deprecating laughter. "But I sure don't know what I'm going to do every minute of this one ... I've known Lila before. She rejected me. I have things to resolve with her."

Too carefully, Helen asked: "Do you remember details?"

Reluctantly Brook told her about the Dutchman. "We lived in the Netherlands on rolling farmland. She ran away from me and took our little girl. I don't remember why she ran away."

"Maybe you made brutal love to her and told her obscene things. That's a fair guess, I think."

"I'm sorry." Brook buried her hot face in Helen's shoulder. "I feel so destructive and — furious, somehow. Like you're making me love you. And I don't want to."

"Isn't that rejecting me?" Unconscious of her flowering labia, Helen sat cross-legged.

But Brook was more lost in the shock of a complex of memories than she was responsive to her desire. "You comforted me before. I used you to get over her then."

"Charming little bitch," Helen said breathlessly. "What do you mean by 'using me' to get over her? Did you dump me afterwards?"

Brook stiffened, wishing she could prevent the images in her mind, which were falling like jigsaw pieces into place. "No. I lived with you. We never married. It was a scandal to the Church."

"So? I repeat. How is that using me?"

"I never said I love you. I worked you hard. And once, I struck you."

"And I stayed?" Helen sounded incredulous. "No wonder I'm a feminist in this life." That other time must have moved behind her eyelids also. With little sense of volition she said: "I miscarried, more than once."

Brook's eyes spilled over. "You died in childbirth. You were just twenty-four years old."

Helen put her forehead to Brook's as though to pick up or sustain the sputtering flow of images. "You kept calling me to come back. Too late. I remember thinking I got even with you."

"At what cost." Feeling crazy, Brook covered Helen's eyes.

"Aren't you lucky?" Helen said, grimly removing her hands. "You get another chance."

"At what?" Brook said flatly. "Loving you both? What are the odds of either of you allowing that?"

Helen rocked uneasily back on her haunches. "About the same as the odds of us being here again, in this place and time. I'm glad you're not a man. You can't control me now. At least not in my womb."

"No." Brook whispered. "I never could. It makes me as furious now as it did then."

Helen parrotted her words. "Let me in. Let me in, Brook. Don't try to prevent me."

Brook heaved a shuddering sigh. "Why do you want in? I'm no better now, it seems, than I was then."

With an attempt at humour, Helen shrugged. "I dunno. Maybe I need the excitement."

"Like a monsoon needs more rain," Brook muttered.

CHAPTER THIRTEEN

Lila donned shorts and a bulky cotton shirt and went to make coffee. Sunlight spilled on the oak table, highlighting the varnished grains of the wood. A gentle wind rustled the curtains; the sky was cirillian blue, bright enough to hurt her eyes.

She poured juice, thick with the pulp of oranges, glad that she had not bumped into the lovers in the kitchen. She felt tenuous and raw, the sounds of their lovemaking having kept her sleepless. It was her insomnia, however, that she felt was unreasonable because it was unnecessary. The women had not been thoughtlessly loud, they had just been — vocal.

That she was upset by their spending the night together was hardly a feeling she could express. After all, Helen had often stayed over, sometimes in a guest room and sometimes sharing a bed with Lila. So she could hardly be expected to realize that her being there would disturb Lila in any way.

Still, Lila had been very clear with Brook about not wanting to deal with overnight guests. Surely she had the right to feel affronted that Brook appeared to have ignored Lila's wishes simply because desire superseded any agreement she felt had been made.

How ungrateful Lila felt, after sapping Brook's energy to deal with her dark and harrowing confessions. Why shouldn't Brook comfort herself in the arms of someone whose life was not a morass sinking into a quagmire?

The crows were disturbed by something. Their jeering cries almost made her wince. Lila glanced out to the lawn. Sun and shadow chased one another in the leafy branches of the oak. Brook was barely visible, reaching slowly around the trunk and coaxing. Lila heard the lilt of her voice, saw a grey squirrel dart forward and retreat to a safe perch. Around and around circled tiny paws, making short work of the nut. Then Brook offered husked nuts to the crows. She seemed to be mediating between species, reassuring them that they would all be fed.

How kind Brook was, and how giving. Was that what their kiss had been, a kindness on Brook's part — compassion and not passion at all? Alone in the kitchen her ears reddened. Is that what her "scruples" amounted to, jealousy, even rivalry with her dear friend over a common object of desire? Lila would believe so, if not for the memories of Helen as gazelle, hands and feet clamouring for footholds in jagged rocks on challenging winter hikes. Helen, who had taught her how to halt a headlong plunge down white walls of snow, to veer on skis away from gorge and crevass, whole trees and boulders hurtling nearer and faster than any car, on the rim of the terrifying, frozen world ... literally trusting Helen with her life.

Learning to confide, on nights when the stars blinked cold and aloof, eons removed from anything human. Trusting Helen's skin on a narrow mattress in some chalet, her warmth radiating into Lila's chill dreams like a space heater. Moon shadows nestling into Helen's thighs and breasts like a reverent lover ... Oh, for the courage, for the safety of shadows to trace Helen's pelvis with the rim of an open and hungry hand ... Letting sleep come, reluctant and sad.

And now Brook was Helen's lover. And Lila didn't know which one of them she envied more.

Like a call to arms the phone rang. In the moment it took Lila to pick up the receiver, she was swamped by an illogical fury that her peace was always interrupted, that there were so few unstructured moments in her life. Every exchange she had felt truncated, choppy. It was probably the school board, however, offering her a half-day's work. She dared not ignore the call.

Even as she answered, Lila knew that it would not be the school board. It was her doctor, Judith Kranston, with the results of Lila's mammogram. Dr. Kranston wanted to schedule her for a biopsy, to be done by a specialist in breast cancer. Colour drained from Lila's face. Carefully she sat down, her voice studiedly even. "Will this biopsy determine whether or not the cancer is malignant?"

Dr. Kranston sounded hesitant but determined. "There is reason to believe that the growth must be removed."

"Oh." Lila said. The door opened and Brook stood smiling in the kitchen. Lila turned an open face to her, mutely begging her to stay. "So tell me what I do now. "

"I've arranged an appointment for you with Dr. Kline. Her office is quite near you, at — " Dr. Kranston gave the address and phone number. "What you 'must do now', as you put it, is be calm. It's probable that we detected the growth in its early stages."

"Probable. You don't know for sure?"

"Lila, I'm a lowly G.P. I leave those decisions to specialists. Dr. Kline is highly regarded as a surgeon and very knowledgeable. She'll let you know exactly what is needed."

"Thanks," Lila said, feeling most unthankful indeed. Making note of the appointment, she put down the receiver, aware of the tremour in her hand as though observing it in someone else. The sense of choice, of even minimal control, was gone. Her mouth felt full of wood chips and very dry.

She finally released Brook from her silent question. "Apparently you were right about my breast."

If Brook was surprised she did not look it. "I have a book in my room, about vitamin and herbal therapy. Shall I get it?"

"I'll come with you." Suddenly Lila did not want to let Brook out of her sight. She, too, might disappear, like everything else in her life that Lila took at all for granted.

On Brook's window ledges seedlings sprouted: tomato and pepper plants, chives, marjoram, basil and thyme. Bemused, Lila went to touch the teeming plants. Through the open window, she was aware of earth smells, of sap running from the bark of trees. The earth was renewing itself. And she faced death.

Silently Brook thumbed through Witches Heal. Trying for humour, Lila murmured: "Adera said you were a witch. I should have listened to her."

"Ummm ... There are obvious problems with your immune system. It is not fielding abnormal cell growth. Teas, like red clover, comfrey and violet would be good for you. I can get you some echinacea root, at Folk Lore. You'll also need to 'up' your intake of vitamins B and C and absorb extra calcium, magnesium and zinc."

"The homeopathic route? I'm not sure, Brook. Maybe I should just listen to my doctors."

"If you believe they can help, they will. Still, they will probably suggest one or two methods of treatment, if the growth is malignant: chemotherapy and radiation. Hard on the body, my friend. And doctors won't tell you about vitamins or herbs to compensate for the effects. For example, drinking miso soup can help leech radiation."

Lila nodded, although Brook's words came to her from a distance, garbled. "Isn't all of this unscientific? I don't think you have the training to diagnose what I need."

From the edge of her desk, Brook studied Lila's face. "None of this will harm you, Lila. If anything, these things may help you to control this disease."

"Control cancer." Lila smiled without humour. "Sometimes, Brook, you are very fanciful."

Brook seemed to gather up her scant five feet and some, even her voice taller than usual. "You've been giving yourself messages that you want to die. Just how soon are you programming that to happen?"

Lila stifled a sharp disquiet. This was the second time that Brook had made a connection between cancer and the power of the mind — the power of guilt to act as her executioner. "Are suicidal thoughts uncommon? Surely I'm not unique in feeling sorry for myself."

"Suicide is a very angry thought. And a deadly one."

Lila blinked. Having confessed her sense of responsibility for losing Jack, she did not feel like examining the more fundamental level of her responsibility to live. If she had one. She whispered: "Do you actually think we're given any choice over how and when we die?"

For a small eternity Brook seemed to be considering a private dilemma, one which kept her silent. Then her strange eyes cleared and she looked fearless again, if somewhat troubled. "I think that we choose every scene in the drama of our lives. There are no accidents. What would have happened if you left Jack when you wanted to? Staying didn't change anything. It only made leaving his decision."

Lila was beginning to come out of her numbness, to feel provoked if not actively manipulated. She heard her voice going up, sharply. "Don't confuse the issue by bringing Jack into this. You imply that the victim of cancer becomes a victim by her own choice. I will not assume that I'm complying with getting this disease so that I have something else for which to feel responsible."

"Lila, thoughts create reality. And thoughts can change it. There is a link between getting cancer and feelings. Repressed emotions affect the body."

Lila tried not to feel both judged and indicted but she did. "Is this what happens when I share with you? Brook. I thought you were different, somehow. Less emotionally manipulative than you're being."

As if to clear away smoke-filled air, Brook waved her hands. "If by now you don't know me well enough to trust me — "

Lila leaned on the radiator, dangerously close to upsetting the flat of herbs. Her tone was deceptively calm. "You mean because we're supposed to have shared a past life — or since we support the mutual fantasy that we do." Behind her even tone was the hostility of a physical attack.

Brook's expression became unreadable. Slowly and evenly she murmured: "I was concentrating on far more current events, myself. If you feel bullied or reproached, forgive me. I don't know the balance between concern and cruelty. I'm just going on instinct here — the instinct that you need either to be very angry or to cry. You're safe to do both, you know. I do love you." She came to stand in front of Lila and loosely held her wrists.

Love. Like a decrepit wall, Lila's face crumbled. Love had nothing to do with logic or the argument between them. Brook was not an evil person or even a stupid one. But how could she believe such dangerous things? Was the illusion of choice Brook's crutch in the world, just as logic was hers? They both needed crutches, then, to deal with life's imponderable and permanent cruelties. Still, she had to be guided by her own intuitions. Brook's premises certainly could not be trusted. Pulling herself free, she said stiffly: "I'll take care of myself. Dealing with things alone is all the honesty of which I'm capable."

With a frustrated gesture, Brook raked through her wavy brown hair. "I'm here for you, Lila. You are not alone."

"Here for me ... " Lila repeated, her breathing jagged. "No, Brook. Each of us is here for herself. And by herself."

Brook seemed momentarily stymied. "Is that what you did with Jack — close him out and then wonder why he went away? What are you afraid of, Lila? That someone will see through your defenses? That you might — oh, horrors — need someone?"

"I *need* my defenses," Lila said tartly. "You seem to use whatever information you get against me." Deliberately she turned her back on Brook.

"So your solution is to hide every time you have an angry thought. Do you think you hid from Jack that you didn't love him? Or did Jack somehow lose your respect because he loved you enough to marry you. And how, Lila, could anyone love you when you do not love yourself?"

Many times Lila had been told that her eyes were gunbarrel grey. Now she levelled them at Brook as though she held a rifle to her head. Contemptuously she snorted. "And then I gave myself cancer. Just to punish myself. Really, Brook, this amateur psychologizing is offensive."

"You'd rather die than make a choice. Wouldn't you? Is divorce so unspeakable to you? People begin again all the time."

Don't listen, Lila thought. *Salt pellet words, that's all they are. Some of them are bound to hit and sting.* "I'm not like Helen or like you, off to replace men with women — as though your relationships are any easier. Examine your own motives, Brook. You may come up with a dark mirror, too."

"Oh, Lila." Brook seemed almost ready to let Lila push her away. "Is that it? Are you afraid of being a lesbian? Is that worth dying for — or staying married?"

Lila felt the collapse of her last line of defense. Why was Brook playing for power? And where was Lila's own power to command? "Brook," she said darkly, "let it go. Let it — and let me — be!"

"No. Jack let you go. I don't intend to." Standing at least six feet away from Lila, Brook crossed her arms. So why did Lila feel embraced by her in some binding way? It shocked her to see Brook through a film of tears. Her own vulnerability made her cruel. "Don't make me run from you again. You're quite a jailor, Brook — in either lifetime." The shock of hearing her unpremeditated words made her realize what she was remembering from that other time. She blundered out of Brook's room and away from this distressing confrontation between worlds no longer held apart by the dimensions of time and place.

Responsibility for cancer. Resentment carried her legs faster and faster down a steep hillside, until her muted senses conveyed to her that she was heading for the beach. Yes, there was a biting wind from the ocean and salt spray dampened her face and hair. Breathing fast, she hunched into her collar, slowed enough to take note of where she was. The sky was alive with the flight of gulls; on sand and water, ducks and geese waddled and bobbed. Around her was the cycle of life and death, carrion crows feeding on refuse flung from the ocean to die under the pitiless sun. And other life, merely carried by the tides towards a less immediate dying.

Agitated, Lila shook her head, walking down and down towards the waterfront. She felt weak-kneed as she descended. Gulls screamed loudly, forlornly wheeling over the invader in their world.

To the north the green mountains were being steadily forested; logging companies poured their deadly wood preservatives into the inlet. Vancouver the beautiful, with a high incidence of cancer despite its reputation for clean water and air and soil. How many others would become victims of environmental cancer, exchanging health for the conveniences of a modern life style? "Development" and "progress" —

double-edged, cutting blades. Every evolution both in technology and in life dearly bought.

Lila stopped walking, horrified by Brook's belief that her own attitudes could affect or halt cancer. Asbestos and lead, mercury and PCBs. The planet was being inexorably poisoned, with very little concern for the future of any species, including that of humanity. Cancer was just one symptom of prolonged human plunder of the environment. The earth was a living organism. Nourishment had to be returned to it as nourishment was returned to the individual body. The need to replenish was as cyclic and continuous as summer and winter.

And what about the gene "pool" she shared with her mother? But that death was nearly two decades removed. There had been many advances in the treatment of cancer since then. Lila certainly would not — did not expect to — die at the age of thirty-seven. But time was passing like a great blade through a field of wheat. Death — her death — would come, just as inevitably as had her birth. If not now, then soon enough. Even assuming that desire didn't somehow trigger a belief in the illusion of eternity, how could she face this particular death, meet it with courage? Would dying be any easier just because she had done previous dress rehearsals? She certainly didn't feel ready to bring down the curtain. Did she?

There's a link between cancer and repressed emotions. Just enough truth in that to rob Lila of her righteous anger. Brook needed to control Chance by believing that willpower was stronger than dumb Luck. That was all. Yet Brook could be struck by something falling out of the sky, or assaulted by a mugger or — to use a more "down-home" example — raped by a person like Lila's father. Her mouth twisted. *I call such things random and incidental. Brook calls them predictable.* How invidious and punitive were such beliefs. Brook had the audacity to talk about Lila's guilt and then dump more guilt on her.

What stubborn dishonesty. Industrialists were spawning genetic mutants as prolifically as fish spawn. Better that Brook should take responsibility for her own part in allowing the earth to be made into a festering cesspool.

Putting the blame "out there" in the world outside her skin made her uneasy. In at least one respect, Brook was right: Lila could choose to take care of her body. Whether her precautions would be enough, sufficient unto the damage already sustained in her cells, she could not be certain. But if Brook wanted her to make tea and drink miso and meditate every day as she had long ago stopped doing, Lila could recognize that as caring. She supposed that Brook didn't have to be logical about the reality of disease and death; she needed only to think that she was doing something. Like Lila needed to keep putting one foot down in front of the other until today turned into tomorrow. Until this desperate time was only history and something else was happening in her life at last — presuming that life was a progression between birth and the grave, and not an eternal circle.

She turned, plodding back up the steep incline to the tarred pavement. Climbing tired her, inordinately. Uncertainty, like sediment riled in a clear river basin, was clouding her energy. Still, she could not expect serenity until she knew what her options were. Time she would lose, absorbed by her treatments for cancer. And time taken away from teaching was literally money. For now, though, Jack would send enough to pay the mortgage — after all, he would need to assuage his guilt for leaving Mark and Cyndi.

How cynical of her. Jack was basically a decent man, selfish perhaps in his need for physical satisfaction, but reasonably fair. It was his sense of responsibility that Lila had to fear — that he would learn she had cancer and feel obligated to return to her.

Never, Lila thought. *If our love is dead, Jack's pity would be putrescent.* Impatiently she rubbed tears away from her mouth.

She did not know at what stage in her ramblings she decided to dial Helen's number. Then the receiver was picked up and Helen's beloved voice electronically invited Lila to leave a message. She let the receiver find the cradle, blundering away from having to ask for something inchoate and blind.

CHAPTER FOURTEEN

The waiting room was filled with balding children and young women, some of them skeletal. Draped over tabletops and spilling from large bins were stuffed and plastic toys, doll houses, trucks and building blocks. From the coatracks and the umbrella stand came the smell of damp and rain. Comforted by Helen's hand, Lila eavesdropped on receptionists who were scheduling biopsies and surgeries, engaged in delicate negotiations with various hospitals. Then Lila saw a slender, grey-haired woman identified as a doctor by her stethescope. The woman handed a file to one of the receptionists, mumbling instructions in technical language. After her retreating back, the receptionist called cheerfully: "Yes, Dr. Kline. I'll get on it right away." Lila's pulse jumped. So this was the woman upon whose judgement Lila's life depended.

However competent Judith Kranston might find the good doctor, Kline was quite obviously overworked. In less than fifteen minutes, four patients went through her doors. Then it was Lila's turn.

"Do you want me to come in with you?" Helen whispered.

Lila hesitated. "If it's bad news, I'd rather have time to create a poker face. Sorry, Helen. I'd feel naked otherwise."

Helen's clasp steadied her. "Hey. Just don't forget, you hold the chits."

With a precarious smile, Lila turned her back and marched into Kline's inner sanctum, feeling that she was facing a firing squad, not a card game.

Dr. Kline was businesslike in a way that an efficiency expert would have envied. Even her voice was clipped. She confirmed Kranston's belief that Lila's cancer was malignant. "We'll do the biopsy. You needn't fear waking up without your breast. Even if there is need to do radical surgery

— a mastectomy — the operation would be scheduled after you consent to it. You will also need surgery to remove the lymph nodes under your left arm. The lump you have is at one o'clock and there may be nodal involvement." After dropping that bombshell, she said: "You can get dressed. I have surgical rights at two hospitals. My office will call you once they've arranged for an operating room."

With bare civility, Lila drawled: "Hold on. I have a work schedule, too. If I'm hospitalized my employer — and I — need to plan around that. Will I be?"

"Not for the biopsy. From that you should be conscious in a couple of hours. Arrange for someone to drive you home. You will be having a general anaesthetic and cannot legally drive for twenty-four hours afterward. The lymph surgery is more involved — allow about four days of hospitalization, depending on how much fluid you drain."

Lila stared. She hadn't the slightest idea of the function of her lymph nodes, let alone comprehending how she would be affected by their absence. Resentfully she thought: *The cancer business is definitely booming and I'm just one more carrier.* She struggled to be fair.

Patricia Kline's waiting room was filled to capacity. Of course she was peremptory. Still, Dr. Kline could defend herself, very well it would seem. It was Lila who needed protection: against a medical establishment which would, as Brook had warned, act *on* her and not necessarily with her. Like a proud person will who must suddenly depend upon others of only precarious generosity, Lila felt acutely embarrassed, even a sense that she had been betrayed by her own body. The cold hand of wariness twisted in her gut.

"What about chemotherapy or radiation? Is it too early for you to know about that?"

"I'll know more about the levels and types of treatment you need once I find out how far the disease has spread."

"There must be an alternative to chemotherapy," Lila said doggedly. "Do I have to take chemicals into my body if I don't want to?"

"You don't have to do anything if living is not important to you. A combination of chemotherapy and radiation increases your chances of survival by far. Don't worry about any of this now. Leave your treatment to the experts. Okay?" Cursorily, Dr. Kline patted Lila's shoulder. "Good girl." The door closed on her exit. Good dog, Lila thought. Sit. Wag. Dress. She joined Helen in the waiting room, avoiding her tender glance.

"Lunch, or home?" Helen asked. "How much time out do you need, before facing the domestic inquisition?"

Lila's smile felt like a nervous tick. "Lunch, thanks. Don't count on my appetite, though."

"She took all of a minute. I wonder what she earns per hour."

"Multiply the rate by sixty patients," Lila grumbled. "Let's get out of here."

"Be glad she's not a gynaecologist," Helen wisecracked. "She'd be sued for not taking time to warm the speculum."

"The chilling cost of health," Lila punned feebly.

"Well?" Helen looked strained, reminding Lila that keeping her friend in suspense was not kind. "How serious is it?"

Lila shivered. "Not serious enough to send for Jack."

"Well, he's an actor, isn't he? Maybe if he pretends to care, he'll come to believe in the role."

Lila enunciated through stiff lips. "He'd bring pity, not love. Helen, you mustn't tell him. Promise me."

"You need my word?" Helen drawled. "No one but you has the right to tell or not to tell. As you like."

"I'm sorry, Helen," Lila murmured. "You wouldn't even confide in Brook, would you, if I asked it."

"No." Helen nodded. "I wouldn't. Not that I'd advise you to be that secretive. Let someone share this with you." Lila said nothing, reassured of Helen's loyalty.

Athene's on Broadway was cheerful, Greek music spilling over the loudspeakers. The volume emphasized Lila's headache. Once they were seated by a maitre d', however, Lila asked Helen if she wanted to share some retsina.

Briefly Helen scoured her face. "Sure. Are you having something else or will this be a liquid lunch?"

"Greek salad. And saganaki — if you'll split it with me." Wearily Lila covered her eyes with her hands.

"Saganaki it is — and a small order of callimari." Helen nodded to the waiter, who took their order. "A half litre of Botrys should be enough?"

Lila nodded, aware that the Greek wine would improve neither her headache nor her health. Right now that did not seem to matter. She was too busy feeling sorry for herself, thank you, and damn it, she was going to enjoy her self-pity while it lasted. Her sense of irony made Lila grin.

Perhaps encouraged by Lila's smile, Helen probed: "Will you tell Mark and Cyndi about having cancer?"

"They still haven't recovered from Jack's zinger. I'm afraid to give them more than they can handle."

Warningly Helen shook her head. "Lies and omissions protect no one but the perpetrator, don't you think? Certainly not the children they are designed to protect."

"I know." Lila looked more than a little glum. "I'm sorry I've made it impossible for them to turn to their father for help." She forced a philosophical grin. "God knows, nothing is permanent. But you — and Brook — must seem solid as the Rock of Gibraltar to both of them."

Briefly Helen touched the pale band of Lila's finger where her wedding ring used to be. Self-consciously Lila drew back her hand. She still felt awkward without her ring.

"I don't feel it," Helen said wistfully. "Though it's nice of you to say so. What I called familiar in the world has been rearranged. I can't locate myself in the new territory."

Lila's brows contracted. "Is there something bothering you, Helen? Something I don't know about?"

Helen's eyes glimmered with tears. "Not really. It's not everyday that someone I love gets cancer. Forgive me if I go through angst about it."

With unusual demonstrativeness, Lila cradled Helen's hand between both of hers. "Don't try to be all things to me. Let me develop my own resourcefulness, Helen. Emotionally and otherwise."

For a moment Helen clung to Lila's fingers as if to a lifeline. Then she let go, enbarrassed by her own panic. "I know. It's about perspective. Still. Divorce is trying enough, but cancer too? It's so unjust."

Lila's smile was bleak. "I find being calm less exhausting than rage. Or tears. Don't you?"

Helen glanced away from the greyness in Lila's tone. "I don't like the sound of resignation, Lila. Mine or yours."

Lila was sharply reminded that being ordinarily cheerful was an act of courage. Such a daily act would at least keep despair at bay. Perhaps it would even help her to get well again. Like an approving crescendo, Lila thought satirically, music from *Zorba the Greek* poured from the loudspeakers, evoking images of street dancing and communal celebration. After all, Lila was far from alone — whether or not she was able to accept the diversity of help offered to her. She didn't want to think right now about her quarrel with Brook. Even if Lila's pride was foolish, she had the right to make — and certainly the motivation to pick up after — her own mistakes.

Frowning, Lila clicked her glass to Helen's. "Perhaps we need costumes and carnivals, to deal with divorce and disease and the inevitable — death. Anyway, for now let's drink ... To life."

"Le chaim," Helen murmured.

"Don't worry, Helen. I don't plan to go gently into that last goodnight." Involuntarily Lila shivered. Was her survival really so simple as wanting to live? Is that all Brook had been trying to determine — that she did want to?

St. Vincent's Hospital was narrow and ancient, with photographs of Pope John Paul II, ornate crosses and pictures of Jesus, His bleeding heart pierced through with thorns. A kneeling St. Vincent raised an illuminated face to a cloudy sky. Obviously Patricia Kline was a practising Catholic. It was fortunate for Lila that she did not need an abortion, she thought. Try as she did not to be cynical, Lila abominated Christianity. To her it was a two-thousand-year tribute to human ghoulishness and blood lust. Why else would one elevate a dying man on a bloody stick and encourage others to imitate such a dubious model of brotherly love?

Protest Lila had, but Helen insisted upon accompanying her to surgery. "But there's no need for you to do that. Brook has offered to drive me or I can call a cab."

"Hush. Brook is keeping the kids from freaking out. I'll wait right there the whole time. Bureaucracies are too big not to bear watching."

"But surely Cyndi and Mark would be better off at school. They'll have nothing to occupy their minds at home."

"But but but. You sound like an outboard motor. Lila, stop trying to control how other people show their love for you. None of us is going to get any work done until we know what's going on here." There was no arguing with Helen when she used that particular tone. Nor did Lila really want to. It was reassuring to know that her friend would be on stand-by if anything at all went wrong for her.

The two women huddled on a crowded bench in the alcove, neither of them bothering to scan the dog-eared and outdated magazines for something of dubious topical interest. To keep butterflies at bay Lila looked carefully around her. Nurses kept shooing non-patients away from the make-do waiting room which was really the entrance to the hospital. Stolidly, Helen withstood the nurses' efforts to get her to move. She crossed her arms and looked so imperious that Lila nearly laughed. Levity, however, would be highly inappropriate here — or would it? At any rate, fear seemed to darken the room, spreading like shadows out from so many anxious faces. With gallows humour, Lila watched the attempts of intake staff to get people in pain or shock to part with socio-economic information, so that they could be stored directly in the computer's memory as bytes of data.

"Why do these questions reduce to 'And how will we be paid for this?'" Lila whispered irascibly.

Without missing a beat, Helen whispered back: "Got a wad of bills? 'Twould hasten the process, methinks."

Lila's snicker was interrupted by an aide who promptly wheeled her into the elevator, ignoring her protest that she could walk. In the moment before the doors closed, Lila realized that Helen was again under duress from the staff, who would have preferred to telephone her when this one of many outpatients was ready to go home. With a conspiratorial motion of the thumb, Helen indicated that she would do her waiting from the cafeteria.

The aide chatted with a male porter all the way down to the ward, prevailing upon him to assist her in dumping Lila onto one of four cots. Almost immediately a nurse bustled in and handed Lila a pill and a green gown. With a thick Scottish accent she told Lila to wash her chest thoroughly with antiseptic soap. Her name tag read — predictably — "Margaret." With chirpy cheer she waited for Lila to swallow the tranquillizer and then gestured at a sink in the corner of the open room where a plastic container rested. Left alone, Lila took a facecloth from the rack near the sink and wet it. The liquid soap was drying and abrasive to her skin.

She touched the furrow in her breast. It was sensitive to her fingers and fibrous as spaghetti squash. How could she not have noticed so clear a sign of the intruder beneath her skin? Censure, however, would win her nothing but more guilt. Concretions of guilt, like the accumulated droppings of pigeons on a much-used perch. That Mark and Cyndi could become victims of the failure of her body; that she had involved her friends and her mother-in-law in this debacle too. Washing vigorously, she made the mistake of looking in the mirror ...

Suddenly she was pacing outside the open door to her mother's hospital room, worried that her father might visit while she was there. But her worker had arranged for that not to happen. After three long years of not seeing her mother, could Lila go in? What would she say to this woman behind chrome bars, this stranger who had suffered a stroke and had little remaining power of speech?

A middle-aged doctor entered the room followed by an entourage of medical students. Although a nurse partially drew the bedside curtains, Lila saw all of them reflected in the mirror, like pawns on a chessboard. Carefully the doctor lifted her mother's bandage, which came away spotted with pus and blood. Where her breast had been, there was only a flat place raw as red meat. With deft movements, the doctor sterilized the wound and bound it with clean gauze. His departing words sounded patronizing. Without a nod, he brushed past the young girl in the hallway.

So this was the sight for which her social worker had tried to prepare her; an overdose of cobalt to her mother's breast. Skin cancer, eating vociferously into her mother's heart and lungs. A second stroke paralyzing her on one side. Knowing that did not prepare Lila for the sight of her mother's limbs lying wooden and immobile as logs. Paralysis had frozen some of the muscles of her face into a grotesque smile, as at last she became aware of her daughter hovering indecisive in the doorway ...

Eventually her mother fell into a coma, her cornflower-blue eyes perpetually surprised. Every winter she had had bronchitis. But now her breathing was more tortured and racking than a bronchial cough, each breath struggled for and dearly bought. Finally her father asked the hospital to withdraw the intravenous keeping her tenuously alive. "Let her die with dignity," he whispered hoarsely. "Can't you see that she's no longer here?" By then he shared with Lila the vigil at the bedside. By then Lila's worker was there with her and besides, her father's attention was far away from anything to do with her. Bristling with days-old beard and rumpled in his over-sized clothes, he would look through Lila as though she were not even there.

It took her mother more days of pain and slow starvation to die. That was called mercy killing. Might Lila never need such mercy to be shown to her.

Spooked by the memory, Lila climbed into bed and waited. She began to read *Getting Well Again*, by the Simontons. Brook had bought it for her, since it was about visualization techniques in the treatment of cancer patients. Avoiding Brook made Lila unhappy, but she did not know how to unmake their quarrel. Until she resolved the contradictions she felt about Brook saying that one was "responsible" for cancer, it was better to avoid her than to argue with her. Though better for whom, Lila wasn't sure. Right now she deeply missed Brook's certainty. Convictions, even when one does not share them, are very reassuring.

At last the pill Margaret had given her slowed her mind. Words jumbled and blurred on the page. All too soon, an orderly was there to take her to the operating room. The anaesthetist prepared a large needle and attached it to a jumble of paraphernalia in case there would be need to give Lila a transfusion. A sharp jab in her vein and Lila began to count herself down ...

When she regained consciousness, she was back in the ward with gauze bound tight across her breast and ribcage. She tried but could not lift the bandage to check the results of her biopsy. There was no pain. The mound of her breast was apparently there. She let herself breathe, deeply, as Brook had taught her to do during massage.

Soon Margaret appeared to ask Lila if she wanted tea and toast. Caffeine and white bread for cancer patients. Like all protocols in the hospital, this one seemed to be designed to suit their expediencies and not for the welfare of patients. It was offered with the bribe that Lila could then dress and go home. Gratefully enough, Lila drank the tea and left the toast. Around the rim of the cup the tea wiggled — her hands were shaking.

Deliberately, she put on her watch and a gold necklace, reclaiming the loose blouse she had been warned to bring and pulling it down over her slacks. Awkwardly she tied the laces of her running shoes. Soon enough Helen was standing in the room, looking curiously hesitant. So Helen had kept her promise that she would not go home to wait.

"Rise up and walk!" Helen drawled, in her best imitation of a faith healer. She touched Lila's fingertips with her own and then kissed her tremulously on the forehead. She seemed afraid that a frontal embrace would hurt her.

Reassuringly Lila smiled. "I'm not in pain," she said. "Just anxious to get out of here. I can't stand hospitals."

"Let's take you home," Helen said firmly. "You can walk, Lazarus?"

"I can, but I'll be given a wheelchair. They can't risk a lawsuit, after all." No doubt Lila sounded normally sardonic. Her face, however, felt white as hospital linens.

What would this surgery mean to her? She may not be breast proud, but it was a breast-fixated culture. A woman's bosom was the focus of many eyes. If she had to, she could compensate for disparate breast sizes with a padded bra, or with one of several cosmetic illusions. Whether she would need to compensate, Lila could not tell. The thick dressing beneath her blouse gave nothing away.

Feeling suddenly weepy, Lila met Helen's eyes. "My mother had a mastectomy," she said slowly. "Her cobalt treatment activated skin cancer. It ate down into her heart and lungs until she literally rotted away."

Alerted by her tone, Helen sat beside her on the bed. "You are not your mother," she said frostily. "And cancer treatment is more and more sophisticated every year."

Lila's voice was flat. "I know. I have to be very careful about identifying with her. Still, in my case and in many others cancer is hereditary. Kline told me that daughters develop it sixteen years earlier than its appearance in their mothers. Did you know that?" She stared unseeing at the lockers. "At twenty, Cyndi could have to deal with cancer."

Helen reached for Lila's hand, becoming aware of the bandage across her vein and tracing a light finger around it. "And if she does, you'll blame yourself. For passing on those faulty genes." She did not bother to disguise her sarcasm.

Taken aback, Lila blinked. "I know. I blame myself for everything. I always have. Actually, I'll be glad when Jack takes the kids for the summer. I've got to stop feeling so responsible."

Helen reached carefully around her bandages to hold her. "Did you feel responsible for you mother's death, too?"

Looking out the window, Lila nodded. "I didn't know what to feel. Resentment, love, pity? The absolute certainty that she knew what my father was doing. That she could have prevented him and did not."

"So you blamed her for not protecting you. Did you hate her?"

Lila's mouth twisted. "I thought she never loved me. Sometimes I just wanted to scream at her until she could."

"Cyndi's more fortunate, isn't she? You're alive, for her to love — and hate. And whatever else, you're more of a parent to her than your mother was to you."

Her eyelids twitching, Lila glanced at Helen's knees. Even her corneas felt bruised. "At the time my mother died, I was living with foster parents. The social worker thought it was a good idea for my mother not to know where I was, in case she told my father. At first we met at the Children's Aid, until she got tired of being treated like a criminal on my father's behalf. Then I didn't see her until she had the Society notify me that she was dying."

Helen whistled softly. "Following no contact, that must have been some information."

Lila's breathing was uneven. Images of her mother's comatose face, of her paralysed body, were seared in her brain. She felt like a cheap Kodak camera developing instant photographs. "I feel very tired. Take me home."

Helen did not move. "Before your mother died, you must have wanted desperately for her to say she loved you."

Lila's face buckled. "No. Nor could I tell her that."

"And I bet you feel guilty." There was no answer. "How guilty, Lila? Enough to think that you, too, should die unloved?"

Lila fastened her gaze on the ceiling tiles, which were water-stained and warping. Revealingly her mouth quivered. "I wanted to be in control ... "

"Hey. She abandoned you. You can't make yourself love someone — even a mother. "

"You sound remarkably like Brook. As though it's guilt that could kill me, and not cancer."

"Let's hope that neither will kill you. Lila, leave 'shoulda-coulda-woulda's' alone. How useless they are."

Worry gnawed at Lila like an enflamed tooth swells the gums. "Helen, do you think that cancer is linked to the emotions?"

"I think depression is bad for the health. Don't you?"

Lila gaped. All of this sounded remarkably like Brook telling her to clean up her attitude. But from Helen the words sounded non-offensive and logical.

Before she could share her ponderings, Margaret was there with a wheelchair and Lila was being trundled to the front entrance. Soon Helen drove up in her Mustang and assisted Lila into the car. Smiling tenderly, she buckled the seat belt around Lila's chest. "You have a home, Lila — and a safe one. Would M'Lady like to be there?"

"M'Lady would," Lila said, relaxing gratefully into the seat. "Thank you."

With feathery lightness, Helen kissed Lila's fingers. "No," she said. "Thank you, for sharing something so personal. I love you, Lila Tennant. I always have."

For some bizarre reason, Helen's remark made Lila's throat tighten. "Me, too," she said ungrammatically.

CHAPTER FIFTEEN

Shadows of leaves dappled Brook's white shirt, danced along the exposed skin of her arms. Firmly she clasped the balcony with her feet, feeling the stretch of her stomach muscles as she did sit ups. Then she leapt upright, placing her palms flat on the cedar railing. The wood was cold and damp. When would the days be warm enough so that she could take off her shoes and let her toes directly contact the ground? She certainly needed earth energy: her prized serenity was fracturing.

Impatiently she sighed. Beltane, May Eve, would soon be here. This time the witches' circle would include Helen. The coven would offer flowers and seeds to the ground; send ululations and chants to the thickening moon. Then they would do a healing for Lila and celebrate their joy in life, their resilient optimism. The time to honour the renewal of life is most certainly in the face of death.

Brook shivered. Lila wouldn't die; she didn't really want to. *What if she does want to?* The thought stung like angry wasps. Brook was opening herself to morbid speculations. A sure sign that she needed to meditate.

At her elbow Mark waited to be noticed, his bony wrists protruding from the sleeves of a shirt he was rapidly outgrowing. Sunshine glinted from his glasses; he reached up to shade his eyes. With an attempt at a smile, he murmured: "I adopted Mom. Do you know that?"

"I guess you're glad you did." Brook waited. It was up to Mark to let her know where he was heading.

Like a turtle he pulled in his neck. "I will be if she doesn't leave me."

Brook jack-knifed into exercises for her back, gazing up at Mark from the sleeping bag. If Lila did "leave," no doubt Mark would view it as willful abandonment. After all, for a child there is no transcending death or rationalizing it away. "That sounds like you think she wants to leave you."

Pouting, Mark shook his head. "If she did, I'd go find her."

Spontaneously Brook laughed. "You would, too." Oh, for the elusive balance between light and honest. It was crucial to Mark that she exude the confidence that said everything was and would be all right. Mark was lonely for his father and so angry with him. With Lila's illness his need had grown huge. Sometimes Brook felt swamped, pulled into a thick sludge from which she could extricate herself only by extricating Mark. She was neither mother nor father to him, but she was a hinge-joint in his life, beloved because she was there.

Too near her head, Mark stubbed at the balcony with the toe of his running shoe. "If anything happens to Mom, will you go away, too?"

A question as loaded as the chamber of a gun. So much could happen, if Lila decided not to repair her quarrel with Brook — the worse-case scenario being that Brook could be asked to leave. She catapulted from the deck to give Mark her full attention. "I'm here for just a while, Mark. You know that."

Mark clenched his fists. He turned around as if looking for his way out of a maze, turning again to stare directly at her. "So you'll just move out. And we won't see you again."

Brook had worked hard to win his and Cyndi's love. It now seemed that with Mark, at least, she had succeeded all too well. With deliberate camaraderie she drilled her fingers into his shoulder. "There is a very scared boy making up a play in his mind, called 'what if the worst happens and I'm left alone.' We're pals, Mark. Pals see one another, whenever they can."

Resisting a tenuous hope, Mark searched her eyes. "I wish this was a play," he grimaced. "Then I'd know the ending in advance."

Gently Brook stroked his hair. "Hey. Lila went for a simple biopsy. She'll be home in a few hours. Why don't we ask Cyndi if she wants to go to Capilano Rock and Gem and poke around? They have some crystal-making kits there. Perhaps we can pick up one for you."

The sun peeked momentarily from behind his lacklustre eyes. "Crystals. Oh yeah! I could grow them." Then the clouds rolled back into his face. "I want to be here when Mom arrives."

"So do I. But time passes a lot faster when you're not paying any attention to it. Come on, Sport." Playfully she placed her hands in his back and pushed him along.

When Cyndi opened the door to them her eyes looked puffy and red.

"Yeah?" she said gruffly. "Whad'ya want?"

"You," Brook grinned. "How would you like to add to your collection of polished stones? Do you have tourmaline yet, or lace agate?"

Visibly Cyndi brightened. "Why? Do you have some for me?"

"Remember the book I showed you called *Crystal Enlightenment*? I'm scouting for rhodochrosite for Lila. Sugalite, which is a beautiful purple, and malachite, which is bright green."

Cyndi screwed up her nose. "Oh! The book that says stones cure people. Really, Brook."

"Really, indeed. Stones have been on earth far longer than we have, my dear. And they will survive us, by eons."

Cyndi flounced her shoulders. "So will plutonium. That doesn't mean we should bring it home with us."

"Oh well." Brook dangled a baited hook. "I thought you might like to come but I guess I was wrong. We'll be back by one." Wrapping an arm around Mark's shoulder, she turned to leave.

"Wait! I'll come. It's better than being alone here."

"Isn't it? And you don't have to believe in the healing power of stones to enjoy them. Do you?"

"I guess. But if you're getting me something, I prefer topaz to tourmaline ... "

Brook hid a smile. Her sense of the magic of stones might be regarded as a superstitious remnant from another time. This age, however, lopped down trees at a fast pace and killed off one species every week. What would happen to the so-called "paragon of animals" once humans grew completely beyond Nature — i.e. killed it off? Hearing the voices of stones or trees or water depended upon listening for them. And being open to natural influences.

In the Datsun, Brook distracted Cyndi with sights along the route. Or tried to distract her. Cyndi turned to the window and mumbled. After several fruitless attempts, Brook said jauntily: "Okay, Cyndi. Out with it. What's bothering you?"

"You are," Cyndi parried. "I dunno. Mother. Dad. Everything." She rolled her eyes at Mark who sprawled in the back seat, humming to himself.

"It sure is a tense time, " Brook agreed heartily. "How do *you* want the story to end?"

"Story? This ain't fiction, this is life."

"Listen to old Methusalah!" From the back Brook heard Mark's responsive chuckle. "Have you ever heard someone say 'if life hands you a lemon, make lemonade?' I know there are many things that seem written in stone — as though nothing that we can do will make them better. But sometimes we bring on the worst just by expecting it."

"If I got what I want, Dad would smarten up and come home ... Brook, do you think it's right that Mother won't tell him she's ill?"

"Are you thinking of telling him? I thought you were 'down' on snitching."

"Ha! Mother finds lots of ways to snitch for my 'good.' How is this any different?"

"Suppose she tells — or you tell — Jack. How do you think he'd feel?"

"Well, he married Mom. Doesn't he have an obligation to care for her — for us?"

Brook cranked her head towards the blind spot in her rear window. "Is that how you want to be treated? Like a debt?"

"Yeah. I mean — no. Brook — " If words were stones Cyndi would have tripped over them. "In the library I got out a book on breast cancer. It said that one out of four women die of it. Do you think that's true?"

"Die!" Mark squeaked. "Whuddar you talkin' about?"

For their sake and her own, Brook was optimistic. "At Lila's age? Don't go writing her obituary. Besides, if it comes anywhere near a crisis, Lila would tell Jack. And he'd be here — for both of you."

Cyndi squirmed in the seat. "I don't ever want to get married. Not if people end up alone when they're going through something like this." On the pronoun her voice broke.

Gently Brook reached for Cyndi's hand. "Hey. You're pretty young to be disillusioned. Try not to be cynical about Jack — or Lila. Beyond doubt, your parents feel like hell about doing this to you."

Determinedly Cyndi tugged her fingers away. "Dad should feel like hell. He's prob'ly the only one of us who's happy."

Sighing, Brook leaned into the head rest. No wonder wisdom was valued beyond rubies. "It's easy to blame the person who leaves first, Cyndi. But — pardon the cliche — it takes two to tango." Across from Capilano Rock and Gem she parked, feeling that it was inappropriate to leave this conversation dangling. Mark certainly had his fears, too, and might be better off for dealing with them.

But Cyndi now stood beside the car. "Well, who am I supposed to blame? My mother? At least she stays with us."

"Are you saying that Jack doesn't give a shit for you, because he left?"

Cyndi raised an uncompromising chin. "Yeah. In a nutshell."

"That's not true," Mark interjected. "You're the one who's full of it, Cyndi."

"Easy, fella," Brook squeezed his shoulder. "Don't the two of you start in on each other."

"Oh, let's look at rocks," Cyndi said impatiently. "*Adults* can't talk in front of *babies.*"

Brook's smile was grim. She would be the last to deny that Cyndi needed to express her anger. But Mark certainly should not be the object of her pique, shoved away in the box of childhood. "Cyndi, you and your brother are in this together. And you're both afraid. What makes you presume that Mark should deal with his fears alone?" Too loudly Brook slammed the car door.

"Don't break the windows," Cyndi quipped. "Isn't that what you tell us when we slam the doors?"

"I do indeed." Sheepishly, Brook laughed. She, too, would have to learn how to express aggression.

Just inside the cluttered store were ammonites, trilobites and fossilized plants, their shapes perfectly imprinted in rock. Along the back wall were shelves containing pieces of petrified wood, inconspicuous looking geodes hiding their crystalline beauty, yellow and blue coral from ancient seas and chunks of black, shining obsidian. In cardboard boxes were polished stones: tiger's eye and lace agate, goose-sized jasper eggs and slices containing tiny landscapes created by some natural force. Then there were the slabs of agate — orange and brown, blue and red — which reminded Brook of the lamp Helen had on Mayne Island. Suddenly Brook missed Helen acutely. Perhaps she could make a lamp like Helen's for her own bedroom. Soon they must create time to be together, she and Helen — just the two of them with nothing to do but rediscover what they shared so easily and with such pleasure. A unique sympathy of minds and bodies. Even thinking about her made Brook feel soft and warm ...

Safely locked under glass were rotating trays of precious stones: green emeralds, blue topaz, purple lapis lazuli, gleaming in the florescent lighting. The trays also contained rose and phantom quartz, and single and double-terminated smoky crystals from Brazil, Madagascar and Arkansas. Glittering beside them were several clear crystal pyramids. Like the pyramid at Giza, the triangulated shape emitted inexplicable frequencies, its mathematical dimensions having some ageless and odd power to effect healing. When the shopkeeper was free to show it to her, Brook would ask to have a closer look at it. Meanwhile Cyndi and Mark were too quiet. She pointed to a display case containing selenite roses, pale pink stone "blooming" into unexpected flowers.

"How can rock do that?" Mark exclaimed.

"Selenite is a chameleon. It takes on all kinds of shapes and colours. See those pointy needles? And the pieces that look like coral? All of them are selenite."

Cyndi folded her arms across her budding chest. "Okay. According to your weird book, what is selenite supposed to do?"

Amiably Brook met her challenge. "Have you read anything about the witch burnings in the Middle Ages?"

Cyndi shook her head; anticipating a story, Mark's eyes went round.

"Once upon a time, women were healers and some men did not like that. So they called these healers witches and put them to death in a variety of ways. The women who were left began to program what they knew about herbs and medicines into selenite crystals, which can store human knowledge. They trained others to receive this information so that their knowledge would not be lost, even when many of them were taken away to be burned."

Mark looked confused. "Programming a crystal? Oh! The crystal in a computer is like that. Right, Brook?"

"Yes. Or think of a telephone carrying what someone says to you across a distance. Only selenite does that telepathically."

"Kinky." Apparently uncertain about Brook's sanity — or her seriousness — Cyndi winked at the store owner. "I don't know who these people are. They only came in with me."

Unperturbed Brook continued. "Once a thief robbed the home of a witch and left behind the selenite crystal, thinking that it was ugly. The crystal recorded telepathic pictures of the robbery. When she got home, the owner of the stolen jewels held the selenite and was able to find out where the thief had taken her belongings and get them back — much to the surprise of the robber."

Still engaged with a customer, the owner of the shop elevated his eyebrow. "I should buy more selenite," he drawled, opening the halves of a geode and displaying it. One side of the Thunder Egg was loaded with amethyst crystals, the other with quartz.

Cyndi drew an incredulous breath. "On the outside it looks like a silly old stone. On the inside it's beautiful!"

Softly Brook chuckled at her. "See what you notice when you look? Some people are like geodes, too."

"Spare me," Cyndi retorted. "Like you say, Brook, you do like cliches."

"Well, la de da." Brook said. She was not at all offended.

At last the owner was free and she could ask to see the pyramid. Strongly it pulsed in her hands — her brain was soothed by it as though she had fallen lightly asleep. This crystal would do very nicely for Lila, especially once Brook showed her how to program it for healing her breast.

Well aware of the approach of afternoon, Brook wasted no time at all in securing the stone Cyndi wanted — which was quite modestly priced — and placing the crystal-making kit in Mark's hands. Possessively he carried it towards the door. In Brook's own hands were small boxes containing a green triangle of malachite, a striated piece of pink rhodochrosite and the precious, shining pyramid which Brook must somehow get Lila to accept from her. It was, for Brook's budget, a most extravagant day of giving. She wanted to share with all of them part of the essence of who she was, a person who believed in magic as a focused act of will. What people called magic was nothing more than a concentrated form of energy directed through objects towards spiritual goals. Lila might call Brook's belief in the transforming powers of magic nothing more than "esoteric bullshit." But pain was bullshit, too. And there was no need to live with it.

For Helen she had gotten a phantom quartz, its smoky wings raised as though a small butterfly struggled to break into flight from within it. She would set it carefully in copper wire with peacock feathers and place it in Helen's window, where the sun would make a rainbow of colours on her living room wall. *It's time I cooked dinner for that beautiful woman*, Brook thought sadly. *I want this biopsy to free all of us, so we can go back to dealing with simple things — like work and play and love.*

Then she was back in the traffic. And any concerns Brook had, either about her extravagance — or her priorities — had to wait for a less hectic time.

CHAPTER SIXTEEN

Wearing a bandage. For two weeks Lila could do little more than dab water on her back and chest. Sitting in a bathtub made her feel like she was recycling her own body dirt. Sometimes Cyndi would volunteer to help her wash, no doubt out of curiosity regarding her mother's wound. Brook, however, maintained a stoic distance from the bathroom, perhaps worried that any overtures on her part would be categorically rejected. Perhaps? She was right. But Lila missed the tenderness the two of them had shared, before she herself pushed Brook away with both hands. Now pique and pride seemed hollow. Now both were being eroded by a wild, if very private, grief over the loss of a friendship more precious than she had ever known.

Just when Lila felt closeted away in her grieving, objects like echinacea root or taheebo mysteriously began to appear amidst her toiletries. Or Brook would peek around a corner to say that she was (quite coincidentally of course) on her way to a health food store and would Lila like her to pick up any vitamins while she was there? When Lila said no, Brook nodded and went away. But in the mornings when Lila appeared in the kitchen, Brook would be taking vitamins and casually offer to share them with her.

By the fourth such "coincidence," Lila handed Brook thirty dollars and told her that she could stop pretending to be innocent. In future she wanted these vitamins listed under household expenses to be shared in common. The enigmatic Brook smiled, not bothering to defend her motives. But then why should she, when Lila was now contributing to what it was that Brook wanted her to do in the first place. She felt like checking her shoulders for hidden wires — Lila the obedient puppet and Brook the skilled puppeteer.

Finally the days of not being able to itch ended and it was time to remove the dressing. At Dr. Kline's office, strips of adhesive tape pulled at Lila's skin. The work of a fortnight of oxygen deprivation had made her breast grey and covered it with sores. Even more startling were the metal staples joining together the puckered lips on her breast, making Lila feel like a human canvas for some avant-garde artist.

Dr. Kline's nurse left her with a bottle of antiseptic and several pieces of gauze. Vigorously Lila scrubbed at the adhesive gum which clung to her breast. The solution burned into pus-filled sores. The incision itself, however, looked competent. Lila was left with a scar perhaps three inches long, and a breast that seemed almost normally fleshy and round. She breathed a sigh of relief.

In came the taciturn Dr. Kline to check the wound. She was still unable, or unwilling, to clarify the method of treatment which would follow Lila's lymph surgery. "You have thirteen nodes. The cancer may have spread to all or none of them. The real danger is whether your lymph system is generalizing the cancer to other areas of your body. The lungs and stomach are particularly susceptible, so we'll be sending you for x-rays and scans."

Lila blanched. She felt a sense of jumping through medical hoops like a trained dog. She sincerely hoped that her body, unlike her mother's, would not be increasingly maimed by efforts merely to postpone the inevitable. Chemotherapy, Lila had learned, could catapult her towards an early menopause. In an attempt to destroy this invader, toxins would be poured into every cell, leaving none unaffected. Aside from making her bald or thinning her hair, the chemical overkill would lower her white blood count and make Lila far more susceptible to infection of all kinds.

This information Lila had garnered from a brochure in the waiting room, certainly not from the close-mouthed Dr. Kline. Though the good doctor did ask Lila if she wanted to be part of a study on women's responses to particular regimens of treatment.

"No," Lila said loudly. " I don't think I'm quite ready to be 'studied.' I haven't even reconciled myself to receiving chemo — or radiation."

Kline frowned very slightly. "We'll discuss your fears later, when all the facts are in. Okay?"

Her tone reminded Lila of how adults sometimes sounded with "difficult" children. Lila was far from okay but Kline was gone. The door to the examination room closed firmly behind her.

Adding to Lila's sense of being carried by implacable forces, her lymphectomy was scheduled for April 28. She would celebrate turning thirty-seven from a hospital bed. With some irony, Lila thought: I may not believe in God but someone is toying with me. One. Destroy in this petty human the sense of the predictable and the expected. Two. Remove from her all sense that she can influence her own life or control what is done to her. Not, of course, that Lila or anyone else needed such lessons in the already generalized and specific chaos of living ... What if she asked the receptionist to reschedule the date of surgery — would that place her own survival at risk? And how common was it, to be undergoing a second operation only three weeks after her first? But if Dr. Kline did not deign to answer her questions, her receptionist certainly was not qualified to do so.

Feeling only superficially resigned, Lila drove home, a curve of sorrow around her mouth. The rearview mirror cautioned her not to take her expression into the house. Still there was not very much about which to smile.

Not wanting to be alone, she followed the sound of music to Brook's sitting room. Wearing a bright yellow sweater, Helen was stirring at the embers in the wood stove with a poker and jitterbugging slightly to a song about tight black jeans. She threw another log in the fire and closed the cast-iron grate. From the floor Brook gazed at Helen, her amber eyes openly sensual.

For a moment Lila felt like an Icarus figure whose wings were suddenly burning. But the warmth of the room as well as the warmth of the women intrigued her. Nor was there any reason for Lila to skulk away without sharing in their steadying comfort. She didn't even have to say that she was terrified or angst-ridden, only let herself be cared for by both of them. She stared into the room, searching for a clue about whether to stay or to creep away.

The austere walls of Lila's sitting room had been transformed by bright-coloured tapestries and paintings by Indian artists, some of these so powerful as to draw Lila right into the canvas. One, of a figure in a black ceremonial robe standing on a wind-tossed shore, seemed to lead her farther into a darkness evocative of dreaming and death. With effort, she glanced away from the painting, only to notice that subtle track lighting had eliminated the windowless dark of the room. Crystals hung suspended from the ceiling. Bookshelves and bright filing cabinets gave the room an atmosphere of loving and frequent use. Small speakers piped in sound from the stereo in Brook's room. Large, inviting cushions, royal blue and bright orange, were strewn invitingly over white, hand-constructed benches.

Pegged to the brick wall was a shaman drum, decorated with a stylized frog and a raven. The side of the drum featured beads, white and blue and bright red, portraying mythological birds. Fastened to these beads were the feathers of eagles and wild turkey, dangling like a fringe around the base of the drum.

No longer were Cyndi or Mark avoiding this room, although Lila herself steadfastedly persisted in regarding it as Brook's private lair. But the children were not here today. Adera had taken them swimming at the community pool.

As she hesitated in the doorway, Brook reached up with a soft laugh to draw Helen down beside her. Feeling excluded, Lila turned to leave the women, but Helen noticed her standing forlornly in the light. "Lila. Is the bandage off, love? And can we see the breast?" She sounded both jocular and serious. If Lila would show her the scar, she knew that Helen would very much want to see it. Though it was not the kind of thing Lila wanted to show off.

Brook's forehead puckered. Was she unhappy that Lila had disturbed a lover's tableau? For a moment her strange gaze drew Lila and she had the unpleasant sensation that she was dissolving into Brook's eyes. Helen cleared a place near her and Lila sat down gladly by her friend, although her movements were precipitate and clumsy. With gentle fingers Helen unbuttoned Lila's blouse and moved her bra strap aside, examining the surgical scar with a kind of rapt attention.

From her cross-legged position on the rug, Brook, too, looking small and ageless, attended to Lila's breast. To Lila she seemed both too wise — and too cryptic — to be genuine. That was not a compliment to Brook, surely. And maybe it wasn't intended to be one.

"When is the next surgery?" Brook's tone was like the sound of a waterfall. Perhaps she intended to soothe Lila as she would soothe a skittish horse, firm hand on the bridle. Lila's mouth curled back. How defensive she was being towards a woman who shared with her the daily and pragmatic acts of child care.

"On April twenty-eighth," she replied. "I'll be hospitalized for a few days."

Helen's eyebrows arched. "On your birthday? Okay." With rough delicacy, she fastened Lila's silk shirt, twisting each button in her hands. Lila wished she could disappear into her blouse and become merely colour or design. At least then her life would have a pattern and not be subject to other people's interpretation that it was melodrama. Certainly Brook must find Lila's dilemma self-induced.

Frowning, Brook handed a small box to Lila, a box which she obviously wanted her to open. "An early gift." Brook's voice shook.

With her fingernails Lila sliced through the scotch tape sealing the box. Swathed in cotton within it was a winking crystal pyramid.

"I'm sorry, Brook — but what is this for?" Lila hoped she didn't sound as naive as she felt.

Brook's ears reddened. "It's a pyramid. When you hold it, visualize your breast healing — several times a day if you can, if only for a few moments. This book will explain the technique. I've marked the section for you."

Feeling skeptical Lila began to read. She was to imagine that the pyramid was large as a tent and that she was inside it. *You are complete within, feeling safe and tranquil. Like a plant you reach deep into the soil for nourishment, like a tree you reach to the sky. Imagine that you are drawing upon green, healing light and directing it towards you. Even asleep, you program your cells to repair and to renew. Picture them healthy and resilient. As a plant is nourished by soil and water, so are you nourished. Imagine it, so it shall be.*

Positive thinking would help, whether or not Lila held a crystal or a cow pad. Still, the pyramid was beautiful — a gift selected and given with care.

Clumsily Lila reached for Brook's hand. "Thank you. Meditating should calm me down."

"That's the idea." Brook cupped her hands over the pyramid Lila held. "I promised Cyndi and Mark that they wouldn't be farmed out to their grandmother's while you're hospitalized. They asked to remain here, in their own space."

Lila smiled somberly. "I will talk with them about it, Brook. I know they'd be in good hands with you, but Adera also wants to feel useful. She may be willing to come here if necessary."

Helen reached for Lila, with an embrace that was a banquet to Lila's senses. "Give me some way to be of use, too."

Tentatively, Lila spread Helen's black shining hair into wings and let it fall. "Of course," she murmured. "Meanwhile, don't let Cyndi or Mark write a doomsday scenario for me. If they do, they'll succeed only in frightening themselves."

Brook cleared her throat. "Hey. You and I need to check out what's real from what's feared as much as they do."

Uncertainly Lila nodded. "We'll talk, no doubt. But weren't you and Helen supposed to head for the art gallery?"

Brook glanced at her watch. "I guess. Would you like to join us?"

"Thanks, but I've scheduled a heart-to-heart with the kids when Adera brings them back. Later, Brook." Tenuously she embraced the shorter woman. "Thanks for the gift, and the attempt to clear the air."

She turned quickly, and past the lump in her throat freed the two women to enjoy their afternoon alone.

A middle-aged nurse checked to make sure that Lila had shaved in preparation for surgery. Once again, she was handed some pills. Normally, she didn't even use aspirin for fear of becoming dependent on drugs. Now she was being handed tranquillizers like after-dinner mints. She took them feeling that her calm was odd. She didn't trust her apparent serenity.

"Remove your jewelry and put it in the drawer," said the very English nurse. "Or give it to me for safekeeping."

Lila declined to surrender her watch and ring. She put them at the back of her locker, as talismans to her safe return. Methodically she washed, this time reassured by being treated as though she could fend for herself.

Swiftly she got into bed and tried to block out the sight of a crucifix of Jesus on the wall. Once again the sedatives interfered with her concentration. She tried to keep her eyes from closing. Then an orderly was there with a gurney. And the English nurse was drawing up the bar so that she would not fall out. "They're ahead of schedule today," the nurse said, with false cheer. "You get to have this over with sooner."

Lila also got to look at the ceiling all the way down the narrow and poorly lit corridor. The orderly anchored her against the wall among others. Before long Dr. Kline was there.

"Hello, there," she said. She was already wearing a green hospital gown and had a mask tied to her neck. "How are you?"

"I'm fine." Lila smiled, glad to see her surgeon at last. Perhaps if they could talk even briefly now, Lila might feel more confident about the surgery and the surgeon.

"Good," Kline patted her on the arm. "I'll see you later." Yeah, Lila thought. When I'm unconscious and can't see you. Hands rolled her from the gurney to the narrow table and strapped her down. A surgical team hooked her to the intravenous. Again the needle, large and sharp. In this day of AIDS-contaminated blood, Lila sincerely hoped that nothing would go wrong to necessitate having a transfusion.

As though she had spoken aloud, her anaesthetist said cheerfully: "It's just a precaution. You probably won't need blood. Start counting backwards from ten to one ... "

Now familiar with the procedure, Lila counted her way into oblivion.

When she woke groggily, she was in the recovery room, post-op patients lined up on either side of her. With her fingers she probed at another padded dressing, which reached from rib cage to sternum. Tubes ran into a plastic bottle at her side, which was filling with watery, red liquid. She was still hooked to the intravenous.

Nurses clattered instruments and directed the lifting of patients. It was a while before someone realized she was awake. An orderly wheeled her back to her room, where she fell instantly asleep.

In another surge of consciousness, Lila looked out at the lawn. A gardener was methodically planting orange and yellow marigolds. One side of the entrance to the hospital was littered with rolled-up turf. Bags of grass seed sprawled on their sides. Farther to the right was a green tractor and a machine which would powder clods of earth beneath steel blades.

Suddenly she heard her mother, saying: "*I never want to die in winter. The earth is so ugly then and so ungiving.*" Whatever her mother's choice in the matter, it was mid-January when she died: a rare and bitter wind keening while mourners scattered from the grave like rats seeking shelter from a pouring rain. Within seconds, wreaths of flowers were flattened, leaf and blossom. Even the pallbearers had slipped precariously on the slick ground.

Tears blurred her vision and then sleep carried her mercifully away from her own regrets. She did not see Brook enter with a vase of sturdy white carnations which she placed on the sill, or stand momentarily at the window as though she wanted to throw it open to fresh, not forced, air. A nurse wrote on Lila's chart and hurried away, competent and impersonal. Rigidly scheduled temperature and blood pressure readings. Routines and medications ruled by the clock. With slight hesitation, Brook placed the crystal pyramid in Lila's hand and closed her fingers over it.

Briefly Lila opened her eyes. "Hello, beautiful ... " She smiled at Brook, lips pale and cracked. "I'm so thirsty ... "

"Perhaps you shouldn't drink."

Determinedly Lila shook her head. "Bring me a glass," she said. "I'll only sip at it."

She sipped. But the water affected her and she vomited, surprised at the force and suddenness of the propulsion. The liquid was clear; there was, after all, nothing on her stomach. Lila was too surprised to be embarrassed.

Gently Brook dabbed at her mouth, helped her onto the pillows. She found paper towels and cleaned the floor and then her own hands.

For some reason Lila didn't even care that she had vomited. She was so glad to see that Brook was there. "Will you be here when I wake?" she muttered drowsily.

A smile in her voice, Brook answered. "Of course. Now go to sleep."

Her sandy lashes drooped. Lila slurred something that sounded to Brook like "Promise." Every time Lila awakened Brook was sitting by her bedside in the unwelcoming chair. It was certainly not designed with consideration for the contours of the human body.

Continually Lila woke from her drug-induced sleep, forgetting that she had seen Brook here. Her voice filled with shy pleasure and wonder, the voice of a child who feels undeserving but very glad. Again she would ask "Brook, when did you get here?" If Lila did not remember her reply, that was not what mattered to either of them.

CHAPTER SEVENTEEN

"Lila is coming home today, Mark. I'm going to need some help blowing up balloons. And you haven't yet wrapped your present to her."

"How do I wrap a panda?" Mark wisecracked. "The nose pokes up." From narrow sticks he was shaping the fuselage of a model airplane. At this stage of construction the carriage resembled the skeletal remains of a sun-bleached bird.

Good-naturedly, Brook slapped the seat of his pants. "Be inventive," she said. "Cyndi is making chocolate cake. If you're quick about helping, maybe she'll let you lick the batter."

"Oh God," Mark grimaced. "She'll probably poison us all." Nonetheless, he headed with alacrity towards the kitchen.

In a moment the shattering clamour of silverware made Brook about-face to investigate, following the aroma of baking as much as she was led by the din. In the kitchen Cyndi sorted through drawers made even more disorganized by her search. In a blackening funk, she looked up to see Brook at her shoulder.

"Oh, Brook, do you know where the cake decorators are? I want to make sugar roses."

There was no point in spoiling Cyndi's efforts by telling her that sugar and chocolate were anathema to cancer. After all, who could expect children to separate the word "cake" from the word "birthday"? It was Lila who would have to limit her own consumption. "You can make roses? I'm spastic at that sort of thing. Oh, well. I don't like icing anyway."

" 'Oh well,' it's not your birthday," Cyndi retorted. "You don't have to like it, do you?"

"You mean I get to have what I want on my birthday? How nice." She fished out the decorating kit from its obscure location on the lower shelf, handing it with a flourish to Cyndi. Then she felt Helen's presence before she turned to see her leaning against the doorframe, red-lipped and rosy-cheeked and smelling of fresh air and flowers — the delicate perfume of lilacs with which her skin was imbued. Brook's beloved and edible woman was wearing an open-necked red shirt, the outline of her breasts hinting at pleasures rather than revealing them. She was clad in beige slacks with a thong belt. Out of consideration for Cyndi, Brook kissed Helen sedately on the mouth. Cyndi, however, squealed and embraced Helen far more enthusiastically. So much for the idea that she objected to witnessing their displays of affection.

"Is the kitten in your car?" Cyndi asked anxiously. "Or did you already bring it in?"

Helen put a finger to her lips. "Shh. It's in the basement. I think we should surprise Mark, too — unless we want the cat to be let out of the bag, so to speak ... Where is he?"

Cyndi shrugged. "Licking the cake bowl in the living room."

"Well!" Brook pretended to be piqued. "Am I to be included in this secret?"

"Oh, love." Helen waved her grumbling aside. "Come with me — I'll show her to you. I think Lila could benefit from giving herself permission to pet someone, don't you?"

"No comment," Brook chuckled.

Cyndi whispered sotto voce. "I'll stay here so Mark doesn't get suspicious."

From behind the washing machine the kitten peered at them, small tail twitching. She was half-Siamese, with light brown stripes running through orange fur, testifying to the other half of her gene pool. Two white paws at a diagonal and a white chest made her look as though she wore tiny socks and a bib. Lint had already hitched a ride in her whiskers. In the semi-darkness, the kitten's purple eyes shone. As Brook bent to coax the tiny animal farther out of hiding, Helen kissed her arousingly, in the small of her throat.

"Ummm," Brook leaned into Helen, lingering on her lips and tongue until she felt both soothed and very actively seduced. Choosing that moment to be bold, the kitten waddled over to them, purring loudly, sniffing and rubbing back and forth across their legs. Laughing, Helen scooped up the round furry ball and cupped it between her hands.

"What a good idea for Lila," Brook said, still feeling weak in the knees.

"You don't think she'll resent the kitten — see her as just another dependent?"

Brook touched a finger to Helen's lips. "Frankly, I don't think Lila stands a chance of getting rid of her. Look at those eyes."

"Yeah, except that the kids will blackmail her. She may not be able to give it away."

"Why agonize over a gift? You're not responsible for how Lila reacts to getting it."

Helen set the kitten gently on the rug. Still purring, it made a beeline towards the litter box which nestled near the dryer. "You're right. Anyway, we still have food to prepare. The hospital is going to call when Kline deigns to tell Lila that she can go home."

Brook shook her head. "It seems that doctors choose to be efficient or to be humane. Kline's choice is clear."

Helen tickled her under the chin. "And to hell with shades of grey. Did you make the cheese ball? I picked up candles and unearthed Lila's damask napkins."

At close to noon Adera arrived, carrying huge gladioli and purple irises. Brook helped her find vases to display the bouquets in front of the wall-length mirrors in the dining room. Adera had just recently evacuated Lila's room where she had been installed throughout the week, keeping her eye on the children — and on her, Brook bet.

Adera and Cyndi arranged place mats, napkin rings and serviettes. The table cloth was the deep purple of ribier grapes. Tapered pink beeswax candles sat elegantly in the middle of the table.

Brook measured the excitement in the house by the tension in her own gut, as she garnished devilled eggs with fresh parsley.

Adera removed a sprig and put it promptly in her mouth. "It was a good idea of yours, to have a party for Lila."

Brook responded with equal courtesy. "I hope this will make up to her for being in hospital on her birthday, not just tire her out." She set down pink china plates and a pile of silverware. From there Cyndi took over.

"I'd rather be tired than forgotten," Adera murmured.

"I'll try to remember that." Brook put on Tret Fure's *Terminal Hold*, listening to Adera hum softly as she put the finishing touches on her own entree. The woman seemed quite liberal, after all, proximity having removed her fear of the Big Bad Lesbian.

When the hospital finally summoned her, Helen left to pick up Lila. "Catch you later, beautiful," she murmured. In another rare moment of privacy she ran her hand sensuously along Brook's buttocks.

Along with Mark and Cyndi, Brook wore paths in the carpet checking the window at the sound of every motor. At last Helen drove up. Too excited to be demure, Cyndi raced to the door with Mark in close pursuit. Feeling suddenly shy, Brook waited in the kitchen, rewarded soon enough by the sight of Lila's slate-coloured eyes. Without the drainage bag and intravenous, she looked denuded. Her shirt was the colour of rain-wet violets, her slacks a pale mauve with stylish tucks at the waist. She was noticeably thinner and a little flushed.

For Brook the impact of her eyes was visceral. Something in her solar plexus clamped down hard. She was relieved when four voices swung into the "happy birthday" chorus. She definitely needed time to recover her equilibrium. Helen's blue gaze nudged her and slid away, tactfully.

Lila looked more embarrassed than moved by the attention. She swept the room with a graceful bow. "Thank you all. The place is so clean — do I live here?"

"Thank Cyndi for that," Adera drawled. "She's been cleaning since you left."

"So?" Offended, Cyndi trounced over to the sofa and slouched down.

"So you must really have missed me," Lila teased, draping an arm over her daughter's shoulder.

Cyndi visibly tensed. "Is that your bad arm?"

"Other side. And I'm supposed to use my 'bad arm,' Cyndi. It's good for me."

By the trajectory of Cyndi's eyebrows, Brook knew that there was no chance that Lila would not use her arm. Cyndi would have her exercising from the time she got out of bed in the morning. She stifled an amused smirk.

"You'll never find your presents, Mom." Far too tentatively, Mark nudged alongside his mother.

Tenderly Lila took his face between her hands. "You'll help me, I bet. Though I'd rather anticipate them for a while, if you can stand it."

Gingerly Mark sat next to Lila's injured arm. Tactfully Brook left them to establish their own rapport.

Helen stopped her from over-filling the salt shaker and took over the grinding of peppercorns. "*You're* distracted," she said, her tone not quite light.

Brook did not answer.

"Do you have something to prove to Lila? Is that why you're making so much of an effort?"

"Oh, Helen. Beyond a certain point, I'm scared of taking care of someone. My mother manipulated me far too much that way; tried to control all of us by making us feel sorry for her. In this situation, I know the reverse is true. Lila hates depending on others. And yet I keep inviting her to need me. Do you understand it?"

"I'm not sure I want to. Everyone needs to give, Brook. And — this is not a reproach — sometimes each of us needs to take."

"Do you doubt how I feel about you?"

Helen did not smile. "I know you'll be spending tonight here, in case Lila needs you."

Brook frowned. "Well, she is just out of hospital. Can I make it up to you by meeting you for tennis tomorrow morning?"

Before Helen could answer, a satiric voice broke in on them. "I need to feel useful in my own kitchen. Let me help?"

Wondering how much Lila had heard, Brook gestured at the counter, where Adera had arranged hors d'oeuvres on a tray garnished with radish roses, Brie with pepper cheese, fancy crackers and red grapes. Slices of kiwi fruit surrounded the ball of sharp cheddar that Brook had liberally powdered with walnuts. With a flourish she opened the fridge door to display a tomato aspic impregnated with slices of apple and carrot, and a leafy salad heavy with raisins and nuts. "I hope you're hungry," she said.

"Oh! And I was feeling sorry for myself for having a birthday in hospital."

Silently Helen placed a grape in Lila's mouth and closed her friend's jaw around it.

"Ummm," Lila murmured. "Whatever hospitals serve, I swear, is regurgitated so no patient has to chew."

"Regurgitation is for the birds," Helen deadpanned. Brook swatted her. "Punny, but not funny ... Birthdays deserve to be marked with friends. Not with bedpans."

"Until you're my age," Adera said grimly.

Lila sounded stern. "Especially at your age. And Brook — I hope you've been putting as much attention into your writing as you evidently have into this."

"Yes, mum," Brook drawled. "Do you want to check my homework?"

"You two," Helen said thoughtfully. "Don't rile one another. That's not what you want."

Adera chuckled. "Don't order them to kiss and make up, for God's sake."

Angry words leapt to Brook's throat. But Mark crept beneath his mother's elbow, pressing his head against her stomach, and from the dining room Cyndi impatiently summoned them. Thank Goddess for the loving tyranny of children. Least said, soonest mended, as Adera herself might say.

Dinner was far from leisurely. Mark gobbled his way through the meal and sat waiting for Lila to finish her dessert. Long before she was done he excused himself to pile gifts one by one in the archway to the dining room. For Lila's sake Cyndi pretended that she did not notice, but cast Mark stormy looks for spoiling the treasure hunt. Lila herself seemed studiously oblivious to Mark's shenanigans.

At last it was time for the gift-giving. Mark produced his panda bear, with two green ribbons sitting atop its glass eyes. With a smile Lila freed the bear of its celluloid prison and promptly named it Barrington. Perhaps because she did not want to seem like a child who could not wait her turn, Cyndi asked Adera to give Lila her gift. Adera's envelope contained a season's subscription to the ballet.

Then it was time for Brook to present her gift of stones — sugalite and malachite and rhodochrosite — though she wished that she could do so in private. Explain the power of stones in front of skeptics.

"What a beautiful shade of purple." Lila lifted the knuckle-sized piece of sugalite and admired it under the candles. "Yeah, Mom," Cyndi chuckled, "Brook thinks it will cure you."

With dignity, Brook met the barrage of enquiring eyes. "Sugalite amplifies feelings of wisdom and understanding." She fished out her own bag of gems which she usually wore hidden in her bodice. "See — I carry sugalite, too."

The contents of the rainbow-coloured bag were examined with sharp attention. "The other two — malachite and rhodochrosite — work together. When you meditate, hold one in each hand. Any disease is the result of emotions which are considered too dangerous to express. The stones will help you to let them safely out —" Brook stuttered into silence. Oh, what had she done? This gift would only reactivate the quarrel from which neither one had yet recovered, about the psychological roots of Lila's disease.

Inexplicably Lila left her chair to kiss Brook on the forehead. "It's a beautiful thought, Brook," she said huskily. "You make me feel treasured, and quite undeserving."

Perhaps to rescue Brook from digging herself in further, Helen stretched her arms in an lazy arc over her head. "Cyndi, why don't you see what you can find downstairs."

Satisfied that Mark had not spoiled that surprise, Cyndi vanished. She came back carrying a small lump under her sweater, a lump which meowed and twisted free, landing — quite by accident — on Lila's lap. This time Lila's eyes were wet. Shakily, she reached out to stroke the kitten so gently that it settled, purring where it was. "Oh, Cyndi," she said. "How did you —?"

"It's from Helen, too. She said that you would probably want the kitten neutered and she'd pay to have that done. Do you like her, Mom?" Cyndi's anxiety about her possible rejection of the cat was obvious.

"Do I." Lila's voice arched. "I had a kitten, when I was about five years old. She got run over by a car ... We'll have to keep this one away from Mark's fish."

Helen squeezed her shoulder. "So you're planning to keep her. I wasn't sure she'd be welcome."

"She's welcome," Lila whispered. "Thank you."

Outside the window daylight had fled. There were shadows under Lila's eyes and she leaned more heavily into her chair. Gift-wrap was strewn around her, and open boxes. Adera cleared away the remains of the cake and the dirty glasses and prepared to wash the dishes.

Across the length of the dining room table, Brook's eyes danced with Lila's, their mutual attraction all too obvious to Helen. With an armload of plates she pointed her nose towards the kitchen like a tracking dog, making her audience titter. If Helen felt insecure Brook did not know it. Her tact gave Brook the room to sort through her emotions in private.

"I need to faze out for an hour," Lila said wearily. "Brook, perhaps we can talk later this evening?"

"I'll be in my room," Brook said noncommittally.

Unwillingly, Lila handed the kitten over to Cyndi. "Don't torment the cat, the two of you. By the way, is she trained?"

Brook removed the litter of food and gift-wrap and took the garbage out to the bins. She heard Cyndi promise to keep the animal off the carpets until they were sure of the feline's habits.

Before much later Helen left, shrugging away Brook's bear hug and her whispered promise. "Tomorrow morning for tennis, lover ... "

Upstairs in her room, Brook lay down with her back to the door; realized with astonishment that her cheek was wet. When someone tapped on the door she sat up, startled. Lila crossed over to the bed and nestled against her back, the padded bandage rubbing along Brook's scapula. Her heart thudding, Brook turned to her.

Lila was whispering. "I'm being as responsible as I can, Brook — for everything."

Brook murmured. "I know that. " Desire ran like a current through her irises, making her glance down at the floor.

"You keep saying that the body listens when we tell it we don't want to live. You may be right about that. At any rate, it was your saying that I would rather die than love a woman that made me so damn mad." She lifted her chin, tremulous and bold in one and the same motion. "After all, I've loved Helen for years now, and from time to time have even felt that I could be in love with her ... " Embarrassment flashed briefly in her eyes.

"I mean — the idea of making love with a woman doesn't feel immoral or offensive. It just seems like one more thing to deal with, one more complication in my already complicated life. And what if I tried that and it didn't work either — " She shuddered visibly.

Brook felt the rasp of an impatient anger. "Nothing comes equipped with guarantees. Not lesbianism and not heterodoxy, either."

"I didn't say that my feelings were — or are — noble. But they are my feelings, in themselves neither good nor bad. Isn't that what you keep telling me, Brook?"

"But you'd rather die than love a woman. Oh! I know, we've been through this already." Brook had the sudden and rebellious urge to kiss her fully on the mouth. Oh, great. A careless kiss and this woman would never confide in her again. Careless? As "careless" as she was about her writing, about meditating or about Helen ... *Yes, Brook,* she groaned inside. *Think about Helen. And about helping Lila through this.*

"Besides, shouldn't you be telling Helen if you're in love with her?"

Lila's laugh was jagged as the edge of a saw. "No. That moment passed a long time ago. I'm not ready to make love with a woman. Right now, I'm just afraid of dying. And so tired of being afraid."

"You're right about being tired." She touched the shadows that were like bruises beneath Lila's eyes. "Go to bed, Lila. I have my share of regrets for how I approached things with you, too. Honestly."

Lila stood, feeling summarily dismissed. Nothing prepared Brook for her next question. "Brook. Do you think that you could lie down with me?" Her voice wobbled uncertainly. "I feel so much in need of holding." Brook's jaw dropped.

"Forget it, Brook. I'm way out of line."

Narrowly Brook kept from blushing. "If you're sure that you're not complicating your already complicated life."

"It was a bad idea. I'll find my balance without leaning on you." Suddenly as Lila had entered the room, she was gone.

Brook did not know how long she sat or even about what she thought. In what might have been five minutes or an hour, she let herself into Lila's room and stretched out behind her. Lila lay on her side, her injured arm elevated by a pillow. She was facing the wall.

Brook did not speak. She felt cold and very afraid.

Some time between midnight and morning Lila whispered for Brook to get under the covers; reached carefully to embrace her so that she would stop shivering.

In the grey light of dawn Brook woke with her lips pressed against Lila's neck. She jerked back, embarrassed. But Lila slept on, her breathing slow and deep. Her injured arm held Brook where she was.

CHAPTER EIGHTEEN

Helen stood in light, blue sky and birdsong around her. Flexing her long limbs, she tossed a tennis ball into the air and sent it slamming against the clubhouse wall. It ricocheted back; effortlessly she sliced at it.

"Honing your advantage, Winters? I'm already handicapped playing with you."

Helen jumped. She had not seen Brook approach. "So you say," she retorted. Only by sheer reach could she monopolize the court, since her arms and legs were longer than Brook's. She also played to the line or lobbed just over the net, to keep her opponent running and off kilter. Nor did she have an obvious preference for left or right-handed returns. Still, Brook was agile and wily. What she lacked in reach she made up in speed and intuition, anticipating problem plays without giving herself away. If anything, insouciance was her secret weapon.

With unremitting diligence Helen played. A slight hesitation in Brook's serve and almost imperceptibly Helen adjusted her balance. Her racquet streaked where it should not have been able, lifting the ball almost from the floor into a stunning return. She won the first game and lost the second only to chance. The ball hung suspended between her court and Brook's and she misjudged. Groaning, Helen watched it roll down her side of the net.

"Thanks," Brook said to an invisible deity and shook Helen's hand. They could play no longer. There was time only for a swim and a quick shower before Helen went to class.

Brook's mouth wrinkled in distaste for the chlorinated pool as she held her nose and plunged. She came up and dog-paddled, watching

Helen's strong arms propel her through the pool, her feet kicking away from the edge as she completed several fast laps. Stroking far more indolently, Brook enjoyed the visual distortions of her legs and the refraction of light beneath the water. She did the dead man's float and opened her eyes just as Helen jumped on her waist like a playful mermaid. Down she plunged and gasped for air, wrapping her legs around Helen's pelvis as she ascended. Helen's arms held her there as though Brook were nine years old. She felt the caress of water at her labia as Helen paddled to keep them both afloat.

Impulsively Brook kissed her, then drew away coughing. "I can't stand this pool," she grumbled. "The chlorine makes me feel like I'm swimming in bleach."

"I'm glad you explained. I didn't think kissing me was repellent."

"It isn't. Helen, can you forgo the Olympic tryouts and talk to me? I feel really mixed up."

"Olympic — well, it's good to know I look serious." Helen projected herself unto the deck and found their towels. She waited until Brook stood dripping behind her and draped them both in a single towel. "I haven't seen the lifeguard yet," she said huskily. "Why don't we retreat to the sauna."

Gingerly Brook settled on the hot wood. Fortunately, it was too early in the day for the sauna to be an oven. Obviously more heat tolerant, Helen ladled water over coals before she climbed up to join Brook, her damp towel protecting her from the temperature of the bench. Brook winced away from the tenderness in Helen's eyes.

"What is it, Brook? You haven't invented a new source of angst — about Lila, I mean."

"Damn it, Helen! I hate being so predictable ... Lila asked me to sleep with her last night. And no, it wasn't sexual, at least not on her part."

"Oh," Helen sounded as though Brook had punched her. Then she laughed. "So we still have crushes on Lila. Just how bad is yours?"

Again Brook heard Lila's voice saying: *From time to time I've even been in love with Helen.* The three of them were walking in a minefield with one another and any one of them could be seriously injured by a misstep. What a ridiculous fear. Certainly all of them were able to deal honestly with one another. Nor should her love for Lila mean that she would — or could — withdraw her love from Helen. She chuckled uneasily.

"Crush. You mean like the night we showered together, when I lusted over your perfect legs and striking eyes."

Looking neither flattered nor placated, Helen leveled Brook with those celebrated eyes. "So maybe I'm the crush."

"No. Crushes don't evoke so much tenderness. I respect and admire you. If anything Lila is the crush. There is no logical reason for me to love her. We don't think alike about anything. Healing the mind is a strange idea to her — like my other strange ideas about stones and magic. She accepts my beliefs only because they are my beliefs, not because they're hers."

"So? Is it logic that made you choose me?"

"No. And yes. Chemistry is certainly a part of it. Sometimes I think there is no love without lust. But some needs are sheer masochism and should be lopped off like the blighted branch of a tree in order to save the healthy part of it. I'm happy with you, Helen — excited by the workings of your mind and deeply grateful for your acceptance. You give me a lot of room to grow. And you're probably more patient than I am with my neuroses."

"Maybe I accept too much about you because I'm infatuated — and foolish."

"So you think it isn't reasonable to love me." Brook tried to sound teasing.

Glumly, Helen rested her chin on raised knees, her blue eyes suddenly hard. "Well, you did tell me about your philandering father. I didn't realize how much you were like him."

"Helen," Brook let her hand slide along Helen's knee, "that shot is unworthy of you."

"Like I'm unworthy of you? We can't all be 'together,' Brook. Some of us are insecure. I told you at the beginning: I need to feel special. You can't say I misled you."

"Did I breach some rules for my behaviour? I was acting on the understanding that both of us want to be open with one another."

Helen sent her a blistering glance. "Are you thinking of Lila in any of this? She's dealing with enough, Brook, and certainly would not appreciate a lesbian coming on to her."

"I won't ask her to deal with me as a lesbian," Brook said, doggedly. "But she may be asking herself to deal with lesbian feelings, Helen."

"You mean that she's coming to love women. Or that she loves you?"

Soothingly Brook put her hand in the small of Helen's throat. "She'd never say anything of the kind. Lila knows that you and I are lovers. Furthermore, she'd probably be horrified to know how I feel about her."

With a shudder Helen shrugged off her hand. "Is it Lila's loyalty that you're counting on to protect me?"

"You make me sound like an opportunist. You know I'm committed to you."

Helen snorted. "One 'commits' prisoners or mental patients."

"Whatever. We both know what you expect and what you won't tolerate ... Rules. Like stone tablets handed down to Moses at Mt. Sinai. Who cares about rules? It's love that matters, the rare and uncommon miracle of love. For one person or more than one, love is always the unexpected and ineffable gift."

"That's very nice, Brook. Still, rhetoric aside, I'm waiting to hear what you want to do about Lila. Are you asking me to share you with her, if she can be persuaded to love you?" Sarcasm spread towards Brook like squid's ink in water.

"You're as good at verbal serves as you are at tennis. I concede. To risk jeopardizing our love, I'm a fool. And I'd be challenged, too, by the way, if you told me that you wanted to sleep with Lila, whether or not she reciprocated that feeling."

"'Challenged.' Don't analyse me, Brook. You may not know me as well as you think you do."

"Please. Let's not quarrel. You're right, of course. Lila has enough to deal with."

"Oh. Resignation. You don't believe you can win her, so I win you by default." Helen wiped at her eyes as though to dry off sweat and clasped the towel determinedly around her shoulders.

"I don't know that I want to 'win' her. She would probably make me very unhappy. Helen, I'm thinking of moving out. I need to get some distance from Lila, for my own sake as much as for yours."

Helen gaped at Brook as though the latter had just developed webbed feet. "And how will you explain that to Lila? 'Oh, your cancer has become inconvenient to me? I prefer to run away from problems, despite my promises to the contrary'?"

With leaden eyes Brook gazed back at Helen. "You make me feel unjust, like a child faced by reasonable parents. Isn't it obvious what will happen to us if I continue to moon over Lila? And how can I be objective enough to help her if I'm off centre? No. Moving out may cause some immediate problems —"

"Yeah, three of them, named Lila and Cyndi and Mark. Don't you think they need you right now — need some stability in their lives?"

"Helen, what kind of friendship becomes a series of obligations?"

"So don't move out. Let's be evolved. I'll make up a chart for who gets Lila on which nights and on what holidays. After all, why *should* three emancipated twentieth-century women be caught up by silly things like monogamy? After all, it's so — limiting." On the brink of crying, Helen struggled for words. "I hear you resigning yourself to less than you really want. And your moving out would jeopardize Lila as she begins to reach out, to try your methods for healing — for helping herself. She doesn't trust easily, Brook. You'd have to tell her why you're really leaving, not just some cockamamy story about avoiding 'ought-to'—"

A woman opened the door to the sauna and backed out, murmuring to the person behind her.

Despairingly, Helen glanced at the wall over Brook's head. "I've got to get ready for work. No matter how fascinating this is to you, it is a conversation which will have to be finished later." Head down, she stumbled past the women on the other side of the door.

Brook followed her, almost looking forward to the shock of the pool. After the unnatural heat of the sauna she gasped, hoping that her heart would not fail as she hit the chilling water. Helen bypassed the pool entirely and headed for the shower. When Brook joined her, she was already hurrying into her clothes and making a point of not being able to talk over the noise of the hair dryer.

As she headed for the exit, Brook said anxiously: "We are having supper tonight, aren't we? Helen, I am sorry to hurt you just because I didn't deal with this one alone — "

But Helen was walking away from her, fast. Over her shoulder she carolled: "I'll call you."

When Helen came home, daylight was fading. Afraid of the silence, she turned on the television, oblivious to the images and sounds of male-centred drama. With a grimace she changed from a dress and heels to baggy pants and a loose tee-shirt.

From the stove her kettle screamed. She took it off the burner, glad for the shrill reminder. Otherwise, only her nose would have recalled her: the smell of buckling metal activating the memory of putting water on to boil.

She poured scalding water over mint leaves, the aroma reminiscent of clover in a summer field. The smell evoked her longing for the cabin on Mayne Island, for the grand flight of eagles, wings spread to pockets of wind. At night even the stars spoke to her there, light and shadow on the rocks and the sounds of seals harping, noisily social in their remote colony.

Thinking about the island was a mistake. Immediately she heard wood crackling and the pop of cinders flying up the chimney. Saw Brook resting on her elbow, the pink glow from the flames highlighting the gleam of her naked skin — Brook's whimsical and hungry eyes caressing her.

Even in the midst of that idyll Lila had intruded, Brook's dream calling them home to account to Lila for their love. Her resentment embarrassed Helen, the pettiness of her jealousy. Sexual competition had no right to divide friends from one another. After all, it was Brook who was the interloper in Helen's life, the recent development, the glitch. Lila was years of yoga and aerobics, of concerts and late night conversations — of desire spiralling through her intestines even when Lila had fallen soundly into sleep. Longing that could not be requited, for at first there was Jack.

Not only Brook was attracted to Lila's vulnerability, to the absence of guile and the quixotic hopefulness which ran through her smoky irises like clouds before the face of the sun. Jack had been a reason for restraint, certainly, and Helen's own habit of caution whenever she found herself in love with a heterosexual woman. Jack might have been a temporary twist in a widening road, but Lila's innocence was more inviolable. There was only one way to deal with wanting someone so badly. And that was to avoid occasions for touch. It was then, however, that Lila began touching, her trust and tenderness so open that Helen could not forbid her merely in the name of protecting herself against her own lust.

Impatiently Helen drank, the tea scalding her palate. She put the cup down sharply. Early this evening she would call Brook. They could go to dinner and try to avoid the kind of heart-to-heart they had had this morning. Perhaps, just perhaps, Lila would not have to come into the conversation. Helen's conscience pricked her. It was Lila who needed Helen's reassurance, not Helen who should be seeking Brook's. Helen after all was in the full bloom of a flowering love, and certainly healthy.

No. She did not and she would not pity Lila for having cancer. That was an emotion with which Lila could not deal. Ironically, Brook's loyalties seemed to have as little to do with pity as did Helen's. They both loved Lila, that was the simple and profound truth of it.

Helen rubbed at her eyes. She wanted to call Brook and tell her that her sulking had fizzled to its natural end. Brook would accept that; she would come to see her and spend the night. Brook, after all, was not saying that she was confused about sex with Helen, she was confused about the thought of sex with Lila. But possessive or not, the idea of sharing her lover jolted Helen like a cattle prod, maddened her in a way she would not have thought possible.

Still, how could Brook protect Helen from her feelings? To do that would be for Brook to admit that her feelings were "wrong," that she was "bad" to feel what she did. And Helen knew very well that that denial was crazy-making. One loved or one did not. One was loved or one was not.

Yes. This was crazy-making. Surely she could summon a little garden variety trust, some confidence in her own ability to hold Brook's love. But Helen's self-confidence was evidently a thin veneer and easily torn. By the violence of her reactions, she recognized that her distress had as much to do with her feelings towards Lila as they did with her love for Brook.

Helen closed off the chattering television and the light by her arm chair. She rested her head against its broad back. For a while there was chaos in her brain, a kind of buzzing, background noise. Then she was drifting, a leaf on a light breeze towards a current of water. The channel looked clear and cold and then grew deeper and dark, pushing her onto a distant shore.

She saw a woman in a long dress, her gestures agitated, and another woman leaning back, watching with amusement. The woman was asking: "Are you telling me the truth, Chloe? Is he unfaithful — and with you?" Chloe. The name slid into her psyche as one's own name does, provoking identification. "With my own sister?"

Chloe's eyes were carefully veiled, but Helen felt her deception, the manipulation behind her lidded face. Felt it, as though she were Chloe and fully aware of the woman's motives.

"Oh, how will I leave him? He loves little Nadia so much." The woman's grief was tearing and palpable.

Helen bolted forward in the chair, blood pumping in her ears from an agitated pulse. So. Now she knew her full role in the scenario of the Dutchman. Her responsibility for driving a wedge between husband and wife. No wonder she had blocked her awareness, and flown into panic and angst. Brook's need to move away from Lila revealed that even after centuries Lila had not lost her love.

There was a taste like bile in Helen's mouth. To lie to her own sister so that she could have her husband ... No. She, Helen, had not done that. Someone else had; someone of despicable opportunism. Chloe. Helen could be responsible only for what she did now. She couldn't drag this other life into this already complex present.

Still, she could not deny that she was manipulating Brook. She wanted

Brook to feel her hurt, to blame herself for having a wayward heart. Why couldn't she be content with the love of one woman?

Could Helen keep Brook if she did not manipulate her? Keep. No one kept another person. That had driven her wild in her marriage to Tony — that sense of being someone else's possession. Yet she was forcing Brook to choose between her and her own best friend. That power play could lose her Brook's trust and then Brook herself. Unless she freed Brook to do what she needed to do. What she wanted to do. Win Lila's love.

Maybe Helen was here this time to experience what Lila had experienced then — the utter desolation of losing someone she deeply loved. Her thoughts scrambled, as though someone had thrown a wrench into speeding machinery. Darkness surrounded her chair, enveloped her between the gateway of two worlds.

CHAPTER NINETEEN

Lila took off her rain-misted Cowichan sweater; ran her fingers along the outlines of stylized ravens. Buying the sweater made no sense. She had several warm and durable woolens and the price was sheer ransom. Then why had she been so excited by buying it? Oh, oh. The shaman's drum in Brook's sitting room. Her mind had tricked her into devising a way to "wear" Brook's spirit.

She shook her head. *What is wrong with me anyway? Throughout that restive night, she held me so tentatively that it was difficult to fall asleep. Why? Is falling asleep like losing control over all the changes in my life? Whatever my motives — loneliness or fear of dying — I do not intend to prevail upon Brook's pity again. Nor will I give myself something to regret.* Lila swallowed a lump of bile in her throat. *Some integrity I have, motivated more by shame than by ethics.*

Fear of increasing dependency on Brook made Lila insist that she would take a cab to the clinic. Because chemotherapy might make her nauseous, she had been warned not to drive her own car. Helen would see her home, since her Mustang needed a tune-up. Her garage was not very far from the clinic.

Being an outpatient had its advantages. At least the time for dealing with Dr. Kline was temporarily over. Now, if only Lila could push down this feeling of being passed from one specialist to another, like a plate of bloody liver.

At the lab, she was tourniqueted and slapped across her vein, which was narrow enough that the technician worried about finding it. A sharp jab and blood was drawn through a needle into three vials. These vials would be analyzed and the results forwarded to Dr. Aziz. Every three weeks the lab would determine whether or not Lila's white blood count was high enough for her to receive chemotherapy. What an idiotic treatment. First it wiped out her white blood cells and then counted on them being there in high enough presence to wipe them out again.

A blend of chemicals was prepared especially for her. She sat in a reclining chair, a needle taped to a vein in her hand, and toxins dripped, innocuous and clear as water, into her blood. She tried not to regard the drugs as an assault, leaking their way into every cell of her body. Well, this had better work, this conveyor-belt medicine which made her feel so totally depersonalized. She wished that pride had not made her come alone. She needed comfort.

After a chest x-ray, she was sent with the film to a holding tank for several doctors. She placed the bulky envelope beside her chair, out of the way of human traffic. Aziz would want to see this along with her blood results. Oblivious, Lila flipped through countless articles, far too aware of these others with whom she shared cancer to be conscious of the meaning of words printed on a page. Women fat or thin wearing very obvious scarves bound tightly over their balding heads. Men resigned to waiting, fingers circling around thumbs or elbows, knees swinging or shoe leather scraping across the floor.

Eventually, Lila was led to an examining room, weighed by a nurse and told to put on a hospital gown. Trusting another stranger did not please her. To Aziz she would be only a body, after all, not a person with feelings. *If he isn't nice,* Lila determined, *I'll upset the clinic's precious routines and ask for someone else. Dealing with Kline has given me some practice in standing up for myself.*

The door opened to a man in his fifties, wavy-haired and greying. "I am Dr. Aziz," he said. His accent was — Czechoslovakian? Firmly he shook Lila's hand. Pale green eyes surveyed her. His smile, though tentative, was calming. In painstaking English, he asked whether Lila was anxious: were there other factors in her life which were unsettling?

"You think my recovery could be linked to whether or not I want to live," Lila said satirically. He was obviously a man of Brook's bent.

"In a way," he answered cheerfully. "I have personally lost patients I had no reason to lose, while those I diagnosed as terminal made a full recovery." He chuckled. "I suppose that is to remind me to pay attention to more than my patients' bodies."

"I suppose," Lila said guardedly.

"You do know that your odds for survival are excellent. Only one of your lymph nodes has been affected by cancer. Still, there are no guarantees."

On the contrary, Kline had given her to believe that each moment had the potential to be her last, unless she could be gotten through another and another treatment process. She resented Kline's lack of information so bitterly that she said nothing.

Aziz thumped at the hollows of her back, took her blood pressure and listened to her heart and lungs. He said reassuringly: "I know that you must be worried. It never does to compare one person with another, but in the scheme of things, your need for nine chemotherapy treatments means that your cancer is minor. You will be able to come here only as an outpatient. After you have chemo five times," he held up the fingers of his right hand, "we will interrupt your treatment for radiation. You cannot receive both at the same time as their effects cancel one another out." He was thorough: was it those Old World manners which made him appear humane?

Reflecting his calm, Lila asked: "Can you tell me how long this rigamarole will take?"

Aziz smiled, revealing crooked incisors. "This 'rigamarole,' as you call it, will probably be over in nine months. Every three weeks, from now until November you will have chemotherapy. Take care not to become pregnant while you are receiving it — a foetus would be damaged. You will notice changes to your menstrual cycle. Some women become menopausal permanently. Your period — if and when it comes back — could be irregular, your bleeding spotty or heavier than normal. There are probably as many variables as there are people. At your age — thirty-seven? — you have had your family, yes?"

"I have had the children I'm going to," she said, with barely disguised resentment. Men often supposed that women were dying to have more children.

"Your husband is not here?" Aziz sounded careful. "It would be nice if he could arrange to be with you. Chemotherapy might make you nauseous — not that I want to implant the idea that you must be. Not everyone is."

"My husband and I are separated," Lila said. "I'm being met here, about three."

"It is good to have friends." Aziz was non-committal. "There are different pills I can give you to treat nausea. One is a synthetic of marijuana, and very powerful. It could affect your dreams; make them vivid and perhaps frightening to you. It might also make you sleep for the rest of the day, which might not be a bad idea. Sometimes cancer follows too long a period of stress."

Lila did not want to drop into a dark hole led by an unknown agent. Her dreams were already frightening enough. "Not that," she said brusquely. "If I must take yet another drug, it will be something else."

"We can try you on Prochlorperazine. You can pick it up from the dispensary before going home. I'd advise that you take it after each treatment and every four to six hours, or as you need it. You can try to 'tough it out,' as they say, but my concern is to make you as comfortable as possible. Until your stomach settles, do not eat lettuce salads and avoid orange and tomato juice for several days. And no alcohol until at least three days after each treatment. Now. Do you have any questions about your surgeries — what you can expect as you heal?"

Lila had a hundred questions. That they would finally be answered was encouraging. "Yes. The back of my arm feels numb. Other nerves tingle. How long will it be before the arm returns to normal?"

"You are fortunate to have had Dr. Kline as a surgeon. Five years ago lymph surgery would have involved completely severing all of those nerves. Someone could stick a huge needle in you or burn you with a cigarette; you would not feel it. Kline piloted a technique to avoid cutting some of the nerves, so that you will regain partial sensation. Over most of the year to come, however, your arm will prickle like sharp needles. That is better than being numb, yeah?"

Lila blanched. "Oh, great. Is Dr. Kline above considering that I might have wanted to know this before surgery?"

Aziz looked disconcerted. "Perhaps she forgot," he said lamely. "Breast cancer is her specialty you know. In Vancouver that makes her immensely overworked."

Lila struggled to be fair. If blame was due, it belonged not with Aziz but with the taciturn Dr. Kline. "So. What else have I not been told about my breast?"

"It will be affected — not so much by the surgery, which is very well done. The nipple may always feel harder than the other and spiral towards the top — like an orange peel? The skin will have somewhat large pores, also like an orange. Radiation will give you permanent sunburn. For the remainder of your life, you must not try to tan, front or back — since we treat your shoulder also, not only your breast."

Lila had never been a "bronzed goddess," but she enjoyed the warm, vital rays of the sun on her naked shoulders. There was nothing like losing that freedom to make her covet it. Her eyes stung. Dubiously, she glanced at her breast.

Aziz touched her shoulder. "So far as the size of your breasts — even you will come not to notice the difference between one and the other. You are lucky. Forgive me for emphasizing this, for you must not feel so lucky. But even a few years ago you'd have been given a mastectomy — automatically."

"Like my mother."

"No. Not like your mother. I read about her in your file. The treatment of breast cancer is not what it was. Now we can link it to diet, to animal fats and caffeine, even to moderate alcohol consumption. Avoid drinking coffee and eating fried foods. Get your vitamins from green and yellow vegetables and from lean meat — no hamburger or pork. Cut down on cheese and dairy products."

"Well, in case I needed a diet — " Lila shrugged, trying for a philosophical smile.

"You don't need it. Try not to lose weight. Women don't like to be told to eat more, but you should. Lots of protein, fibers and brans. We will keep a very close eye on you for two to three years. If your cancer stays in remission for that time, it will probably never recur. You have your age going for you."

Aziz followed up with questions regarding Lila's work, and assured her that she would be able to keep her job. When she left it was with the feeling that she — Lila Tennant — really mattered to this man. Bemused, she made her way to Chemotherapy, still feeling a bit like a prisoner on death row embarking on her last journey.

Once it began, the treatment itself took little enough time — a mere half-hour. But sitting still for it took all the willpower Lila had. She occupied her attention by reading posters which made fun of various clients and their styles of receiving treatment — the anxious client, the impatient and the resigned. Was that what was meant by having gallows humour? To their credit, the nurses were everything a scared person could have ordered — vivacious and caring. Surprising herself, Lila responded with an astute interest in what these women shared with her about their personal lives.

Finally it was time for the saline drip. Lila could barely contain her restlessness. She felt goaded to do something with the rest of her life. Perhaps that was a positive result of contemplating her own mortality. In the scheme of things, what did it matter if she finished her thesis on the bi-sexuality of Anaïs Nin? After meeting Helen — with her courage to leave a husband because she loved a woman — Nin's and June Miller's cowardice about loving one another made them seem remote to Lila.

What had she been searching for, after all, except the record of women's devotion to one another, which she had by more immediate example in the lives of Brook and Helen? No wonder Jack had resented her absorption in Anaïs Nin and pointed her — irritably and repetitiously — towards Helen Winters. But that was another bucket of worms.

When she got home today she would head upstairs to her office and search for the poetry she had put aside for too long. Her files were well-organized. In moments she could find what she was looking for, a loose-leaf binder with typed pages. Reading the manuscript she might rediscover her poetic voice, feel the power of her words — if, in fact, they were so poignant as she remembered. Single poems of hers had been published in several anthologies, literary magazines and quarterlies. If Lila were to submit these and others not as odds and sods, but for the consideration of a single publisher ... The idea shocked her. Then she no longer felt fanciful or afraid to do such a thing. One poem could be refused just as easily as a volume. She had gotten rejection slips before, but she could also point to published work.

Tied to the point of this needle, she felt like a skittish horse, circling and nudging against fences. Cancer was a sharp burr which must be dislodged. She must at some time have known how to play. She could not always have been such an unwavering source of constraint in her own life. Sharply, she veered away from self-hatred.

Eventually she would find an editor willing to work with her, someone who believed as she did that her poetry would sell. No doubt that would mean promoting herself in a professional manner. Dimly Lila became aware of Helen's smile shining.

"I'm not sure why you look delighted, but I'm glad." Helen glanced pointedly at the paraphernalia to which Lila was strapped; cradled her carefully around the bulk of the armchair. With a happy sound Lila leaned into her. Almost afraid to say it out loud, she whispered: "Helen, I don't know why it took cancer to make me serious again about writing."

Helen came around to sit on the foot stool. "The silver lining behind all things ... " She sounded tired. "Sorry. The school is in the midst of rehearsals for a concert. My students are literally hanging from the rafters."

Lila clucked sympathetically. "Your eyes are shadowed. Is that the fault of the concert?"

"Oh —" Helen collapsed her long legs and gazed down at her feet. "I'll tell you about it away from here. And you can tell me about your writing project — though I hope you're not trying to be Super Woman, taking that on now. Are you well enough to come to my place?" Helen sounded deeply troubled.

"I may be quite nauseous. Perhaps I should go home."

"Come on," Helen coaxed. "If you go home you'll only have to reassure the kids. Besides, I need to talk in private." A shadow flitted across her eyes. Lila nodded wordlessly.

On their way out of the clinic they picked up her prescription. With annoyance, Lila glanced at her watch. "Wonderful. This took only four and a half hours out of my day."

"Speaking about time — are you imagining that your poetry will be the legacy you leave behind? Is that why you have a sudden and burning desire to be published?"

With deceptive calm Lila turned to face her. "I need a legacy. I will not be obliterated, Helen."

"Are you sure this is the only life time each of us has? I'm not, any more." Helen pulled sharply into the traffic. Whatever was bothering her seemed to be making her unduly aggressive.

Without looking at her, Helen blurted: "Brook told me about a lifetime when she was your husband. Lila, I believe I was responsible for your leaving him. I was your sister and I lied to you about his fidelity."

Lila shivered uneasily. "Hey. Offer me the ritual courtesies of tea and small talk first. This is heavy ... sister."

Helen clasped Lila's fingers hard as if she did not dare to let them go.

At her apartment she made tea and put on Linda Ronstadt. With unusually jittery movements, she sat down at the piano to accompany the invisible orchestra. For a long time Lila watched her play. Then she felt almost like a voyeur who was witnessing something she should not be. Whatever Helen was feeling she was not yet ready to talk. Quietly, Lila left her to have a shower. Then, wearing Helen's robe, she padded over to join her friend at the piano. Hesitantly, she put her damp head in the small of Helen's back. Ever so slightly Helen stiffened.

"Are you telling me that Brook — as my husband — was unfaithful to me with you? I find it hard to believe that you could have been such a schemer. You aren't now."

Helen exhaled deeply. She apparently needed to be told that Lila did not see her that way. "As friend or sister," she whispered, "I seem to have a habit of meeting you before Brook does. Maybe in this life time my love for her won't lead me to love you less. This time I owe you."

Lila's smile was uncertain. "It's hard for me to believe in guilt beyond the grave. Tell me, what prompted this revelation of yours?"

"What prompted it is jealousy. Brook, my dear, wants to be given the chance to love us both."

Nervously, Lila poured another cup of tea, shaking her head as though that would help her to think more clearly. With trembling hands she passed the cup to Helen. Automatically Helen drank. "If 'Brook' and 'I' were married in a past life, wouldn't that explain her attraction to me? We all want to think that we can go back and do something again, with different results. But — even if you, as my sister, stole my husband, do we really want to do this again?"

"Lila, are you attracted to Brook? Please don't protect me from the truth."

Uneasily, Lila laughed. "Brook is with my best friend. And I think that I'd rather swallow kerosene than discuss this."

"I see." Helen looked disconsolate and grey.

"I don't believe Brook wants to leave you. And I have a more recent separation to go through — in this lifetime." Lila's tone was deliberately satiric.

Exasperated, Helen asked: "Doesn't cancer make you feel that you should act on your feelings — not only write emotional poetry?"

The shaking in Lila's hands spread to her knees. Quickly she sat near Helen on the piano stool. Her shaking continued until she herself was alarmed by it. With all the courage she had, Lila turned to gaze into Helen's eyes.

"Maybe the problem is that I'm simply not sexual, that I can't respond to man or woman. How would I live with that knowledge? Would I even want to?"

"What's wrong with the word 'stop'? All sex doesn't lead to marriage, you know. Or to orgasm, I might add."

"Maybe not. But all love may lead to hurt. Even if you could share Brook with me or I could share her with you ... " Lila halted lamely.

Helen's eyes sent the strangest beam of blue light, like a cat hypnotizing potential prey. Then her back slumped and she looked very disillusioned. "Ah. So loving Brook is something only one of us can do. Thanks for making that clear to me."

"Oh, Helen! I need friends far more than I need a lover. Friendship is more secure."

Helen's laugh sounded hollow, almost echoing. "I'm jangling with energy that has no place to go. I need to clean an attic or play tennis or—" her smile flickered briefly and went out. "Dance ... " In the background Linda Ronstadt began singing *Straighten Up and Fly Right*. "Now isn't that song appropriate?" Helen said dryly.

"Come on," Lila said restively. "I'll dress and let's go for a walk. After all, if you're right, we have hundreds of years to solve this. That should be time enough."

"When I was your sister I wouldn't have said that. Oh, well. There is no sense in dwelling on my previous crimes."

Lila's smile was suddenly ambiguous. "You could have waited, you know. Brook came to you anyway."

"And to you." Without looking at her, Helen stopped the tape.

By the time they walked, the sky had cleared. After the rain, mist emanated like steam from the ground. Feeling contrite, Lila took Helen's hand and placed it inside her Cowichan sweater to keep her fingers warm. "To hell with past lives," she said grimly. "I love you, Helen — here and now. And this is where my loyalty belongs."

"Loyalty." Helen sounded dubious. But she let her hand rest, strong and warm, right where it was.

CHAPTER TWENTY

Through Brook's window the air came swollen: a potpourri of flowering scents and the excited cacaphony of starlings, towhees and flickers. The smells and sounds of dawn gave the lie to Brook's sluggish reluctance to begin the day. She raced downstairs to the bath, sprinkling rose petals into the water. Seated in the steaming tub, she checked each of her energy centres as though reading a map. An accumulation of emotions clustered in her solar plexus, her heart. For the past several months she had been caught up in Lila: her separation, her illness, her children. Maintaining the barrier between "friendship" and desire was sapping Brook's energies.

She needed to raise power. Long ago, people would have done that with ritual dance and chanting until dawn, sitting in sweat lodges or walking into the wilderness on a vision quest. Now Brook found power in a coven, where vitality was also raised through dance and chanting, hour after hour, until the energy of each was transmuted into group power. On this Summer Solstice, it was Brook's turn to serve as High Priestess. She, especially, must come from a centred place.

She dried her body with a huge towel, taking the time to touch breasts and pubic ridge, belly and buttocks with her fingers. It had taken Brook years to rid herself of the strangeness of ritual hands placed on her. One lost a child's pride in the body, began to take on the guilt associated with sensual pleasure. This body had been given to her in all its complex simplicity by a creative life force. Today she and her coven would honour that gift of life and the Mother from Whom all life came.

At Beltane, Helen had celebrated the first of the Quarter Days with the Coven of Bridget. Brook had prepared her for the ritual shedding of clothes. Naked one came into the world and naked one dealt with the sacred. Helen answered evenly enough. "I guess I can handle it — so long as a group grope isn't compulsory."

Reassuringly, Brook grinned. "The coven is freeing energies, not seeking a free fondle." She grasped Helen's hand. How precious it was to share the religion of Wicca with Helen, one of many things to share. Their natures were interlocking so that together they were greater than either of them had been alone. Remembering their recent and unusual conflict, Brook's throat tightened. That they could be content, that they could be still. That they could simply open to one another once more.

Wrapped in a kimono, she searched for red and green candles, found them and a pair of scissors and went to the garden to snip red roses, her fingers cautious of thorns. The vibrant flowers were laden with scent: she buried her face in the dew-wet roses. Monogamy and love may not be identical — but for Helen they were paired, in the same way a bird needed two wings if it were to fly. For now Helen needed these "wings." Only confidence in Brook's love would make the fear of losing it go away.

Brook drank a specially prepared blend of herbs, the tea and the heat of the bath opening her heart.

Legs pumping fast, she made it to Spanish Banks in record time, the spokes of the bicycle gleaming in the sun. Leaning against a maple tree Helen waited, her dark hair violet in the morning light. She wore yellow shorts and a bright lavender top that displayed the attractive bones of her shoulders. With a groan, Brook turned her face into Helen's neck. The world without the touch of those hands. Without Helen, irrepressible and ingenuous. There was no way even to imagine it.

In silence, Helen freed a sleeping bag from her bicycle and carefully stuffed it into Brook's pack. In the folds of the bag were the red and green tips of candles, and more roses, their buds curling tightly like crimson labia.

Brook touched Helen on the shoulder and led the way down the steep incline, until her lover's long legs surpassed the reach of Brook's short ones and Helen drew ahead. Winding through the woods were countless log stairs. The sharp descent was a strain on the tired muscles in Brook's legs; she was happy when they came to a clearing and waited for the others.

Seated on the grass, Helen opened a can of guava juice and shared it with Brook. Happily Brook rested her chin on Helen's knees. Long fingers smoothed stray curls away from Brook's windblown forehead.

"Come on, Sober Sides," Helen sounded uncertain, "let's plan where we want to go this summer. We need a change."

"Ummm," Brook leaned into her. "Why don't we go to Witches' Camp or to the Michigan Womyn's Music Festival? Which appeals to you more, Helen?"

"Either sounds fabulous. Or we could retreat to Mayne Island." Hesitantly Helen whispered. "Spend time alone with me. Give me physical comfort to remove my doubts. That's what I need to feel secure."

Sunlight sent shafts through the Douglas firs, turned Brook's hair red as burnt sienna. "As much time and comfort as you're willing to share," she murmured huskily. "Loving you is not a favour or an act of charity. You know I'm more selfish than that."

Suddenly four women circled the grove, cardinal points in a living compass. East, South, West and North. They rotated around Brook and Helen like a wheel in which the two women were the axis, the indefinable centre of Spirit. Feet came rhythmically to earth and up again, motions synchronized to the beating of a rawhide drum. Brook and Helen joined the chant. A soft breeze came up, smelling of sap and rot, of new and old wood.

Ruth. Tracy. Tabatha. Arlan. Their faces painted with swirls of red and green and white. In a smaller and smaller spiral they circled clockwise, until Tracy stepped forward to touch the bones of Helen's face. Having been coached in her role, Helen knelt. Brook saw goosebumps rise on her neck. With pots of dye Tracy painted Helen's cheekbones, nostrils and ears and mouth. Her eyes she rimmed with charcoal. Helen's senses were being consecrated to the use of the Goddess. Accelerated by the beat of the drum, the chanting rose, higher, louder. Keening like gulls, the women swooped. In one synchronized movement they lifted Helen above their heads. Brook stepped beneath her and placed her hands in the small of Helen's back.

"Like the coming of summer we welcome you to this coven," Tracy intoned.

"We welcome you with the coming of summer," five voices said together.

Gently the coven set Helen on her feet. "The heart of summer is the soul of winter. It is the law of the Goddess." With a finger in one of the pots, Brook drew forks of white lightning down Helen's cheekbones. Above each of Helen's sinuses she made a red dot. From her dashiki Tracy brought forth a small mirror, held it motionless in front of Helen's face.

Brook's voice rang out in the clearing. "Light and dark are twins. At this time when daylight is longest, we know that we shall return to the day when darkness reigns. Our lives are as candles and we as wax, burning our individual ways to death."

Behind Helen at cardinal points the candles flared. She saw them only as reflections of light in the mirror. As she had been coached, Helen said: "I am of woman born. I prepare for death with many small deaths."

The mirror swirled with sudden mist. In its shadows Helen saw an infant rising out of the bosom of an ancient crone. The crone had Helen's cornflower blue eyes, staring into the invisible. She lay in a queen-sized bed, her arthritic hands going suddenly still. With a plaintive lament, a woman climbed into the sheets and held the crone as though to lend her the heat of her body. Even beneath white hair, Helen recognized the bone structure of Lila's face ... So Lila would survive cancer — and be present at the moment of Helen's death!

"You have seen your dying?" Tabatha asked.

Helen gasped. "I am very old and I appear to die at home ... Brook isn't there."

"The Goddess has blessed you then with the gift of long life ... It is not Brook's fate to see your death," Tabatha said.

"There is a child rising out of the crone's chest," Helen stammered. "Does that mean that I am to be reborn?"

"We are not yet done with the cycle of rebirth," Brook answered.

Behind her Tracy kicked at the dirt. Being reborn, like having past lives, defied her sense of reality. One life and one particular death was all she was prepared to accept. Sensitive to Tracy's old quarrel with the coven and with the woman serving as their High Priestess, Tabatha brought the mirror to Tracy. Once more the women stood at cardinal points.

What Tracy saw in the shadows of the mirror sucked the colour from her face. With dry lips, she whispered: "I die by water. I simply swim out too far and get a cramp ... In the boat Arlan is fishing and does not see — "

Arlan moaned and slumped forward. Eyes glittering with unshed tears, Tracy drew close, rocking her lover back and forth in her arms. Her voice was guttural. "It's a peaceful death — It's so peaceful and so easy — Overhead there is a hawk, wheeling like a spirit guide ... "

"How old are you when this happens?" Arlan croaked.

"Perhaps a decade older," Tracy answered.

"You have chosen an easy death," Tabatha whispered. Around the coven an excited murmur rose.

"And if I have," Tracy said pluckily, "I can obviously unchoose that death by never going near the water."

"We are always remaking our lives," Brook said gently. "In extraordinary situations we may remake our deaths. Still, some deaths we have already chosen. They are to be."

Tracy looked from one to another of them. "I too have grown in this Circle, learned from you at least half of the healing techniques I apply to my clients. Resist as I might in my head, in my heart I cannot break the ritual ... At least I see nothing to suggest that I will live again." She smiled with some strain. Four in the coven answered softly. "You cannot see what is not real to you. It is the Law."

The mirror found its way to Ruth: with a small shake of the head, she refused it. "I prefer not to know," she said gently. Like spokes in a wheel the women reached out to touch her hand. The mirror rotated to Arlan, who stared into its depths a long time. At last she muttered: "I see nothing but my own image." She handed the glass to Brook.

"I have dreamed my death many times," Brook whispered. "It is for Helen to discover both the method and the moment." She passed the mirror to Tabatha.

Calmly, Tabatha said: "I am thrown by a black stallion ... So be it."

"So it is," they responded. Helen's voice was more shaky than the rest.

Clear-eyed, Tabatha spoke again. "Let's cleanse ourselves in the ocean. Like the tides we ebb and flow."

"We flow and ebb," said a litany of voices.

The walk to the water was silent. Each woman except Tracy placed her arms in an "x" across her shoulders and chest. In trance, Tracy beat the rawhide drum with the flat of her hand. Tabatha shook a gourd, the dried seeds making the sound of maracas. At the shoreline they took sage and sweet grass out of their packs, burning it to welcome the protection of the Spirits. By the shore they abandoned their clothes, painted one another's forehead, throat, heart, solar plexus, and genitals. The designs were unique, the colours prescribed. They strewed roses on the beach and stepped over them with naked feet, going backward and forward as though through time.

Humming the sacred "om," the coven raised their arms. For a long time they hummed, until Brook felt her heart open. Her emotions were purged as though by a diuretic.

They gestured for Helen to begin her walk into the ocean.

Holding a rose in front of her, Helen walked into a series of waves. Looking at Brook for courage, she said softly: "I am born in the womb-water of the Mother. Water and my blood are one."

Clearly Brook answered. "Your blood records all you have been or will be, through many lives. We honour your woman's blood."

Like dolphins the women plunged, water splashing silver from their heads as they rose from it again. Each let go of a stemless rose, listening to the waves and watching until the flowers were out of sight. What they wished for was for each of them to know. They were pledged to serve only as channels of love. Bad energy sent by any one of them would be returned to the sender many fold.

Whooping, they splashed out of the frigid water, stood hopping like children in the sand. Out came blankets and large towels. Six women massaged one another vigorously to get warm and dry. Everyone, with the exception of Helen, started laughing and talking at once.

Was this coven too strange for her lover, too threatening for Helen's continuing involvement with it? Even as she wondered, Brook realized that she was not protecting Helen from emotional trauma, she was protecting herself as a witch from being rejected by Helen. Yet painful emotions where not something to be avoided. Sometimes pain made people grow when comfort did not.

As though Brook had spoken, Helen said: "This is some weird celebration of summer. If this is how you celebrate, what do you do to prepare for winter?"

"Look forward and back," Brook answered whimsically. "What else can one do?"

A big grin spread across Helen's face. "Ah, the paradoxes of Wicca. Interesting, at the very least ... " With a laugh she reached out her arms and five women came rushing to embrace her.

CHAPTER TWENTY ONE

Reaching into his chest of drawers, Mark came up with an armload of socks and underwear. Grimacing he charged, butting his head none too gently into Lila's stomach. The load of clothes was strewn willy-nilly over Lila's lap and unto the carpet. Mark's feet scuffed as he pushed. Teasingly Lila wrestled him down on the mattress, pelting him with his own undershirts. She followed that up by tickling his feet. Twisting away, Mark squealed, his laughter catching suddenly like a bone in his throat. Eyes closed tight, he flopped unto his stomach, small shoulders heaving.

For a moment Lila stood by the bed, letting him cry. She felt frozen as a glacial lake. Then a heat lamp went on inside her, melting the snow she needed to keep her from evaporating into a puddle right there on Mark's carpet. And then she wasn't water at all, she was blood, a pulsating heart open to the rasp of a saw blade. Within hours, Mark and her beloved daughter would be gone from her. Like an automaton, she stooped and began folding Mark's clothes, packing them neatly into his suitcase. She could not stop her hands from shaking.

With an act of will she sat beside Mark, stroking the nape of his damp neck. Tears were wrenched from him, like the death of his childhood, begrudged and unwilling. A soundless, dry sobbing. She had to help. No matter how difficult his feelings were to Lila, they needed to be purged. Very well. He had begun with aggression, rage turned back into himself, deflected into grief. That anger did not belong with Mark, it belonged with her. Firmly she pressed her fingers into Mark's shoulders, digging none too gently into her son's chest. Her sessions with Tracy had to be good for something. Low in her throat, she said: "Talk to me, Mark. What's going on inside?"

Flailing arms and feet, Mark broke into a long wail of outrage. The twisting in her bowels gave Lila no distance at all. Her lungs felt squeezed of air. Words jumped from her mouth, heavy and round as stones. "Your father and I, we're changing your world, aren't we, Mark? Changing everything in it that makes you feel safe. That must not seem fair to you. *We* must not seem fair to you."

Rigid he faced away from her, rubbing fiercely at his eyes.

There was a knock and Cyndi came in. Fresh from an appointment with a hairdresser, she looked sophisticated, older than her twelve years. "Oh Jeez," she said and flopped down beside Mark. "Don't cry. I keep telling you we're in this together. Don't you believe me, Mark?"

Lila did her best to sound firm. "Sometimes people need to cry, Cyndi. Give me a few minutes with him."

Shakily, Cyndi laughed. "Tell me about crying ... There's mold growing in my pillow."

Mark gave a small snicker of surprise, as though he had not imagined that Cyndi would grieve too.

Awkwardly, Cyndi patted her brother on the head. "Hey. Don't you want to fly in a huge jet? At least Dad didn't come to pick us up, as though we're just kids."

Mark peered out from under his hand. "He just can't be bothered," said the voice of an old man.

No child, Lila thought, should sound so world-weary. Still she defended Jack, because Mark needed to believe in his father's love. "That's not true. Cyndi asked him not to come for you."

The bed jiggled as Cyndi surveyed him. "Mark, remember what Helen told me when I yelled at Dad? When I threatened not to go to L.A.?"

Oh yes, Lila thought. The day of the infamous phone call. Lila had barely been home for five minutes when a travel agent called to confirm a flight on June twenty-sixth for Cyndi and Mark Tennant. Prepaid tickets were to arrive in the next day's mail.

Holding the phone in both hands, Lila resisted the impulse to slam down the receiver. Why hadn't Jack asked if that date was convenient for them? Should she — or any of them — have to hear about these arrangements from a travel agent? Maybe he intended to "protect" Lila from the pragmatic details of parting from their children. *And maybe he intended to make chicken stew*, a voice sounded in her head. *Don't worry about other people's motives. All you end up doing is giving away your power.* Carefully Lila thanked the agent and placed the receiver in the cradle. In the time it took her to climb the stairs to Cyndi and Mark, she placed a lid over her anger.

Cyndi did not bother to keep a lid on hers. She had not agreed to spend the summer with her father. After a spate of long-distance yelling and no few tears, she told Jack that she hated him and vowed to stay with Lila throughout the summer.

Downstairs Lila heard Helen put down the newspaper with a sharp slap. Suddenly her face appeared in the stairwell. "There sure is a lot of me-me-I-I going on," she said grimly. "Did you ever wonder how you'd feel, Cyndi, if you and your father were to change places? Buying you a plane ticket doesn't rank with me as an act of harm."

Cyndi gaped at Helen. "Well, excuu-se me," she flounced. "I don't recall asking to be born."

"Be glad you weren't ordered in a catalogue," Helen drawled. "Otherwise, you could be sent back to the warehouse ... If you don't want me to hear you, lower your voice. It isn't fun to overhear other peoples' brawls."

With offended dignity, Cyndi sniffed. "Then go home. You won't be able to hear me from there."

"Indeed?" Helen turned sharply on her heels. "Lila, perhaps Cyndi is right. I'll come back later."

Feeling acted upon from every direction, Lila managed to say: "Don't leave. Cyndi just needs to get this out of her system. Give it time to blow over."

With Latin expressivity, Helen threw up her hands. She emitted a fruity expletive. "Cyndi — I'm sorry for horning in. This feels like the days before my own divorce. My daughter didn't want to see me and I couldn't stand it."

"I remind you of your daughter?" Cyndi queried. "I — I didn't realize, Helen — honestly."

"Don't do this to Jack, Cyndi. You have no idea how much losing the love of a child can hurt."

Cyndi yelped. "I hate it when adults do this it-hurts-me-more-than-it-hurts-you stuff. Mom needs Dad here. And he just doesn't care."

"Your mother does not *want* him here," Helen said, implacably. "Try to accept that."

"But I want him here. Don't my feelings count?" Too late, Cyndi realized what she had confessed. She clapped a hand over the receiver.

In Helen's jaw a nerve jumped visibly. "So go to him," she said wearily. "The mountain can't come to Mohammed, but Mohammed can go to the mountain."

Sounds were torn from Helen's flesh like salmon roe beneath a fillet blade. Flooded by compassion, Lila reached up to embrace the taller woman. Dimly she was aware of Cyndi promising to call her father right back. From the doorway to his room Mark looked on, his expression stoic and removed.

After a pregnant pause, Cyndi mumbled: "So you think Mother wants to be rid of me for the summer."

Quickly and sincerely Lila asserted: "I'll miss you, Cyndi — very much — but Helen is right. Your father needs you, too."

Cyndi started to sniffle. "Shit. Why do people get married, anyway?" Through clenched teeth, Helen laughed. "That's the luck of the draw, kid. Love is like a lottery — we all play hoping to win."

A case of marital roulette, Lila thought. Each of them could have fought to make other choices. But Jack had no stamina for dealing with problems and perhaps Lila had too much stamina for them. Too much of an expectation that problems would always be there. She distrusted simple happiness. That must not be the legacy she handed down to their children. It was not up to Cyndi to mother her young brother when she herself needed to be reassured. "Thanks for taking this on, Cyndi. But you are asking yourself to be too soon old ... I wish I could have protected both of you from this. I wish someone long ago could have protected me. Unfortunately things happen the way things happen. Forgive me, both of you."

Hastily Mark sat up. "Mama, it's not your fault. You're sick."

Lila guffawed, hoping that Mark would not feel like the butt of a joke. "I'm sick. What a handy all-around excuse that is, for hurting you and Cyndi. The truth is that being unhappy *is* being sick and there is only one way to be well again. By determining to be happy. Can you understand that, Mark?"

Grimly Cyndi glanced at her watch. "He better understand it. We have no time to waste. I came to ask you to check my dresser for me, to see if I've forgotten anything."

Cyndi's dresser. How would it look, stripped of hair spray, brush, deodorant, perfume and tubes of lipstick ... Her daughter's chest of drawers emptied of underwear. The closet devoid of those pink slippers with their phony white rabbit's ears — slippers which so obviously belonged to a girl young enough to need a mother. Would Ritt want to be a mother to another woman's children? Within herself Lila struggled to believe that to the lives of Cyndi and Mark, Ritt would bring additional love. That having two mothers was a fortunate thing and would not threaten Lila's bond with her own children. For whatever reason, Helen had lost her daughter's love. But that did not have to happen to Lila. It was not an inevitability, like dying was the inevitable result of living.

So Lila spoke with the conviction she wanted to feel. "What you leave behind is not that serious. You *are* just going for the summer. So please — treat Ritt well. She's probably as nervous as you are."

With a small "tsk" Cyndi strode to the door. "Maybe ... Still, I wouldn't want someone to come to me needing things they should have brought with them. Mark, would you help me sort tapes? Otherwise, I might leave your favourites behind."

In an instant Mark was up, miraculously recovered from his grief. Astonished, Lila thought: *What a lesson in raisng someone's morale off the floor.* She had noticed the maturing of Cyndi's body but she had not noticed the maturing of Cyndi's mind.

During the months that Mark and Cyndi were with their father, what other changes would Lila not share? For surely their children would continue to change, while she and Jack split time with them into boxes that could not overlap.

Her skin crawled with a nebulous expectation that a formless thing was about to be made visible. She wanted to go swiftly down the hall and tap on Brook's door but she knew very well that Brook was "out" — no doubt intending to free this family to deal with parting in their own way. But Brook was part of Lila's family. This home included Brook, more integrally perhaps than it had contained Jack. Her conscience twinged. But a marriage contract made by law had nothing to do with the spirit of love. Nor with the restive and seeking heart of it.

Lila breathed in the faint odour of kitty litter, sweat, granola and footwear. From down the hall came the lilt of Mark's voice, the slightly lower pitch of Cyndi's. She wrenched her attention away from the growing pang in her chest and made a last minute check of things still to be packed for Mark. His toothbrush but not toothpaste. His hairbrush, but not shampoo. Never mind packing towels. After all, as Lila herself had pointed out, Mark was just going home.

Then it was time to drive them to the airport, the car containing the baggage of their silences along with pieces of luggage. At the counter Lila checked in the suitcases, carefully tucked the children's tickets in her handbag. Her purse felt suddenly heavier: what a trick of the mind that was. In the cafeteria she bought them some orange juice; carefully folded a twenty dollar bill into each of their hands. With immense surprise Mark grinned. Never before had he gotten so much to spend by himself. Immediately he wanted to look into all of the shops in the terminal.

Feeling aimless, Lila watched him thumb through souvenirs and banners until with considerable excitement he found his name engraved on a wooden keychain. The vanity piece was enormously overpriced, so Lila insisted on buying it for him. Cyndi found her name spelled in the traditional manner, as "Cindy," which did not impress her at all. In the gourmet foods shop however, she bought a jar of Northern Comfort Maple Syrup to give to Ritt. "I hope she isn't overweight," Cyndi worried.

"Give her gifts like that and she will be," Lila laughed.

"That's an idea," Cyndi wisecracked. "Just kidding. Ha ha."

Then they were at the entrance to security. Lila handed them their tickets, and embraced them for as long as she thought they would allow her to. Their farewells probably had reasonable meaning; Lila heard only a babble of sounds like she was suffering from an aural version of dyslexia. The scanner probed their bodies, looking for weapons more lethal than life.

Then her children were lost to her. Blind, she wandered to the windows, peered at passengers being siphoned into the belly of large planes. Finally she located Cyndi dragging Mark by the hand. Mark tripped; in obvious panic he looked back towards the terminal. With phony animation Lila waved, as though she felt nothing but joy to see them go. "Don't worry," she mouthed. "You'll be met ... " Her words would be gibberish to them. She knew that. For a while they climbed backwards up the steps of the plane, waving. Then her period of grace was over. They walked into another reality, one where she could not follow.

Once in her car, she veered on an impulse to pick up birdseed from a pet store. It would cheer her up, to drive to Stanley Park and feed the birds. Fresh air — and simply time — would take away the sense that her home was a vacant tomb waiting to engulf her.

At Lost Lagoon she was followed by a growing entourage of water fowl which waddled awkwardly after her, honking and hissing at one another as they competed for seed. She strolled around and around the Lagoon long after the grain was scattered. From the footbridge overlooking the pond she watched the graceful ballet of swans, the stillness of the stately heron perched on stalk-thin legs. Darkness settled completely on the water like black ice gleaming.

When Lila came home, the house was dark. She felt along the wall for the light switch, her heart beating too fast. The absence of sound was a din of its own: no rock music, no natural or electronic voices. No doors slamming or footsteps taking the stairs too fast. There was, however, the scuffle of paws and a thin mewling. A white and orange ball piled headlong into Lila's legs. Laughing, she nestled the warm, purring kitten into her bosom. "Tiger Lily," she whispered. Mark called the kitten Tiger — a name more appropriate to its tyrannies. Lila wore these across the back of her hands and along her shoulders, scratches stinging when she showered or did the dishes. Scratches to go with the thin surgical lips on her breast, lips which puckered towards a jack-o'-lantern smile beneath her left arm. These scars would always be a signpost of her brush with death, the thin entrance to the place that could only be entered bodiless ... Lila shivered.

With relief she followed a light to the living room. Someone was home after all. Or perhaps not. Perhaps Brook had merely timed the light to go on. The room was warmer than it was out-of-doors — an oven minus the smell of baking bread. Lila set the kitten down so that she could take off her sweater. Tiger scampered under the couch and batted furiously at a tangle of electrical cords. With effort Lila distracted the kitten with a ball of string so that it would live to grow older. Carefully she lay her sweater across the armchair. Unwary claws could easily tear the knit.

Outside the window the arbutus tree was crowned in darkness. Flickering lights from too many power sources obliterated the stars. Still, there was the aureole of leaves, the shimmering green of a luminescent, new summer.

From far away she heard someone keening, like women do at an Irish wake. Tears ran down her nose and cheeks so fast that Lila thought someone must have turned on the sprinkler in the ceiling. She gulped for air, wondered if this collapse from within her lungs was similar to how a fish felt, dragged helter-skelter into an alien element. The keening would not stop. It rose higher until hands spun her firmly around. Then Brook was shaking her, peering worriedly into her face.

"Oh," Lila said unguardedly. "My darling — you are here." Suddenly she drew Brook within her arms. With soft noises Brook rocked Lila back and forth. She dried Lila's face on the sleeve of her shirt. The gesture was so tender that Lila stared. Then there was only Brook's mouth, her wet tongue and hard teeth: the kiss that Lila did not know she had initiated until Brook gazed at her, incredulous. In Brook's eyes a flame lit like a rag bursting into spontaneous combustion. She lowered Lila onto the couch. Gently she climbed above her, cradling Lila with all the ambiguous tenderness of a mother with her babe — or of a lover, in spirit if not in fact.

That thought was Lila's undoing. She heard her breathing change, felt the clamour of her body reaching like Kali to devour Brook. She kissed Brook's eye brows, her long brown lashes, the tip of her Roman nose.

That soft mouth hummed with current, with bursts of energy that vibrated through Lila's bones. She felt her clitoris swelling, the throb of desire opening and closing her like the tiny hands of a sea anemone, fluttering. How strange. Lila the frigid. Lila the insensiate who was not insensiate after all.

"Goddess help me," she heard Brook mutter. "Please, Lila, I'm not made of stone ... " Brook pulled away, tried to sit up.

The open rebellion in Lila's face stunned her. Through gritted teeth Lila said: "No. No, I deserve love, I deserve *your* love ... Helen has far too much of it." Her own words reached Lila's ears like treachery. She twisted away from Brook, pushed her burning cheeks into the back of the couch. She wondered if she could stop breathing just by willing to, die rather than turn to face Brook's rejection. But her will was a traitor. Without willing this at all, Lila had betrayed herself. Now Brook would not be able to live here. Now she would move out — or worse, move in with Helen ... There must be a way to regroup, to spade dirt over her self-humiliation. Yes, bury it or raise dust so that Brook would be deceived about the source of this self-abandonment. After all, Lila was distraught, deprived of her children and slightly demented as a result ... Disgusted by her cowardice — her opportunism — Lila groaned aloud.

Suddenly hands reached inside her shirt, slid like warm snakes along Lila's skin. Arms encircled her, warm breathing raised the hairs at the back of Lila's neck. Brook curled like a river along its banks, cradling Lila's hips between her thighs. Her kisses ringed Lila's neck like separate beads on a strand of pearls. "It's all right, Lila," she whispered. "You must feel as though Mark and Cyndi are gone forever, not only for a while. Of course you want physical comfort. You can have it, Lila. We don't have to confuse it with sex."

Lila tried to lie still beneath Brook's stroking hands. Goosebumps rose tingling everywhere that Brook touched. Even Lila's teeth tingled. Again her judgement betrayed her. She felt her buttocks pressing hard against Brook's thighs. Passion. There was no way for Brook to mistake the message.

For a moment Brook lay still as the stone with which she had disclaimed any relationship. Longing enveloped her, an inner keening like the sounds of grief that first brought Lila into her arms. No desire without consequences. No consequences without desire. Helen. In both their minds the name was a faint beacon glittering far out at sea. They were lifted and turned towards one another by encompassing waves. The beacon was snuffed out.

Carefully, oh so slowly, Brook removed Lila's shirt. Shamed, Lila's hands went up to cover her mutilated breast, with its nipple made unnaturally hard and large by radiation. Firmly Brook moved Lila's hands. Childlike her fingers traced the dimensions of the scar, climbed the spiral of Lila's nipple. Her expression was strange — sad — and somehow reverent. Leaning on her elbow, she whispered: "You're not afraid to let me massage you — are you afraid of this?"

Lila stammered. "I — I'm not beautiful — I want my body to be perfect for you ... "

Brook pulled at her bottom lip, displaying a crooked tooth. "Nor am I. My nose is too big and my hair far too curly to comb properly. I'm short and my hips are too angular — shall I go on?"

Lila chuckled. "No." She pulled Brook on top of her. The world narrowed to the soft-hard weight of Brook's body, her warm skin and firm, rounded pelvis. Drawn like magnets, they kissed. The world expanded, spiraling bands of colour in a kaleidescope. It was Lila who drew Brook's hands at last and placed them over her mons. Brook stiffened, for a brief moment afraid to cross the arbitrary line she had drawn between sensuality and a far more primal lust. Glancing nervously towards the window, Lila turned off the light. "Draw the curtains," she asked Brook.

In the sudden darkness they blinked. Then they could see one another again, soft white shadows, and touch connected them like batteries of light.

Brook straddled the couch, the weight of her thighs resting lightly above Lila's bare shins. Her hands investigated Lila's belly, lingered with butterfly strokes on her breasts, strokes which became increasingly hard, more urgent. Lila felt her good nipple rise. She reached up to catch Brook's hand, not wanting that kind of pressure on the injured one. But Brook had already moved. A closed fist traced the outline of Lila's thighs, discovering her, skin and muscle and bone. Brook opened her closed hand and with tormentingly light touches retraced where her fist had been. Lila's viscera twisted; there was a flare of pain. So this is what wanting felt like, an aching in the loins so poignant that it hurt ...

Brook kissed Lila's eyelids and the lobes of her ears. She found places in her throat that Jack had never found. Lightly she held Lila's damaged breast as though she wanted to heal it. Unable to endure the love implied by her touch, Lila pulled Brook tightly to her.

Her hand brushed against wetness. With unusual courage she was inside Brook, astonished by the clasp of warm and subtle walls moving to enclose her fingers. She was guided along a living channel, as much part of her as Brook's own tissues. Behind closed eyelids Lila saw red light, throbbing.

An ululation of sound made her aware of Brook's arousal. Lila felt a cupped hand stroking her labia, as though Brook were simply adjusting the volume knob on a stereo. She started to climb the stubborn ladder towards orgasm, struggling to hold back at every rung. Her body was filled with chemicals. They and her fear — her self-conscious, rational mind — doused and strangely re-ignited passion. Her attempts at self-control incited her, challenged her.

Brook was not so ungiving. Subtly she rocked back and forth, her genitals proud and full. Lila's hand twisted, her motions soft, investigatory, then brittle and hard. Thinking diluted her passion, desire intermixed oddly with mercy. How vulnerable Brook was. In this or any act of love one could be destroyed, fired out into the cosmos like a meteorite going wildly out of orbit. Under her curious fingers, vaginal muscles constricted and released, fluttering, the clasp of an all-encompassing world where guilt — or apology — could not exist.

For Lila time stopped, started and stopped again. She heard Brook cry out, a sound like a child plunged reluctant from the womb into life. Was she protesting her aloneness, the queer and stubborn limits of the flesh which bound each one of them to the perverse isolation of their bodies? How strange to use the flesh to come together. More strange, to want to defy any and all of its restrictions ... For the first time Lila's fingers traced the progression of another woman's pleasure, the crazy, strong peaking that she — Lila Tennant — she, together with Brook, had caused.

Her face wet, Brook collapsed on Lila's shoulder. Then she drew Lila's hips suddenly towards her and thrust and paused, thrust and paused again. For countless moments Lila poised on the top rung of her stubborn mental ladder. Helen and their friendship, which must be guarded. Love and an ancient betrayal, being repeated. If she did not come there was no harm. But above her was no blond and square-jawed Dutchman. Nothing flickered from another time, to justify — or to contaminate — this. There were no excuses. There was only sensation — feeling — overwhelming her, overpowering this queer reluctance.

She heard Brook start to cry. And then Lila was crying with her, drawn by a silver thread through the eye of her own needle. Her whole body arched, shuddering and loud, into orgasm. An aureole of lights replaced the black pit in her, where before she had circled aimlessly around and around it. Her stomach felt warm. Full, like there could be no need that was so deep again.

But in that belief, too, she was mistaken. In this collapse of their separate bodies there was no under or over or around. They made love until the light of dawn spilled through the windows and lay like a blessing on their unconfined and sprawling limbs.

CHAPTER TWENTY TWO

She woke to a lioness spitting; reached for the sharpened stick by her bundle of furs. Dressed in bear skins, she scanned the walls of the cave, her senses sharp as the point of the stick she held. In the half-light other hunters rose, silent and ready. Into the dying fire the woman threw a branch. Dry leaves caught, embers encircling twigs like red tongues. In the flare, the woman saw water glisten, drip from the hole at the centre of the lair. The mountain lion might have entered merely seeking refuge from the weather. But she would be hungry and the small bodies of human children would be to her merely the smell of meat.

Leonine the woman loped, her toes more discerning than her eyes, avoiding pebbles and the furs of other cavesmen. At the entrance she paused, sensing rather than seeing the lioness. Felt her hackles rising, like the fur on a wild dog. Then there was the bone-melting scream of the hunting animal. Stick elevated, the woman turned to golden loins descending in slow motion, feeling the splurt of blood as she impaled the brave beast through the heart. Heavy and dying it fell upon her, blue eyes registering the most ancient and primal of traumas. Wide with betrayal, those eyes turned into Helen's, the stifling weight of the body shape-shifted into Helen's, lying mortally wounded above her murderer.

Drained of breath and blood, Lila flailed wildly around her. Through her terror she heard Brook's voice calmly repeating: "Lila, Lila, wake up, you're having a nightmare." Reaching desperately for safety, she woke in Brook's bed; burrowed into her naked shoulder. Her heart was still beating wildly. Slow, rhythmic fingers stroked her hair.

"My dear — That must have been some dream ... Share it with me?"

A dream — yes. Like you, Brook are a dream of desire. But if last night had been a dream, it was the longest and singularly the most erotic one of her entire life. Her muscles felt loose and boneless, and now beneath

Brook's embrace her labia opened and closed in tiny flutters, blatant as the petals in a psychedelic flower. From Brook's skin came the odour of sex, an odour Lila traced back to her own hair and hands, breathing it into her lungs with deep enjoyment. She made the mistake of licking her dry lips. The taste of Brook was a banquet in her mouth.

Lila started to tell her about the wet cave, water dripping from its centre. About the cave woman, filled with primordial energy, stalking the lioness who turned into Helen, dying beneath her spear ...

Brook's soothing turned into a chuckle. "I'm sure my centre was wet, you cave woman."

Lila's ears suffused with blood. "Oh — So that's what the dream was about."

Brook's naked eyes made Lila feel excruciatingly shy. But Brook, too, sounded hesitant. "The lioness — you think you've dealt Helen a death blow ... Is guilt all you feel about making love?"

Lila gazed through her. "No ... But it will be when we tell her, and tell her we must. It would be despicable to lie about this ... " She shuddered. "As despicable as I have been, to demand that you give me the love that belongs to her."

Roughly Brook pulled Lila towards her. Yellow eyes beamed, powerful and oddly vulnerable, in a narrow face. "No one may have the love that belongs to Helen. We — you and I — share the love that belongs to us ... There was no forcing of any kind ... Was there?"

Lila flushed bone deep. "No. I wanted you inside. I needed you inside."

Softly Brook kissed Lila's eyelids. "Can we get close enough — deep enough? There is no end to my need ... "

"Brook. Why are we talking about this? I feel like the loosest and most immoral of women. There is no way Helen will understand. This is — quite simply — betrayal."

Brook's firm hands ran lightly down Lila's arms, massaging. "Not to make love with you would have been my betrayal. At the heart of it passion is simple. If we have a debt to Helen, it's to love her in the way that we do. Simple?"

Perplexed, Lila wrapped herself in a blanket and padded over to the open window. Startled finches flew in hordes up from the hedges. On the trellises roses bloomed, pink and yellow and red. Lila tried to keep the sense of life bursting within as well as around her. But sadness climbed like ivy into her heart, choking the new and tenuous growth spreading there. How could anything as complex as this be kept simple?

Loving Brook was an act bordering on full-scale insanity. There were just too many people who could be hurt by her actions. Mark and Cyndi, for example, who with summer's end would return to Lila's care. What would be the effects on them — what long-term emotional scars would result — if they saw their mother hopping in and out of Brook's bed, sharing that obviously sexual privilege with Helen? If Brook could divide her time and attention between two women. If Lila and Helen could rise above the jealousy of relating to the same woman. If, given that situation, saving their dear friendship would remain possible. No. Like some foolish female version of Don Quixote, Lila was tilting at nothing less than total ruin. Despairingly she gazed at Brook, who lay open to her on the bed, her nudity making nothing but a cosmic joke of Lila's scruples. Scrupled. Her considerations were not ethical, they were pragmatic. Like a jester she was balancing a number of balls in the air to gauge how many she could keep from falling away from her into chaos.

Ending this debacle now was the most moral of her remaining alternatives. Yet, if they must end, what did it matter if they made love just once more? Once, before they turned resolutely away from further intimacy with one another. Lila groaned aloud. "Just once more" and ending this would be an act of self-mutilation, and totally unnecessary. What in the name of heaven was she thinking? Unnecessary? What was more crucial?

Her expression troubled, Brook drew on an over-sized flannel shirt and went to stand at the window beside Lila. She stared out as though her head was filled with nothing but the sound of birds. Then she spoke, neither looking at Lila nor touching her. "You need to think this through, without any kind of pressure from me ... I'm going to leave you for the day — " Lila's sharp intake of breath made her sigh gustily. "And I think — ask Helen if I can see her. She's going to need some reassuring about this ... "

Bald unconsidered words slipped past Lila's lips. "Could you make love to her, after — ?"

Brook's mouth twisted. "Can you be afraid of losing me? We shared not only a joining of bodies but of souls. Don't — please don't — make me feel corrupt for loving Helen too."

Charming. Not twenty-four hours later, the parry Lila had so cavalierly delivered would be riposted by Helen tonight ... Good. Perhaps a chest wound was what Lila needed to terminate her obsession with the lover of her best friend. Even to imagine Helen giving Brook pleasure, finding the os in her ... Graphic jealousy made Lila feel both shame and outrage. Well, this was the result of her disregard for fundamental rules of decent conduct.

Lila watched Brook's lips move, as though listening to a movie with the sound slightly out of sync. "You've got a funny look in your eyes, Lila. Something tells me that you want to end this, now."

Feeling hysterical, Lila blurted: "It mustn't be repeated. I've caused enough harm as it is."

Brook's mouth trembled. "That will always be — your decision to make," she whispered. "If you decide never to repeat this — know how much it meant to be so alive with you in this way ... " Then she clamped her jaw shut, walked stiffly to the door and down the stairs.

Lila heard water running through the pipes. A light breeze rotated a prism hanging over the window. Bands of colour radiated over the bust of Artemis, glowed violet and blue on the elongated ears of Kuan Yin. Cryptic, Her fish bone eyes seemed to follow Lila's pacing back and forth across the room. Restlessly, Lila turned to face the altar, feeling pursued by spirits.

This was not the room of a sexual libertine, of a calculating opportunist. It was a space carved from time, a place from which observances were made to an ancient and humane Goddess ... Humane? Well, was it humane to express the depths and heights of a physical love? Did one have to stifle love in a box and nail down the lid in the name of transcending one's lustful flesh? What sin, what possible sin ... Asceticism was a pile of crap. *Careful, Lila*, she thought. *Think of Helen, think of Helen ...*

That strange afternoon when Helen confessed to stealing Lila's husband — Lila's Brook. Ringing in her ears she heard Helen say clearly: *Lila — Are you attracted to her? Please don't protect me. This time around I owe you.*

Was that true? Did Helen have a debt owing from that other time, a loan which now Lila could call, like demanding payment on a mortgage? What an unfortunate image. In either lifetime, Brook was not coin of the realm, to be bartered and traded. Besides, death should cancel all debts; in each incarnation, one accrued enough of those.

Like an audio tape, Lila's mind played Helen's words. *Maybe now my love for Brook won't lead me to love you less ...*

Could it be so? Admirable. In the name of friendship. No. In the name of love. It was not the act of a friend to offer to share her beloved. Conscience stinging, Lila compared Helen's response to her own proprietorial jealousy. One night with Brook and Lila's temptation had been to possess, to keep Brook like dried flowers pressed in cellophane. In a precious book hidden on the shelves of a private library. Brook was not paper and binding, she was flesh — pulsating, joyous blood, with a heart big enough not only for her but for Lila's children as well. Lila could be as generous, as willing to compromise — couldn't she? Oh what a skill for quibbling desire had ...

When Brook came back her smile was swathed like cotton over a wound. Damp-headed from the shower she dressed, her movements graceful and carefully remote. Could Brook ever be remote enough for Lila not to want her?

Suddenly Lila understood what she must do. "Brook, at the very least I owe Helen an explanation — for initiating this."

Brook started to say something — whatever it was, she must have seen the reasonableness of Lila's suggestion, because she merely nodded.

Lila reached to take courage into her lungs along with the precious air. "I'm sorry for saying that Helen has too much of you ... Brook, I'm so sorry ... Do you know Helen told me that you love me? *She* was willing to share you, if that's what you wanted to do."

Brook's face looked almost heavy. "In the name of my desire — what kind of pressures have I been putting on both of you?"

Lila's smile blossumed like a flower in the desert. "I'm going to find out. This is now clearly between Helen and me — do you agree? *We* have a friendship. And — I will not be shown up by her generosity ... "

Gone from Brook's eyes was the dull, tired look put there by Lila's decision never to make love with her again. Thoughtful, she collapsed on her back onto the futon. "So. We leave the decision to Helen, about whether we go forward or back ... Well, it's not right that I alone have power over two lovers, is it?"

"No," Lila said firmly.

An incredulous smile played over Brook's face. "Why not?" she murmured. "My future rests in the hands of two amazing women ... "

From the balcony Helen called to her, arms already bronzed even so early in the summer. Her short hair caught the light, shining blue-black. She wore a shirt covered with white calla lilies and looked so beautiful that Lila caught her breath. Comparing herself physically with Helen would always make her feel too short and too round and too plain. Well, that was a problem for Lila's confidence, not caused by anything Helen did. Besides, with this humming in her blood, how could Lila not look beautiful?

Joining Helen on the balcony, Lila kissed her shyly on the mouth. Sun-warm, Helen's skin glowed with health. Faintly Lila caught the scent of her cologne, delicate as crushed flowers.

"Your hair cut is beautiful." She ran her hand almost timidly through Helen's crown.

Helen said cheerfully: "In the summer I like wash-and-wear hair." Speculatively, she held Lila at arm's length. "Let me look at you — did things go well yesterday?"

Lila tried not to feel evasive when she answered only a portion of Helen's question. "Mark went into a bit of a crisis, but Cyndi was terrific. She's becoming a very likeable young woman — "

"As though she wouldn't be, with you as a mom ... So separating from the kids was okay then." Helen went inside, returning with a pitcher of iced lemonade and some glasses.

Lila took the glass, smiling like a mysterious and contented child.

"Umm." Helen sounded amused. "Something is making you sensual today — I wouldn't have expected that of bereaved motherhood."

In Lila's throat the muscles tensed. She had not come here on a lark, after all, but to share something with Helen that could only hurt. How to tell her about last night, in a way that would not seem cruel and far too crude for words. Crude like Lila's Trojan-horse smile, while her belly was full of hidden soldiers. Blood drained from her face.

Helen whistled softly. Her loose-limbed walk took her to the balcony; she stared, apparently fascinated, at something on the street below. After a pause, she said: "Lila — I know you like tea and small talk before major declarations. But if one isn't coming, I miss my guess."

"I'm sorry," Lila said, for the third time in as many hours. "Where do I begin ... "

With stately slowness Helen turned, blue eyes hard and bright. "Let me make it easier," she whispered. "Brook isn't the only one who has bleed-through dreams."

"Oh!" Warily Lila placed her hands on Helen's shoulders, wanting to hold her and not daring. Her tenderness now could seem insulting, false like the Judas kiss with which, ironically, Lila had greeted her. What did it matter if Lila's feelings were genuine, when her entire manner must seem degenerate and gloating?

Helen summoned a rag-doll smile. "Your glow is difficult to miss. You act every bit like a satisfied bride ... "

Lila put her hands over her cheeks to hide her heightened blood. Lamely, determinedly, she began to explain. "After I took the kids to the airport, I went to Lost Lagoon and walked for hours. When I came home the house was dark and so — terribly quiet. I started to cry like a baby and suddenly Brook was there and — I was kissing her, like a lover — "

Helen put a finger gently on Lila's lips. "Spare me the details. I can well imagine Brook's response ... " Almost plaintively she laughed. "How funny this is, that you get to be the Other Woman in my life."

"Believe me, I didn't plan this. It simply happened and then I felt so guilty for hurting you — " She covered her mouth as though to stop her cruel words. "Remember when you asked me to admit that I'm attracted to Brook — that I love her?"

Helen sat down, hard. Suddenly Lila felt gauche and far too fanciful for words. In this inglorious world, Helen might not want to be dominated by her emotions, but everyone was. In such circumstances, anyone would fear being deserted and unloved. Besides, even a packrat left something behind in exchange for what she took. What could Lila offer to Helen that would be sufficient recompense for her childlike needs? Childlike? Well, not exactly.

"It interests me that Brook didn't come with you, to make a clean breast of it." Contemplatively, Helen rolled the glass of lemonade in both hands, as though to cool her palms. Her tone also was cold.

Revolted by the vision of herself as one of two miscreants squaring off against Helen, Lila shuddered. "And face you like Romeo and Juliet? I put Brook in this position. I hurt you. It's up to me to deal with that."

Helen made a strangled sound. "How does the prayer go? 'I am grievously sorry for having offended you, not only because I fear the loss of heaven and the pains of hell' — but the loss of Brook in my bed? How odd. Is this the Lila who would not under any circumstances 'experiment with lesbianism'? Obviously you found the experiment to your liking."

"It was no experiment," Lila whispered. "I never thought it would be. But it will be the last time, if you want this ended."

"Why? Brook wants you. Or am I supposed to bow out gracefully, so that things will be simpler for the two of you?" Tears splashed onto Helen's bodice. Swiftly she turned her head away.

Impulsively, Lila went to sit at her knees, rubbing Helen's palms as firmly as she dared. "My God. Do you imagine that Brook wants to leave you?"

"Doesn't she? After all, what is an aperitif— when one can sit down to the entree?"

Lila was genuinely shocked. "Is this how it's going to be, one of us comparing herself with the other in this derogatory fashion? Brook would not even consider leaving you."

"Oh yes? Did you discuss that together?"

"We discussed — I discussed — whether or not to remain lovers, depending on how you felt. It's clear that I was dreaming, to think that you and I could work something out ... " Wearily she placed her head in Helen's lap, feeling lifeless. "Oh, Helen. I do love you. Our friendship means the world to me."

Helen snorted. "It must. No, I won't be sarcastic." She placed her hands in Lila's hair and stroked, gently. "So you honestly think that we can work this out ... amicably, for Brook's sake. She's worth that much to you, Lila?"

Lila gulped, afraid the current might carry her away from Brook; equally afraid of the river that could sweep Helen's love away. "Not if it means losing your trust."

"I see." Cupping Lila's chin, Helen gazed inexorably into her eyes. "Then we need to make some rules here. Rule number one. We all try. When I freak out — and I most certainly will — the action stops and we talk — no holds barred, no matter how painful that is for any of us."

Lila tried to stifle a clammering hope. "Slow down ... Are you saying that we do this?"

"Goddess help me, yes. But no evasions, Lila, no intellectualizing about our feelings, or so-called 'harmless' lies. If you want Brook so badly, you can damn well reach far into your gut and make a place for me ... "

Uneasily Lila stirred. "What kind of a place, Helen?"

"Don't worry, I won't demand ransom like your body in my bed. But I don't think it's fair that Brook should live with you. Both of us should have to come to neutral territory to be with her."

"That's true, I suppose," Lila admitted.

"That's true. Period," Helen said. "That beautiful and crazy bitch has too much her way." She slumped suddenly into Lila's arms, crying. Moved beyond pity, Lila held her. She wanted to crawl into Helen's lap and tell her that nothing would ever get past Lila to harm her. How quaint, when Lila was the source of her friend's pain. The most decent thing she could do for Helen was merely to let her cry.

"And no ogling each other when I'm there." Helen wiped at her eyes. "If I see Brook on your lap I'll push her off it."

"Oh — " Lila whispered. "This is too hard. The two of you should go away by yourselves for the summer. By fall I'll have returned to a semblance of sanity."

Helen tried to giggle. "Maybe you're a lesbian and maybe you're not. For years I've wanted you to be. I won't stifle any part of your finding out."

"If I'm not," Lila said shakily, "I have a funny way of showing it."

"Like my funny way of laughing." Helen blew her nose. "Now let me get up. I've got to go for a long walk. You're welcome to join me at Van Dusen Gardens. But for the next few hours, the first person to mention Brook is going to pay. Handsomely."

CHAPTER TWENTY THREE

Awakened from a sound sleep, Brook fumbled for the alarm as Helen, with a soft groan of protest, opened her eyes. For a few moments they held one another close. Then Brook swung her feet determinedly out of bed. They had a lot of packing to do before catching the ferry, for despite her qualms, Lila and Helen had insisted that their annual camping trip include her.

Lila must already be up. The smell of coffee made its way invitingly up the stairs; on the radio was the clear, crisp notes of a sonata for clavichord.

Brook shared the confines of the bathroom with Helen. She slicked her hair with water to get her morning rooster tail to lie down. Behind her, Helen's reflection looked unusually sober. Did she find their familiar intimacies uncomfortable with Lila in the house too? Firmly Brook reached for her hand. "Come on," she said. "We have a van to pack."

Noisily they clattered downstairs, practically colliding with cardboard boxes in the hallway. Several contained camp pots, thermal cups and cutlery, scratch pads and cleansers for tough campsite tasks. Pragmatically, Brook checked for garbage bags and toilet paper, a flashlight and wind-resistent matches. She put her Swiss knife in the pocket of her pants and checked to see that the long-handled tongs and egg-turner were crossed off on Lila's list. They were. On tiptoe she reached for the large thermos and found that Lila already had it sitting near the stove for the coffee they would take with them on the road. Lila's checklist indicated that coffee and tea had already been packed, as had granola, honey, milk and spices. In a carry-all expressly set aside for the journey was fresh fruit and cheese, bread, boiled eggs and nuts.

Brook turned to meet Lila's bright eyes. She looked expectant as a child and, not oddly, shy. Impulsively, Brook kissed her on the cheek. Remembering Helen's injunction against public demonstrations of their affection, Lila's colour flared. She stooped to pick up the tent and ground sheet, confused between also carrying the plastic water container or the canteen and the axe. Impulsively, Helen kissed Lila on the cheek opposite to the one Brook had chosen and filled her long arms with several bedrolls.

"Thanks for leaving me something to do," Brook wisecracked. She removed perishables from the 'fridge, vegetables and fresh salmon and a bottle of champagne which would be opened at the campsite. The cooler was amply full when she closed the lid on her activities.

Loading the rented van was fast. The three women formed a relay under the bright and welcoming sun. Helen took charge of planning where things would fit in the van. Lila checked the house, making sure that the lights would go off and on when they should. Adera would water Lila's plants and "sit" with the kitten. Watching the frenetic activity of three humans in the process of leaving, Tiger was not at all impressed. Brooding yellow eyes flared from beneath the couch. Lila retrieved Tiger and kissed her small face. Had she not been afraid of losing the kitten to the surrounding woods, she would have brought Tiger with them. With many backward glances, she set the kitten down.

To console her for parting with Tiger, Helen suggested that Lila drive. At seven in the morning on this first long weekend of the summer, traffic was already ferocious. Throughout the winding drive to Horseshoe Bay Terminal, Lila alternated between accelerator and brake. For the last mile-and-a-half from the docks, traffic came to a laborious halt. The women had time to leave the van and gawk like children at scarred, towering cliffs. Trickles of sun-lit water tumbled from porous rock. Tangled roots of trees held against every law of gravity to sloping inclines. Feeling inward and apart, they climbed around fallen rock, gathering pebbles and feathers.

At last they boarded the Queen of something or other, vehicles packed in like mackerel in a crowded tin. They avoided the line of bodies snaking towards the cafeteria for breakfast. On the upper deck they opened the flask of coffee. They breakfasted on eggs and bread and crunchy apples. Food was sweet in the open air.

Brook lifted her binoculars to scour the shorelines of distant islands. Locating an eagle soaring on pockets of wind, she put her arm around Helen's shoulder and pointed. The small intimacy made Lila aware of her jealousy. She turned her head away. Perceptively, Helen circled Lila's waist and with a warm hand held her fast. The quivering epicentre of Lila's envy abated.

"I hope every campsite isn't taken before we get there," she worried aloud.

Brook gesticulated tenderly. "Hey. If Qualicum Falls is full, we'll drive to Miracle Beach. The sites there are beautiful too."

"Okay," Lila said. The need for simplicity was a taste in her mouth more acute than the food they had just eaten. She ached with longing to hear the sound of the waterfall carried on the restless wind all through the night.

Disembarking took forever. At last they broke free to the open road, winding between rain forest and shoreline, cliffs and sand. Blue and iridescent, sky and ocean pulsed in some inaudible harmonic scale.

Another hour and Lila slowed the van in front of the gate to Little Qualicum Falls. Tires crunched over gravel and dropped into potholes. Inching along, they debated the merits of each site: this one had firewood and water taps and outhouses within reasonable access. That one had more privacy from other campers or flatter ground or fewer stones. Pointedly, Brook and Helen deferred to Lila for the final choice of site. After cruising around many, Lila parked the van with a flourish beneath the spreading limbs of a tall cedar.

"Let's put up the tent," she coaxed. "There's something about a home away from home that appeals ... "

"Yeah," Brook teased. "With all the stuff you brought, we ain't roughing it in the bush."

Lila reached to swat Brook's head, then self-consciously withdrew her hand. "Remember that when you're heating water to wash in. Basins are roughing it enough for me."

Brook smiled cryptically and craned her neck. The site nestled in the midst of huge Douglas firs and blue spruce. Sitting as it did on a hill, she thought, the site would drain easily. She jumped from the van, swaying like a sailor until she found her land legs.

Helen handed her the ground sheet. Brook spread it on gravel; dug a shallow channel around its circumference with axe and branch. Rain was probably far from what this weekend would bring, but Brook wanted to be prepared. Helen deciphered the puzzle of interlocking poles and directed the placement of tent pegs. With good-natured insults, the women put up the large canvas tent.

Thoughtfully, Lila wondered if, as they had in other years, she and

Helen should have come here alone. Never mind that they felt the need to prove that they could share Brook in such close proximity — like Lila's insistence that Helen spend the night under her roof with Brook. If they were going to do this, Lila had better know the dimensions of her own jealousy. After all, she had gatecrashed, plunging raw need through the territory of their love. To this point, at least, she and Helen had not competed for Brook's love. And however hard this was, for Brook this parcelling of her emotions must be especially difficult.

A mosquito recalled Lila to the mundane tasks of camping. Idly she swatted, became aware of Brook gazing at her intently. She coloured, supposing that Brook's glance was a query about work to be done. Aware of gravel beneath her knees, she crawled into the tent. Helen handed her foam mats, releasing them from their bunjie cords. Lila hesitated over what to do with the sleeping bags. Zipped into one she felt confined, yet she didn't quite know how to handle the sleeping arrangements.

"Ta-da!" With a happy grin, Brook proffered an arm full of cushions.
"Pillows!" Lila said. "And you tease me about bringing everything."
"Hey, Lila, do you mind if we unzip the sleeping bags? I feel like a mummy wrapped up in one ... "
"Oh, not at all," Lila said, wanting to laugh. She accepted a battery-operated light from Brook and hung it on a hook in the tent wall. With it, they would be able to read tonight, or she could write in her journal. Adding to her pleasure was Brook's suggestion that they fill the thermos with hot tea before turning in for the night. She crawled into sunlight, tossing a prosaic roll of toilet paper into the corner of the tent.

Helen commandeered Brook to help her plenish the firewood. They took the van and backed it up to the woodpile. Lila heard them laughing as they filled a plastic drum with water from the tap. She watched them stack a prodigious amount of wood into the van. Then they drove towards the park gate to pay for the site.

Left alone Lila began gathering dry twigs and branches. Before long, Brook joined her, hands too small for the size of the loads she attempted to carry. With a broad wink, Helen picked up the trail of branches dropped by Brook.

"Big is not necessarily better," Brook drawled. As if to prove the point, Helen caught her hair in the branch of a tree. Brook razzed her, amiably.

The kindling would burn well. It was evident that there had been no rain for more than a week. Just the same, Lila lay a garbage bag on the ground to protect the wood against dew and filled another with some of the wood in the van. Matches she placed in a can with a lid. She hoped that Brook and Helen would not want to build a fire yet. Later this evening would be time for that, when darkness bound them to the campsite.

She need not have worried. Brook offered them a walk along the trails to Little Qualicum Falls. Helen opted for the beach — the trails, she said, could wait until morning when her blood could do with a jump start.

"But the Falls." Even to her own ears, Lila's voice sounded plaintive. Agreeably, Helen capitulated. Dwarfed by giant trees and carrying camera and binoculars they climbed towards the Falls, guided by the roar of the cascades.

Fringing the Falls was a ring of tiny human silhouettes. Tonnes of water tumbled against implacable rock and gushed into whirlpools. In the scarred rock face was the dark mouth of a cave. Lila imagined herself standing in the cave while water cascaded, silver and clear, in front of her eyes. The movement of the water was hypnotic.

A camera clicking recalled her. Helen adjusted the lense of the Minolta and directed Brook to get into the picture with Lila. Squinting in the bright sun, Brook murmured to Lila. "You look caught half-way between pleasure and pain."

Lila blushed. "This place is so — real — that it hurts me … "

From a distance of four feet, Helen said gruffly: "You're that real, too, Lila." Her intensity was more intimate than touch. But she must have embarrassed herself, because she walked swiftly away.

Brook and Lila stood mesmerized by the grandeur of Little Qualicum. Then Brook made her way over rocks to squat near the mouth of the stream. She emptied the medicine bag around her throat and washed her crystals and healing stones. Like points in an isosceles triangle, her friends watched, feeling reverence for this place and for Brook. Her spirit and the light in the water seemed all of a piece. Mesmerized they stood, until the voices of the water became indistinguishable from the voices in their blood and they flowed like simple molecules along with the stream. How long they stood there none of them knew.

Then, under the force of an agreement they had not verbalized, they ambled back to the van. The sun slanted towards late afternoon. There was time to watch the sunset at Miracle Beach. Most of the way they sang together, Brook using the dashboard as a drum to keep time. Lila hummed, knowing that she could contribute nothing but joy to the harmony of voices weaving in and out of tunes.

Lila tackled Miracle Beach with audacity, plunging into tidal pools with rubber boots. Small crabs and schools of little fishes scurried away from her feet. She found purple olive shells, many of them inhabited by fiddler crabs: sand dollars enough for the event to become commonplace, until Brook taught her to tell whether or not the creature was still alive. At first the movement of velvet hairs made her balk, but she soon released the creature lovingly to continue its life without interference. Then she found something quite extraordinary: a sand-coloured spiral which she lifted up with a shout. "Look! An old-fashioned collar," she yodelled, the shape of it reminding her of the time before collars were sewn to shirts. Then she saw that Brook and Helen were walking along the shoreline at a distance. Would Helen think she had deliberately interrupted their time together? Oh damn!

Animatedly Brook waved. "Don't drop it; it's full of eggs."

Lila looked at the collar skeptically. "Whose eggs?" she asked, when they rejoined her.

"The moon snail's. She makes the collar from sand and her own secretions — hence the name sand collar. See, they're all over." The sand collars, previously invisible to Lila, littered the beach. Lila wanted to take one home with her. It was very delicate and would be even more so when it dried. Her desire to keep this anomaly warred with her sense of concern for moon snail young.

Brook waded into a tidal pool. Wiping away moss, she forwarded an empty moon shell to Lila.

"It looks like a large breast with a nipple," Lila said spontaneously. Embarrassed, she handed the shell quickly to Helen, who tucked it inside her shirt without missing a beat. "The Many-Breasted Goddess," she crowed.

"No comment," Brook said. Warm-faced, she tried not to imagine the breasts of either of them. Careful not to rile the sandy bottom with her feet, she found another moon shell.

"Lift this one out of the water for yourself," she coaxed. Lila edged it free. With shock they realized that the shell was attached to a large, sand-coloured foot.

"Turn it over, so the weight of it doesn't pull off the shell," Brook said. Three pairs of eyes examined the snail, which moved with infinite slowness towards retracting its cumbersome foot. Hesitantly, they fingered the rubbery creature and then lowered it gently back into the sand. Without a word, Lila placed the sand collar alongside it in the pool. Brook gave her an approving hug — Brook, who was as unique and precious as the moon shell with its living host. Lila frankly did not know what she would do if — no, when — Brook was no longer living in her home. In her head she agreed with Helen that Brook should move out. But her reluctant heart was another matter. "You make the whole world feel like home, Brook," she said, feeling gauche.

Brook's reply was equally genuine. "The whole world is one."

"A home with at least one more in the family." Helen's wry response increased Lila's sense of having committed a wrong. Of course. How would Helen respond to a statement which so obviously excluded her? The serenity which had characterized Lila's pleasure in the day was snuffed abruptly. The sun fell like a severed tree towards the horizon, bloody swirls of colour reflected in the darkening water. Distraught, Lila stumbled for the van, walking too fast for either of them to keep pace.

Helen caught up with her, resting an arm on her shoulder. She said with quiet apology: "That was small of me. Sorry."

At her elbow Brook said gently, "Lila?"

"What?" She smiled, disguising confusion with bravado. A crevasse seemed to be opening in the ground at Lila's feet, a hole into which she would have fallen if she were not cradled by two pairs of arms. Wind and shadows stirred across the sand, chilled them in their sweat as they huddled.

With determined honesty Lila whispered: "I've felt homeless in the world for so long. Now where Brook is feels like home ... I don't mean to threaten you, Helen, but I've got to be able to tell her sometimes what she means to me — "

With alarm Helen said: "I want to be part of what you call home, Lila."

"You are! Just what makes you fear that I've lost my love for you?"

"I'm more worried about losing the daylight," Brook said with uncustomary roughness. "Let's talk on the drive back to the site."

"Can't you see that walking back in the dark is better than being left in the dark? You know, Brook, you talk about triads, but what happens when you get close to one?" Helen was not joking. There was nothing of the outrageous or the playful in her face.

Lila started. "Triads! I don't — this isn't — " Her tongue would not obey her. She could think of no words.

The atmosphere was suddenly charged, electrical. "Helen, I don't understand you. Is this a game you're playing with us?" Brook sounded angry.

"Of course she's playing," Lila stammered. "Aren't you, Helen? You're quite right, though, Brook; let's head back."

"Oh, forget it," Helen growled, and started running towards the van. "Even if I were willing to try, no one else would be."

"To try what?" Lila spoke into empty air.

Catching up with Helen, Brook spun her around. "Are you saying what I think you are? That you want to try loving both of us?"

Circumventing Brook's shoulder, Helen spoke directly to Lila. "I know you love Brook. I want to know if you could physically grow to love me —" She started to cry.

Lila felt as though some wedge had opened in the wall of time, bringing with it other-reality. Utopian fantasies were not intended to be lived. Acting on them would bring great danger. She braced to deny Helen's need.

She could not. A simple and disturbing truth made its way to her brain. What Helen did now was an extraordinary act of courage. It would be so easy to reject her; easy but not honest. Words shaped in Lila's mouth, seemingly without her volition. "I'd trust you with my life." Hollowly, she laughed. "I just don't want to ruin things by trusting you with my body."

Brook's anger leaked into the sand. The sun enveloped Lila's face in maddening shadows. She could not read Lila's expression, nor could she allow herself the testimony of her ears. This is what in theory they had talked about so long ago. But theory was one thing and the daily practice of it quite another.

With all of her resolve, Lila stepped within the radius of Helen's arms.

Behind them, Brook tested her soul. What did she feel, that her lovers were embracing? A sense of their beauty shining out from their skin, from their eyes. And — pity. An ambiguous and extraordinary pity — for love, like a garden, needs work. Though she would reach to nurture them both, Brook might not always be a careful gardener. After all, there were few enough models for this kind of farming ... Fences and barbed-wire love. Two against the world, ignoring the cycle of one another's change and growth, the times when feelings must lie fallow. Certainly her mother's pain had not prepared her for this kind of loving ... Or had it?

In silence Brook drove to the campsite, almost too aware of Lila's hand on her knee, of Lila firmly clasping Helen's fingers.

At the site Brook opened Perrier for all of them. Needing time to comprehend this dubious miracle, Lila blew hard at an apex of twigs. She stocked the seeking flames with branches and wood. Then, abruptly, she went to haul the cooler out of the van. It was heavy, and would be awkward to carry alone. Helen and Brook heard her mutter. With raised brows, they exchanged glances. Helen got up to help her carry the hamper to the picnic table.

Hands shaking, Lila cleaned the salmon and placed it in foil. She lathered it with barbecue sauce and fresh basil and placed it on the grill.

Silently, Brook ripped up lettuce and chopped green onions, radishes and tomatoes, mixing her own dressing in an empty mayonnaise jar. She added whole almonds for Lila's fight against cancer. She had never felt so automatic about the idea of eating. Wind layered the leaves; carried sparks flying into darkness. Silently, Helen primed the lantern and set it in the middle of the table.

Wood snapped and sizzled. Helen put peppermint tea bags in a boiling pot of water. "That's enough peppermint to clear sinuses," Lila joked. Laughter broke the tension among them.

Lila began to talk. About sexual love, which she had long ago learned not to trust. If she had a plan, it was not to hurt either of them ...

Suddenly Brook got up, poking with a stick at the coals. Unsmiling she turned to face them both. "Hurts are so ingrained that they don't even come any more from what someone else does. They come from us — from our lacks and our betrayals ... I won't make any promises, Lila. Except that I will try to be honest and to care about each of you."

Cross-legged they faced the fire, chewing at food and their own morsels of that truth. Finally, Lila felt that she must be toppling head first into the flames. She was drained of emotions and nearly asleep where she sat.

Helen cooled enough of the steaming water for Lila to wash her hands and face. Maternally, she crawled into the tent to help Lila change into thermal underwear. For a moment Lila hesitated to strip off her shirt. She was ashamed of the scars on her breast and armpit, of the nipple that radiation had made so abnormally hard. Then she took the shirt and determinedly lifted it. With gentle pity, Helen cupped the breast. In the branches of the cedar a huge moon watched.

Helen lay beside her, stroking her hair until Lila pretended to sleep. Uncertain about the distance that Brook was maintaining, Helen emerged from the tent.

Brook lay on her back, gazing up at a sky crowded with bright, winking stars. Behind her raised knees she could barely see the fire's lapping tongue. She seemed locked in some private reverie.

Helen busied her hands by scraping black off camp pots, rinsing cups and utensils in warm water. Reluctantly, Brook left the ground to dry the dishes, to cart things back to the van. Still she looked immersed in herself.

Then she popped a champagne cork into the darkness. The first cup she poured for the Goddess. Smiling at last, she sat close to Helen and toasted her with champagne. In the woods a nightbird scolded.

"Do you remember the first time we shared champagne?" Brook murmured.

Helen said shakily, "Of course I do."

"I felt we made as much of a covenant then as some people do when they get married. Only I didn't ask you to love only me."

"I asked you to," Helen whispered. "For a while."

"For a while," Brook agreed.

"Brook — do you think I'm pushing Lila too hard?"

"Too fast, perhaps. Give her time to love you — naturally."

Helen laughed, ironically. "Oh, our love is natural — it's just not equal to yours."

With a soft expletive Brook stood. "Damn it, Helen — Worry less about making comparisons between yourself and me and more about protecting Lila. Or we'll both lose her."

"To what, Brook? A flash flood? She's desperately in love with you."

"To her need for simplicity. For her, complications may destroy love."

"Oh," Helen said. "It sounds to me like *you* wish things were more simple, too."

"Well, don't you wish that?"

Helen giggled uneasily. "In some funny way I think I'm throwing dust in my face ... Let me sleep on it, Brook ... I do know that I love you."

"And I know that you love Lila, too," Brook whispered.

In the tent Lila heard the soft murmur of their voices. She felt as though she were spinning slowly towards the giant moon, engulfed in golden light which threatened her with sudden madness. She lay still, trying not to ask to be held. Brook and Helen after all had needs of their own ... Shadows preceded her friends into the tent. In moments Lila was cradled between them like a large infant in swaddling clothes. Their kisses soothed her.

Lila's voice cracked. "I feel like I'm going to be punished."

"For what will we be punished, Lila?" Helen's reply was barely audible.

"I don't know. Hubris, maybe. Trying to be free as the gods."

Stretched out beside Lila, Brook gathered her close. "We are all we know of god," she whispered.

Tremulously, Helen murmured: "I'll brush my teeth."

Lila laughed outright. "Oh, that makes me feel so much better. You're nervous too."

Brook kissed the back of her neck, adding to Lila's trembling.

In a moment Helen lay on the other side of her, curling along her spine like a graceful mermaid. Two pairs of hands explored the slope of Lila's neck and shoulders, her waist and thighs. The women's fingertips moved so slowly that Lila forgot to be anxious and began instead to feel frustrated. Brook's warm breath stirred at her ear lobe. Aggressively, Lila reached for her mouth. In every cell, Lila felt her movement towards love. Tentatively Helen kissed her way down Lila's back to her buttocks, made her way back again to her shoulders. Lila shivered with pleasure and cold. With a small exhalation, she closed her eyes.

Brook kept her eyelids closed with kisses and nibbled on the lobes of her ears. She found those places in Lila's throat that made her tingle everywhere.

Tenderly Helen touched her damaged breast. Unable to endure her own vulnerability, Lila buried her face in Helen's shoulder. She felt as though she were about to arch out and away, shuddering all the way down to wet, dark blankness. With soft delight, Helen laughed. She burrowed her mouth into Lila's blond hair.

Lila felt Brook's open hand edge beneath the covers to stroke Helen's belly. Incredulity swarmed across Lila's body like goose bumps. If they were to make love, would this act among them seem depraved? Depraved. What an inane concept, antediluvian as the Great Flood. To the left of her, she saw her friends pause to touch and cling and whisper. Behind Helen's lovely breasts, the moon continued to rise, smiling. Then, like a woman giving birth, Helen squatted, her breathing swollen. She arched like a bow towards the roof of the tent. In wonder, Lila touched the shuddering arch of Helen's neck.

Such strange and silent dignity in the midst of passion ... For a moment Lila felt confused. Questions vibrated inside her like she was the skin of a rawhide drum under the beat of hands. The fire flickered red through the canvas. Red and dark, passion and puzzlement, shadows and light.

Shyly, her fingers found their way inside Helen. Slowly she rotated her fingers, her thumb, so very slowly, wondering how she could be this tender and open and lost. With a sucking sound Helen's vagina widened; Lila felt momentarily engulfed and far too small. On Helen's cheeks were the unabashed glistening of tears.

When at last she could speak, Helen whispered: "This is so beautiful. Can we really love one another like this?"

All this while Brook lay still along Lila's back, barely daring to breathe. "Can we, Lila?" she asked. She was shaking, like a rabbit trapped by dogs. Lila drew the sleeping bag around Brook, rocking her as though they were all endangered. Helen cradled them both, letting fear seep slowly out of the tent.

At last Lila laughed ruefully. "Teach me how to do this better — though you may find that what you want from me is not so special after all."

"Bite your tongue," Helen murmured.

With small, reassuring touches, Brook left them to stand in the light of a powerful moon. Suddenly she felt green as a sapling, her veins bursting with hope.

Also from gynergy books

By Word of Mouth: Lesbians Write the Erotic, Lee Fleming (ed.). "... contains plenty of sexy good writing and furthers the desperately needed honest discussion of what we mean by 'erotic' and by 'lesbian'." SINISTER WISDOM **ISBN 0-921881-06-1** **$10.95/ $12.95 US**

Each Small Step: Breaking the Chains of Abuse and Addiction, Marilyn MacKinnon (ed.). This groundbreaking anthology contains narratives by women recovering from the traumas of childhood sexual abuse and alcohol and chemical dependency. **ISBN 0-921881-17-7 $10.95**

Fascination and Other Bar Stories, Jackie Manthorne. These are satisfying stories of the rituals of seduction and sexuality. "A funny and hot collection from the smoky heart of the Montreal bar beat." SINISTER WISDOM **ISBN 0-921881-16-9 $9.95**

A House Not Her Own: Stories from Beirut, Emily Nasrallah. "For centuries we've been seeing war through men's eyes. Nasrallah's unflinching yet compassionate prose presents it through the eyes of women." BOOKS IN CANADA **ISBN 0-921881-19-3 $12.95**

Imprinting Our Image: An International Anthology by Women with Disabilities, Diane Driedger and Susan Gray (eds.). "In this global tour de force, 30 writers from 17 countries provide dramatic insight into a wide range of issues germane to both the women's and disability rights movements." DISABLED PEOPLES' INTERNATIONAL **ISBN 0-921881-22-3 $12.95**

Lesbians Ignited, Carolyn Gammon. This impassioned first book of poetry delves into the fiery heart of lesbian life and love. "Gammon's work is a positive representation and celebration of female sexuality." WLW JOURNAL **ISBN 0-921881-21-5 $9.95**

Miss Autobody, Les Folles Alliées. In this celebrated and hilarious play, the women of Anytown, led by a savvy group of feminist mechanics, thwart a scheme to show porn videos at a local bar. **ISBN: 0-921881-25-8 $10.95/$9.95 US**

Without Wings, Jackie Manthorne. In this new collection of interwoven stories, the author of *Fascination and Other Bar Stories* moves her characters out of the bar and into life. With wry humour, Manthorne creates an eminently readable tale of lesbian life today. **ISBN 0-921881-29-0 $9.95**

Woman in the Rock, Claudia Gahlinger. A haunting collection of stories about forgetting and remembering incest by an award-winning writer. Gahlinger's characters live near the sea and find consolation in fishing, an act that allows for the eventual, triumphant emergence of the "woman in the rock." **ISBN 0-921881-26-6 $10.95/ $9.95 US**

gynergy books is distributed in Canada by General Publishing, by InBook in the U.S. and in the U.K. by Turnaround. Individual orders can be sent, prepaid, to: **gynergy books**, P.O. Box 2023, Charlottetown, PEI, Canada, C1A 7N7. Please add postage and handling ($2.00 for the first book and .75 for each additional book) to your order. Canadian residents add 7% GST to the total amount. GST registration number R104383120.